THE FINAL CURTAIN

With shoulder-length blond hair and cornflower-blue eyes, Ronnie Simmons is quite irresistible to his fellow actors — of both sexes — and in the jaundiced opinion of his boyhood friend, TV soap actor Nick Carter, he loses his heart with regularity. So it is surprising when Ronnie's sister, Susan, begs him to talk her brother out of his latest relationship. Being between jobs, Nick sets out for the rural backwater where Ronnie is appearing with an Arts Council sponsored touring company — but behind the idyllic pastoral façade lies a disturbing mystery, and Nick is soon involved in violence and murder . . .

KEN HOLDSWORTH

THE FINAL CURTAIN

Complete and Unabridged

ULVERSCROFT
Leicester

First published in Great Britain in 2008 by
Derringer
an imprint of
Willow Bank Publishers Limited
Cambridgeshire

First Large Print Edition
published 2009
by arrangement with
Willow Bank Publishers Limited
Cambridgeshire

British Library CIP Data

Holdsworth, Ken.
  The final curtain
  1. Actors- -Crimes against- -Fiction. 2. Suspense fiction.
  3. Large type books.
  I. Title
  823.9'2–dc22

  ISBN 978–1–84782–818–7

Published by
F. A. Thorpe (Publishing)
Anstey, Leicestershire
Set by Words & Graphics Ltd.
Anstey, Leicestershire
Printed and bound in Great Britain by
T. J. International Ltd., Padstow, Cornwall

This book is printed on acid-free paper

For three treasured members of my own cast, Paul, Claire and Grant, of whom a Producer couldn't be prouder.

1

Ned Tucker was dead, I was out of work and the traffic on the M6 was nose to tail as usual.

There was a gap in the outside lane. A white van was coming up fast but I wasn't in a patient mood. No, damn it, I was angry! I pulled into the lane ahead of him. He didn't like it and flashed his lights. I floored the accelerator and left him behind. The classic Mini Cooper is probably the best city car ever and after months of crawling around Manchester my little car roared with pleasure to be let off the leash.

Okay, so perhaps I shouldn't complain. I'd been booked to play 'Nasty' Ned Tucker for eight episodes of *Brooklands*, and that's precisely what I'd done. I had hoped for more but the powers that be, in their wisdom, decided they'd had enough of him.

But why, for Pete's sake, did they have to bump him off? If they'd just written him out, there would have been a chance of coming back in a later episode — look how the old stars of *Coronation Street* and *EastEnders* keep popping up again and again — but when you're dead, you're dead, *finito!*

I blame that new writer. She works on the theory of 'more violence, more viewers' and in a couple of months she wiped out half the cast. It wasn't so bad for me but some of those *Brooklands* people were household names, they'd been in the show for ten years or more!

Of course Sam Abrahams claims credit for getting me the job, (Sam's my agent, by the way) but I know I was hired because some bright spark at Granada Television came up with the idea that to have Eleanor Cooper's ex in the show would give their ratings a much needed boost — particularly as the media had cast me as the villain in our much publicised divorce.

Thinking about Eleanor added fuel to my anger. The road ahead was slightly uphill and two huge juggernauts were battling it out neck and neck, holding back all the vehicles behind them. I floored the accelerator and roared past them in the fast lane as if they were standing still.

Eleanor had entered my life during a summer season at Bexhill-on-Sea. She came to replace one of the girls whose pregnancy was beginning to be obvious and breezed in to our little theatre just like the song — tall and tanned and young and lovely — and she singled me out immediately. Imagine, a gorgeous girl like her making a play for a broken-nosed roughneck like me? I couldn't believe my luck. Then, when only a matter of days later she suggested we share a room, I thought I'd won the lottery.

'I want us to share everything, darling,' she had cooed sweetly.

Things happened quickly after that. A registry office wedding with the ladies of the company throwing confetti and enjoying a little weep, an Irish theme pub reception with the men doing their best to get me tiddly on Guinness, and a one-night honeymoon in the best hotel in Eastbourne with Eleanor whispering, 'Wouldn't it be cosy if my money was tucked up with yours in a nice little joint account at the bank?'

It was money that had set me apart from the other eligible young men in the company. I know that now, of course. I stood out in that hard-up little group because, thanks to a small legacy, I was the only one who could afford to run a car.

But Eleanor was talented as well as beautiful and there was no one more pleased for her than me when she landed a major part in a big West End production. The show was a smash hit but I got the biggest shock of my life when, in the midst of all the excitement and celebration, she sued me for divorce, telling the press I'd done nothing to help her in her career. I couldn't understand why she would say that as it was far from being the truth. My incredulity quickly turned to anger when I discovered she'd filched what was left of my inheritance to buy the lease on a swank apartment overlooking Regent's Park.

A reporter caught me just as I'd discovered Eleanor had cleaned me out. I don't remember what I said to him exactly but I do know I called her a few choice names. The very next day his tabloid newspaper appeared with the headline: 'SMALL-TIME ACTOR JEALOUS OF WIFE'S WEST END SUCCESS.' So there I was, the villain of the piece, and a right nasty piece of work I looked in that picture they printed of me. But then I always do, looking mean is my stock in trade.

It was a second or two before it registered that my mobile was ringing. My Mini is quite noisy at high speed and the phone was in the pocket of my padded jacket on the back seat. I ignored it. I needed to stop at the next services anyway and it was bound to be Sam. I'd been badgering him for a new job ever since I knew Granada were not going to renew my contract.

I pulled into the services car park, dug out the phone and found that my missed call

4

wasn't from Sam after all; it was from Susan Simmons. I was intrigued.

Susan and her younger brother, Ronnie, had played a major part in my early life. The three of us had come together as children all of twenty years ago at the Cornish home of Stan and Marjorie Earnshaw. The Earnshaws were a childless couple, well past middle-age and comfortably off, who had decided one year to give some poor kids from London's East End a seaside holiday. Stan was a bluff Yorkshireman who had made a tidy sum of money converting old Cornish buildings into holiday homes, his wife, Marjorie, was an enthusiastic member of the local Women's Institute and Amateur Dramatic Society. It was originally to have been just a one-off but we all got on so well together it went on to be repeated year after year until us Cockney kids were in our teens. 'Uncle' Stan died not so long ago. It was his legacy that Eleanor had helped herself to.

Susan and Ronnie's father was a widower who, although confined to a wheelchair, did his best to run a small photographic shop in Stepney, and me, I was an orphan, forever being bundled from one care home to another. 'Family' was a word I didn't know the meaning of until I went to the Earnshaw's house in Cornwall.

Susan would climb trees with me and p
football but all her little brother did was
follow me around like a faithful puppy. This
irritated me and try as I might I couldn't
shake him off so I began to teach him things,
like how to make rude noises with a blade of
grass between his thumbs and to whistle
through his fingers.

Years passed and Susan was to discover
that trying on pretty dresses in the big stores
in Truro with 'Auntie' Marjorie was infinitely
preferable to scrambling over rocks to catch
crabs with me, so Ronnie replaced her as my
eager confederate and willing accomplice. He
treated me like his big brother and that was
okay but with burgeoning adolescence my
feelings for Susan were not in the least
brotherly. I had a king-size crush on her. She
was my first love and I still remember the
tender moments we shared. Looking back I
must have been a fumbling, bumbling lover
but at the time I was John Travolta and Susan
was my Olivia Newton John. I was thirteen
and, of course, I knew it all.

Marjorie Earnshaw would take us regularly
to the Minack, that exquisite mock-Grecian
amphitheatre overlooking the sea at Porth-
curno. What a place of magic that was. The
music, the costumes and the lighting held me
spellbound. It was there that I caught the

acting bug and back in London I took to wandering around the West End, gazing longingly at the photographs outside the theatres. One day I spotted a crowd of kids waiting to be auditioned for a new production of Lionel Bart's *Oliver*. On the spur of the moment I joined the queue and to my amazement and joy I was offered a part.

I never gave parental consent a second thought. My foster father at that time paid me scant attention anyway, his only interests in life being West Ham United and the local workingmen's club, the latter was a laugh in itself because for as long as I knew him he was drawing unemployment benefit. Anyway, he refused point blank to allow me to accept the part and I was flabbergasted. I begged and pleaded with him to change his mind but he wouldn't budge. Days went by and I'd just about given up hope when right out of the blue — and to my immense relief — he gave permission. I didn't find out until later that he'd done a deal with a national newspaper for the story. I can still see the headline: 'EAST END WAIF IS WEST END URCHIN'.

Ronnie blew his share of Uncle Stan's bequest on a motorbike, a camera and the high life — not necessarily in that order — and much to Susan's disapproval he followed me onto the stage. He telephones me regularly and the two of us meet as often as our respective engagements allow. We have a slap-up lunch, which invariably I end up paying for, talk about the theatre, his latest conquests and taking pictures — Ronnie inherited the love of photography from his father.

Susan, I regret to say, I haven't seen for years. A pragmatist through and through, she wasn't interested my world of make-believe. She studied hard and went to University, using Uncle Stan's legacy sensibly for food and accommodation. She got a first in something or other. We keep in touch but it's very much a Christmas and Birthday Card relationship. She only phones me when she's worried about Ronnie.

Her number rang for a long time before she answered. 'Nicky, hi!' she said eventually. 'Sorry about that, I was in the office. I've come outside; I didn't want everyone listening . . . It's Ronnie. I'm worried about him.'

Luckily, she couldn't see the big grin on my face.

'He's with a little touring company, playing at village halls and the like.'

'Yes, I know.'

There was a moment's silence before she said, quietly, 'He's worthy of better things.'

That was a dig at me. 'Well, at least he's *got* a job,' I retorted irritably.

'You're not out of work!'

'I am.'

'But you're on television three times a week?'

'They shot my last scene yesterday.'

There was another pause while that sank in. Then, completely ignoring what, to me, was a devastating piece of news, she said, 'I always talk to Ronnie on Saturdays. It took me ages to get him to understand that he can't just phone when it suits him — you know what a mobile junkie he is — but now he calls me every Saturday morning at half past ten. You can set your watch by him. He's been doing it for months.'

I was impressed. 'I should try that,' I said. 'He phoned me in the middle of a take once. It was very embarrassing. I was furious with him but really it was my own stupid fault for taking my mobile on the set . . . '

'But he didn't call me last Saturday!' she cut in. 'I've tried calling him but there's no answer. I think his phone must be out of order or something.'

'Did you call his digs?'

'Yes, I did. The company are staying at a pub in a village called Chapel Heath. The people there said he was out. They said he's always out taking pictures, when he's not on the stage that is. He sells them to newspapers. Did you know that?'

'Yes, I've seen his work,' I said. 'He's remarkably good at it. He told me he's toyed with the idea of giving up the stage to become a full-time freelance photojournalist.' I paused expecting her to say that anything would be better than the life of an itinerant actor but on this occasion she didn't.

'I really wanted to have a good heart-to-heart with him after Tuesday.'

I was confused. 'I thought you said Ronnie only speaks to you on Saturdays?'

'By phone, yes. But on Tuesday I was in Cannford on business and being so close I made a point of going to see him.' She sighed. 'Oh, Nicky. He's seriously in debt and he's in love again.'

So what's new about that? Uncle Stan would have described Ronnie as living a Champagne lifestyle on a bottle-beer income — and the good-looking young devil was forever in love with someone or other, his cornflower-blue eyes and blond hair, which nowadays he wears shoulder-length, his slight build and his artistic sensitivity make him quite irresistible to fellow actors — of both sexes.

'He loses his heart with boring regularity,' I

said, 'but who knows, one day one of his romances may actually come to something.'

'Not this one I hope, this is one tough cookie. A female Hell's Angel, if there is such a thing, with a ring through her nose and a tattoo on her neck.'

'Wow! Is she with the touring company?'

'No, she works for her parents who run the pub — and she's a single mother with a young child to look after!'

'He needs a good talking to.'

'Quite, but it will do no good on the phone.'

Suddenly I knew what was coming.

'I know it's asking a lot, Nicky, but I was hoping that if you had a couple of days free? I'd go myself but I'm really tied up . . . '

Well, I still had this thing for Susan, didn't I? And I *was* between jobs. 'Actually, I'm on my way south at the moment.' I said. 'I suppose I could make a detour. What did you say the name of this place was?'

My SatNav took me along country lanes that were uncomfortably narrow even for my small car. Some miles out from Chapel Heath, a tractor towing a lethal-looking piece of agricultural equipment pulled out ahead of me. It took up almost the full width of the road and I had no option but to crawl along behind it, and to add insult to injury, it

11

spattered my windscreen with mud from its huge wheels — at least I hoped it was mud! I suppose it could have been worse, I could have been coming the other way. After some of the longest minutes of my life the tractor finally pulled into a field leaving all of the road to me. With a sigh of relief I accelerated away, passing a sign telling me that Chapel Heath welcomes careful drivers. I rounded a bend and, 'Wow!' Ahead of me was a panorama that was a location finder's dream. Whitewashed, red-tiled cottages with roses round the doors, a grey-stone church spire pointing to the heavens, a comfortable-looking, half-timbered pub with a thatched roof, a duck pond and a village green complete with a carefully mown cricket pitch in the middle. It was a scene straight off the cover of *This England*.

I parked the car in the cobblestone yard behind the pub and went inside where it was everything I expected, lots of oak beams and shiny brass. All very welcoming, which was more than you could say for the po-faced barmaid who seemed to regard each new arrival with suspicion. She had that defiant, me-against-the-world look that I'd seen a lot in the streets where I grew up, women deserted by their partners who were strug-gling to raise a family and hold down a job of work at the same time.

Her blouse had a high collar so I couldn't see a tattoo, but the nose ring was there, plus an eyebrow stud that Susan hadn't mentioned.

'What can I do for you?'

I realised I was gawping. 'Er, just some information.'

She tensed visibly.

'I'm told the Pembroke Players stay here.'

'The theatricals?' she said cautiously. 'Yes they do — but there's none of them here at the moment.'

'Can you tell me where I can find them?'

'Try the village hall.'

'And where's that?'

This was obviously one question too far and she gave an exasperated sigh. 'On the other side of the common.'

A paying customer attracted her attention by banging his empty glass on the bar. She turned away.

'Excuse me,' I said. 'Would you know if Ronnie Simmons is with them?'

She swung back to face me. 'You've not come here to cause trouble like that sister of his, have you?'

'Certainly not!'

She looked away, her bottom lip trembled and she seemed to crumple. 'I can't say

13

where he is,' she said quietly.

I walked thoughtfully back to my car. It looked as though I'd got a lot of straightening out to do. I drove off, turning left out of the car park, my theory being that if I kept the common to my nearside I would come to the village hall eventually.

On the right, I passed the village shop and post office and a small school, while to my left there was just a lot of grass. Eventually, I reached a rather neglected-looking wooden-clapboarded structure with a felt roof and broken windows. I pulled up outside. Surely not, I thought, but there, pinned in a glass-fronted notice board by the entrance doors, was a large notice that read:

THE PEMBROKE PLAYERS
Proudly Present
WAITING ON THE BRIDGE
A play in three acts by
Quentin Minnow
Evenings at 7:30 Commencing
Monday 27th June.
(No performance Sunday)

So, the Players had been in Chapel Heath for four days, more likely five, as they would need a day to set things up. I got out of the car and walked over to the notice board. The small print on the poster gave the ticket prices and went on to inform the paying public that this play was, 'a landmark in drama', 'profoundly moving', and offered audiences 'a powerful and stimulating theatrical experience'.

Ronnie had not only copied me in his choice of career but also in the services of an agent. I could just imagine Sam Abrahams selling him this job. 'It's not everyone that gets a golden opportunity like this so early in their career, my boy,' he'd say. 'You should grasp it firmly with both hands!'

How many touring company jobs had that big, cigar-smoking, wheeler-dealer talked me into? Still, in this crazy acting business you couldn't wish for better experience.

A loud, male voice was booming away inside. I pushed open the double doors and I was back in the world of theatre.

A completely bald man wearing bib and brace overalls was busily working on the footlights. A spiky-haired teenager in black jeans and an *Iron Maiden* T-shirt was sweeping the hall and a tall, elderly, scholarly-looking man in a striped shirt and bow tie was setting out rows of tubular metal and canvas chairs.

Tall canvasses, painted to represent Doric columns screened the wings on either side of the stage, which was set to look like the interior of a room with a pair of large french windows in its centre. A screen behind the windows was painted to represent a garden. It was a universal set, one that could be used for anything, from *Night Must Fall* to *See How They Run*.

The loud, plummy, Donald Sinden-like voice emanated from a smallish, thickset man who was strutting about the stage shouting instructions. His profile was classically handsome, but his hair was a shade too long for a man of his age. His velvet jacket was well cut, but the cuffs and elbows were shiny and from where I stood, I could see that his shoes, although polished to a brilliant shine, were rather down-at-heel.

'Mayberry!' he shouted. 'There's damned graffiti on the garden again! Get your brushes out, there's a good fellow . . . Where the devil's the telephone, Melanie? I told you not to leave anything portable on the stage . . . Dolan! What am I always telling you about booking halls that we have to share with kiddies' playgroups? Avoid them like the plague, dear boy, like the plague!'

This, without a doubt, was Ronnie's boss, Roland Pembroke. When Susan mentioned the name it had meant nothing to me, but the face I instantly recognised. I'd seen it in dozens of films and TV dramas but never in what you would call a starring role. I'd seen him dining on the Orient Express, in a lifejacket on the Titanic and running to a Spitfire in the Battle of Britain. He was playing another part now, that of an actor-manager of a touring theatre company, and I would say he was thoroughly enjoying it. I'd met dozens like him, old actors that just can't stop acting.

'Excuse me, can I help you?'

I'd been so engrossed in watching Roland Pembroke that I didn't hear someone come up behind me. I turned around to discover a slim girl about twenty or so staring at me expectantly. The face behind the large, round glasses wore a worried expression. She was dressed in a shapeless, woolly cardigan, a thick, tweedy skirt and heavy-looking brogue shoes. She held a clipboard to her chest defensively.

'Yes, I hope you can,' I said. My smile seemed to go some way to relaxing her a little. 'I'm looking for Ronnie Simmons. I've tried ringing his mobile but think there's something wrong with it.'

She looked away. 'I'm sorry, Ronnie's not here.'

Roland Pembroke strode to the front of the stage and peered out over the footlights. 'I say! You there!' he bawled. 'Are you from the newspaper?'

'No, sir,' I replied. (Why on earth did I call him 'sir'?) 'My name's Nick Carter. I'm looking for my friend, Ronnie Simmons.'

He leapt down from the stage with amazing agility and strode purposefully across the hall, staring at me appraisingly all the way. He had a large, powerful, upper body but very short legs. I judged him to be a good six inches shorter than me and I'm not tall by today's standards.

'Huh! Aren't we all?' he muttered. He continued to look at me intently and then he had it. 'I know you!' he cried, triumphantly.

Here it comes, I thought. He's going to say, 'You're that nasty piece of work, Ned Tucker, in *Brooklands.*' I get it all the time. I've had little old ladies come up to me in a supermarket and tell me I should be ashamed of myself, I've even had lager louts wanting to take a pop at me. And d'you know what? That pleases me, because I must have made the character believable.

'You're the fellow that married Eleanor Cooper!' he said.

I was disappointed, but then I don't suppose Roland Pembroke gets much time to watch telly.

'Mm,' I said.

He grinned and said jubilantly, 'My dear boy, you are an actor!' He pronounced the last word meticulously, giving each syllable its full value. Stepping closer, he lowered his voice to a confidential whisper. 'Tell me, are you, er, working on anything at the moment?'

'As a matter of fact I'm not.'

'Capital! Capital!' he cried, and began pacing the floor, thumping his fist into the palm of his hand. He stopped and swung back to face me. 'Mr Carter, you are in the unique position of being able to save a theatrical production!'

'I am?'

'Most certainly! You, sir, are an actor currently, er, resting, right? And you are also a friend of young Simmons, are you not?'

I wondered what on earth he was leading up to. 'Guilty on all counts,' I said guardedly.

He turned his head heavenwards and closed his eyes, giving me the full benefit of that classic profile. 'Your *friend*, Mr Simmons, has walked out on us.'

I was stunned! 'He's what?' I gasped. I looked around in desperation. The girl had backed off a few paces but was watching us intently, the clipboard still held firmly to her chest. The old man, the floor sweeper and the electrician had abandoned their tasks and had moved in closer.

'Yes, Mr Carter,' Roland Pembroke continued, 'Young Simmons packed his bags and rode off into the sunset — on that noisy motorbike of his — without a word to anyone.'

'I don't believe it! Ronnie wouldn't do a thing like that!'

The girl took a cautious pace forward. 'It's true Mr Carter, he's gone.' She sniffed and dabbed at her eyes with a ridiculously small handkerchief.

'It's that damned camera nonsense of his . . . ' Roland Pembroke said.

'Ronnie takes pictures for the newspapers,' Melanie explained.

The actor-manager gave her a withering look, 'It was taking over his life,' he said, 'preying on his mind. No man can serve two masters. I told him he must decide between acting and photography — and it looks very much as though he has done just that . . . I said earlier, Mr Carter, that you have the opportunity to save a theatrical production. I'll now go further and say you can save an entire theatre company.'

I couldn't accept that Ronnie would quit his job without an explanation. It wasn't like him to let people down.

'How?' I said automatically. I was only half listening to him.

'By taking over Ronnie Simmons' part in the play.'

That got my full attention. 'You're not serious!' I gasped.

Roland Pembroke drew himself up to his full height. 'I most certainly am. Our budget doesn't run to understudies.' He swept an arm in the direction of the others in the hall. 'Neither Mr Mayberry nor Mr Dolan here is an actor and young Chambers is but an apprentice. Your friend's departure on Saturday has resulted in the cancellation of four performances — four performances, Mr Carter! I've spent all week on the telephone trying to find a replacement for him without success, so it looks as though I'll have to cancel tonight's show as well . . . We cannot go on like this Mr Carter; our sponsors are not happy, not happy at all. Any more cancellations and I fear they will withdraw their support.' He paused and adopted a softer, almost a beseeching expression. 'You, Mr Carter, are heaven sent. I beg you to stay, stay and save the Pembroke Players from extinction . . . What do you say?'

I looked around. All eyes were on me. Roland Pembroke was staring at me tight-lipped, anxiously waiting for my answer. Melanie's hands were folded in front of the clipboard as if in prayer and the other three had crept even closer. For whatever reason, Ronnie had left these people in serious trouble. I couldn't walk away, could I? I took a deep breath and agreed to take over his part.

'But only until you find a permanent replacement,' I added firmly.

There was an audible sigh of relief all round and Roland Pembroke's smile would have given the Cheshire cat some competition. 'Capital! Capital!' he said again. 'When we're back at *The Grapes*, remind me to give you one of those forms to fill in for Income Tax and National Insurance, that sort of thing. Mundane stuff I know but we do have to conform . . . You are familiar with the play, of course?' I said I was. 'Then you'll know that Quentin Minnow saw Seth Cartwright simply as a means of enabling the more powerful character, Sir William Haslett, to deliver the most dramatic lines in the play.'

I'd always thought Seth Cartwright was the hero of the piece but I kept that to myself. 'I take it I'm Seth and you play Sir William?'

'Of course, dear boy, of course. Melanie, go with Mr Carter to *The Grapes* will you, m'dear? We are still paying for young Simmons' room so tell them to put him in there . . . and don't forget to see he has a script!' Turning back to me, he said, 'Brush up on your lines, dear boy. I'll give you a run-through tomorrow morning at eight o'clock sharp, right? Has to be early, we have a drama workshop in the afternoon at the sixth-form college. Come along if you like, the sooner you get into the swing of things the better. You'll be surprised how interested young people are in the theatre nowadays. They have excellent facilities — and they provide free lunch!'

2

It wasn't until I got outside that the full impact of what I'd agreed to do hit me. How the devil was I going to learn the lines of a principal character in a three-act play in one night? I knew the play of course, everybody does, but oddly enough I'd never appeared in it. Roland Pembroke had been quick to spot a patsy, I thought. That man could teach Sam Abrahams a thing or two. Oh, what the hell! I needed a job and it's a nice play with a happy ending — and I do *love* a happy ending.

Melanie climbed into the car beside me, brushing her hairy skirt primly over her knees. I noticed that a large carpetbag had replaced the clipboard, and this she held protectively in her lap.

'Tell me about the other Players,' I said, as we drove out of the car park.

My question seemed to take her by surprise; perhaps she wasn't expecting conversation. 'Oh! Yes,' she replied, a little flustered. 'You've met Mr Roland of course, and Mr Dolan, and Mr Mayberry . . . and young Brian, Brian Chambers, he's a local boy who's with us on a work experience scheme. Well, in addition to them there's Miss Fontaine, Marcia, she's Mrs Pembroke really but she uses her stage name. They met in musical comedy, Miss Fontaine and Mr Roland, although he doesn't sing now. They've been married for years and years and he still thinks the world of her. He'd do *anything* to please her. I think that's *so* romantic, don't you? And then there's their son, Tarquin.'

I turned right onto the road that skirted the common. 'Ah! Shakespeare,' I said.

'Pardon?'

'Shakespeare, *Tarquin and Lucrece.*'

'Oh!'

There was a mounted rider just ahead of me. I slowed to let an oncoming van come by before pulling out to give the horse plenty of room. The rider thanked me with a wave of her crop.

'What's he like, this Tarquin?' I asked.

Melanie didn't reply. I shot a glance at her. She was staring at the road ahead, her lips compressed into a thin line.

'You don't have much to say about him then?'

'The least said about Tarquin the better. You'll find out about him yourself soon enough. Just bear in mind he's Miss Fontaine's pride and joy. In her eyes he can do no wrong.' She spoke with such bitterness I thought it prudent to change the subject.

I asked her why she was with the Players. Her face relaxed immediately and there was even a flicker of a smile. 'I've always wanted to be an actress,' she said dreamily.

She used the word, 'actress,' which I thought charmingly old fashioned. 'I'm sure you'll do splendidly,' I said.

When we got to *The Grapes*, Melanie left me to get my luggage out of the car while she went to seek out the licensee. I caught up with her just inside the entrance talking to a chubby man of medium height with a voluminous white apron wrapped around his rotund belly. The landlord of *The Grapes* turned to see who it was blundering in through his door with a large suitcase and a zip-up holdall. He had rosy cheeks, a seemingly permanent smile and said his name was Arthur.

'If there's anything you want, sir, anything at all, just ask,' he added with a friendly wink. 'And there's a trolley there, sir, for the luggage.'

Stationed just inside the door was a waist high, chromium-plated frame on wheels, into which I gratefully dumped my bags. I like chefs and pub landlords to be somewhat overweight. To me it's a guarantee of quality

— that what they serve up is so good they can't resist sampling it themselves.

My room was behind the pub in a converted stable block. Melanie unlocked the door. She reached inside to turn on the lights and then stepped back to allow me to wheel my luggage in. Immediately inside was a small lobby where a partially open door on the right-hand side revealed a very smart en-suite bathroom. Beyond this was the main room, which was surprisingly big and fitted out with a double bed, an easy chair, a wardrobe and a long dressing table with a stool. On the dressing table was the usual tea and coffee making paraphernalia, a small television set and a plastic letter rack containing stationery and a few colourful brochures.

I was impressed. So this had been Ronnie's room? The expression, 'dead man's shoes' sprang to mind and I wished it hadn't. Melanie made no attempt to follow me but she came in when I called her. She looked so down in the dumps that it was pretty obvious Ronnie had been more to her than just a colleague. My natural instinct was to put my arm around her to comfort her, but as she seemed such a timid creature, I thought it best not to — we *were* in my bedroom after all.

'Have you spoken to Ronnie's agent?' I asked.

She removed her glasses and dabbed her eyes again with the tiny handkerchief. 'The news came as a surprise to him too,' she said with a sniff. '*And* I phoned the hospitals, *and* the police.' Tears started to flow and I began to feel annoyed with Ronnie for making this nice young girl so unhappy.

'Well, it's a stupid thing to have done,' I said. 'I doubt if he will ever work in the theatre again.'

Fortunately I had a clean handkerchief so I gave it to her. She could hardly blow her nose on that silly little thing of hers.

'I don't think that will bother him,' she sniffled. 'It's like Mr Roland said, he's made his decision. Perhaps he loved his photography more than . . . more than anything.'

She began to cry again, and what the hell. This time I did put my arm around her and she nestled into me, her head resting on my chest. She was trembling slightly. It felt rather nice and I had to remind myself forcibly of the vow I made after my divorce never to get emotionally involved with a member of the company again. Her sobs finally subsided and she pushed herself away.

'Ronnie told me that a photojournalist has to be ready to go to the other side of the world at the drop of a hat if need be,' she said, thrusting her little chin forward defiantly. 'And that's what he's done . . . He's suddenly had to dash off somewhere with no time to tell anyone where he was going.'

She said this with such emphasis that I wondered who it was she was trying to convince. Then she turned to leave saying she still had some things to do back at the hall. I offered to run her there in the Mini.

'It isn't far if I cut across the common . . . and a bit of fresh air will do me good.' She stopped at the door. 'Good heavens, Mr Roland would never forgive me.' She scrabbled in her capacious bag and brought out a dog-eared copy of *Waiting On The Bridge*. 'You haven't much time to brush up on your lines, have you? If I can help, my room's only next door.'

She thrust the script at me and fled.

*   *   *

I am by nature a tidy person and having emptied my suitcase and holdall I looked around for somewhere to stow them. The shelf in the wardrobe where extra blankets were stored seemed a likely place and there would be room if I were to put the holdall in the suitcase and refold the blankets.

As I pulled them down something fell at my feet. It was a black, simulated-leather folder about A4 size, with two wide elastic bands crisscrossed around it to hold it shut. I recognised it immediately. It was Ronnie's portfolio: an album filled with big, glossy, eight-by-ten photographs with subjects ranging from the theatrical to the dramatic, from glitzy stage productions to gory shots of road accidents. A freelance photographer's *curriculum vitae* he called it. He found it an invaluable tool for obtaining commissions — and something he would be most unlikely to leave behind, I would have thought.

He'd updated the pictures since I saw it last. Roland Pembroke was in several which I took to be shots of *Waiting On The Bridge*. Tucked between the pages was a large white envelope. There were some loose prints inside. I shook them out on the bed. They were all black and white pictures of churches, old churches, some half-timbered and surrounded by crumbling gravestones, others ivy clad and half hidden by trees and shrubbery. There was a name written on the envelope, something Murray — I never could read Ronnie's handwriting. Perhaps Mr Murray could throw some light on Ronnie's sudden disappearance, if only I knew who he was.

All in all, it had been quite a day so I went across to the pub with the intention of sitting quietly with a drink or two but Arthur had other ideas. He saw me as being lonely and in need of conversation. I could have taken my drink to one of the booths but that wouldn't have been polite and I had a few questions for him anyway so I pulled a stool up to the bar.

He began by telling me he had played professional football in his youth but had been forced to hang up his boots because of injury.

'Footballers didn't get paid like film stars in those days,' he said wistfully. 'And it's not easy getting a job when all you're good at is kicking a ball about. I had to take whatever work I could get. I did everything from working on building sites to emptying dustbins.'

'What brought you into the licensed trade?' I asked.

'The landlord of my local suggested it. He gave me the name of a man at the brewery so I called him, and being something of a local celebrity I got an interview straight away. My name would attract the punters, he said, and with my better half being a trained cook, well, that clinched it, didn't it?'

'But this is a Free House?'

'Yes, it is. This is our fourth pub but it's the first one we've actually owned,' he said, looking around, 'and it will be our last.'

'I'm sorry?'

'This will be our last pub, sir. It's on the market and when it sells we're off, to live in sunny Spain.'

'Do you have anyone interested?'

'I did,' he said, rolling his eyes. 'One of them celebrity chefs on the telly. I got a whisper he was looking for somewhere not too far from London to do gourmet weekends, so I invited him over and showed him my plans for turning the old stables into accommodation. He said if I did that he would be interested, so I went ahead and did it.'

'And you've made a very good job of it.'

'It cost a lot more than I thought it would, but then these things always do, don't they?'

'And what about this chef?'

'The bugger went and bought a place in the Chilterns, didn't he?'

The arrival of another customer put a temporarily stop to our conversation. When Arthur came back I asked him about Ronnie's abrupt departure. His face clouded.

'That rascal? He did a runner ... and bloody good riddance!' He lowered his voice.

'I caught him taking saucy pictures of our Poll, sir, that's our daughter.' He nodded his head towards the tough looking girl with the nose ring. 'She told me he'd offered to let her take his bike out for a run if she'd pose for him. She didn't see no harm in it and she's motorbike mad, she is. I made him take the film out of his camera and hand it over there and then I did. Gawd! If my missus had found out there would have been hell to pay, I can tell you.'

It was hard to imagine Polly in a saucy pose. I was about to ask him if he had seen Ronnie on the day of his disappearance when a man in brown overalls interrupted us by rudely elbowing me aside and demanding a pint of bitter. He was well over six feet tall and built like a rugby forward, with tousled, red hair, bushy eyebrows, a craggy face and a chin you could strike matches on. I was about to protest but Arthur stopped me with a warning shake of his head.

'This is Mr Carter, Caleb,' he said, his genial host smile back on his chubby face. 'He's with Mr Pembroke's Players.'

The giant turned to look at me. His eyes were steel-grey, hard and cold. He gave an almost imperceptible nod of his head, threw some coins on the counter and took his beer over to a booth in the corner.

'That's Caleb Pilcher,' Albert whispered. 'You have to know how to handle him.'

'Does he live in the village?'

'No, the other side of Marshbank, that's the next village going towards Cannford. He's got a garage on the main road.'

I glanced over my shoulder at the booth. 'Is there a Mrs Pilcher?' I asked, feeling sorry for anyone who had to live with such an uncouth monster.

'There's just him and his son, Benny, a lad in his twenties. Not quite a full shilling you understand but he helps his dad out with odd jobs. Caleb's wife left him years ago, got fed up with him knocking her about. She's got a little bed and breakfast place somewhere in the West Country, Devon or Dorset.' He took a glass from the washer and began to polish it. 'They don't sell petrol any more, the big oil companies weren't interested in their piddling orders.'

I'm no expert on the garage business but I do know of some who, although they don't sell petrol, do a good trade in repairs and servicing. I asked why the Pilchers didn't do that.

Arthur shook his head. 'As you saw for yourself, sir, Caleb's not very good with people and his lad hasn't the head for business. They do a bit of light haulage and various odd jobs here and there. Caleb's got a good contract with Cannypots — the plastic flowerpot people on the bypass. He goes over to Holland for them a couple of times a month. Just driving, see. He doesn't have to mix with people.' He tapped the side of his nose with his finger. 'He brings me back some ciggies and wine sometimes. There's no duty-free now but they're still a lot cheaper on the Continent . . . He's into antiques as well, got a shop in the High Street. There's a lot of interest in antiques these days, what with all them programmes on the telly.'

Somehow I just couldn't imagine Caleb Pilcher in the genteel world of antiques. 'I believe old things can fetch high prices,' I said for the want of saying something.

'You can say that again, sir. Eddie Dolan and him have never been so well off.'

'Dolan?'

'Oh yes, sir, Mr Pembroke's stage manager. He's the brains behind it. It was his idea in the first place see, what with all them auctions in Northern Ireland and Caleb having the van.'

'Why go all the way Northern Ireland, surely we have auctions in this country?'

'Eddie's got contacts over there, sir,' he said with a wink, 'and the market for the stuff is over here, see? So, you puts the two together and bob's your uncle.'

'Doesn't Mr Pembroke mind his stage manager flitting back and forth across the Irish Sea?'

Arthur chuckled. 'Oh, he doesn't do that, sir, he does it all on the phone. He does a bit of travelling, delivering the stuff and that, but he keeps well away from Ireland, does Eddie. I'm told he's not the most popular person with some over there. And as for Mr Pembroke, well, he don't mind Eddie having two jobs, especially as he gets a cut.'

My curiosity was aroused. This was far more interesting than hearing about Arthur's days as a footballer. 'So, Dolan has someone buy the antiques for him at auction in Northern Ireland and Pilcher fetches them back to England. Where does Mr Pembroke fit in?'

'He helped out with some cash to buy the lease on the shop, sir. Eddie did ask me but I was a bit overstretched at the time, what with the cost of the stable conversion and everything, so I had to turn him down.' He shook his head sadly. 'I wish I'd gone in with him now though, and that's a fact.'

I asked if Caleb's son worked in the shop.

'No. I told you, he hasn't got it up here,' he said, tapping his temple. 'Anyway, almost all the selling's done on the Internet. But they do have to have somewhere to put the stuff, and if some passerby should be interested in anything, well, Alice is on hand to deal with that. Alice sells artificial flowers. She's a remarkable woman, Alice is. She's no spring chicken but she can do sums in her head quicker than any o'them calculators . . . The shop is called *Flowertiques*, flowers and antiques — get it?' That seemed to tickle him and he chortled to himself as he polished the glasses, his fat belly jiggling beneath the expansive white apron.

'So what odd jobs does Benny do?'

'Well, one is looking after the old church what's in the estuary behind their garage. They has a communion service there every other Wednesday morning but apart from that it's hardly ever used. The Pilchers gets paid by the diocese to look after it, to open it up in the morning and lock it up at night, and keep the grass cut, that sort of thing. Benny does most of that — and he drives the van on Sundays when his dad's not using it. He does work for your lot, shifting scenery and stuff.'

'When the Players move to a new location.'

'That's right, but he has a lot of time to spare, which he seems to spend here. Our Poll's the attraction, if you follow me. Devoted to her he is. He'll cycle all the way here on that rusty old boneshaker of his just to see her.' He raised his voice so his daughter would hear. 'I don't approve of our Poll being too friendly with Benny Pilcher. One child's enough for her to look after, she don't need two.'

Roland Pembroke's fruity voice suddenly filled the room. 'Landlord, a bottle of your finest red for my good lady if you please!'

The little actor-manager strutted into the taproom followed by a tall, slender woman who in her youth, must have been an absolute stunner.

Arthur winked at me. 'That's his wife,' he whispered. 'Buy her a large gin and she'll sing you something from *The Sound of Music*.'

Roland spotted me at the bar and he advanced wagging an admonishing finger. 'Now then, Carter! Playing truant from brushing up our lines are we? Never mind, all is forgiven if you're in the chair.' Turning to his wife, he added, 'Marcia, my dear, this is the young man I was telling you about.'

Marcia Fontaine slid onto the stool next to mine and fluttered her long eyelashes at me. 'Were you really married to Eleanor Cooper?' she drawled, giving me a good once-over.

Melanie arrived with the man I'd seen working on the footlights. He was in his mid forties, slim, of medium height and like many balding men these days he had shaved off the rest of the hair on his head. He looked stern and uncompromising. In my eagerness to escape Marcia's probing eyes I was perhaps a little too enthusiastic with my greeting.

'Ah, the electrician,' I said.

The man's face clouded. 'You think you're a cut above us because you've been on bloody television, don't you?' he said, his accent immediately identifying him as an Ulsterman. 'I'm the stage manager, so I am.'

I grew up in a tough neighbourhood where ladies didn't go out after dark and policemen patrolled the streets in twos. I've met some unsavoury characters in my time and I'm afraid of no one, but the look in that man's eyes sent a chill down my spine.

Roland stepped in quickly. 'I don't know what I'd do without our Mr Dolan,' he said with a patronising smile. The Irishman sniffed and moved farther down the bar.

'You will have to excuse him,' Roland continued. 'He's rather wary of strangers, which is understandable I suppose.' He moved closer and lowered his voice. 'You'll hear it from the others so I might as well tell you myself. He's been in prison.' I must have looked shocked because he added quickly, 'Don't worry, dear boy. His crimes were purely political, something to do with him being a member of an illegal organisation, the IRA or the UDA, I'm not sure which, and quite frankly I don't care. This is his second season with us — and I meant it when I said I don't know what I'd do without him. He's a brilliant organiser and a master in the art of procurement — and you were quite right about his trade. He worked for a London firm of builders before he came to us, the people that converted Arthur's stables. Dolan came with them to do the electrical wiring and didn't go back.'

He was about to say more when Marcia called him over to confirm a point in her conversation with Melanie. This developed into a noisy argument between the two, which left the girl standing on the sidelines looking mildly embarrassed. I beckoned her over.

'I found an album of Ronnie's photographs in my room.' I said, raising my voice to be heard over the Pembroke's vociferous dialogue. I noticed that Arthur was hovering at my side. He showed me a bottle of wine and asked if he should put it on my bill. I shook my head and pointed to Roland.

'Ronnie's portfolio? Melanie said incredulously. He would never have left *that* behind.'

'That's what I thought,' I replied. 'But it had slipped behind the spare blankets in the wardrobe. You said he left in rather a hurry, I suppose he must have overlooked it.'

'I'd love to look through it,' she said

40

excitedly. 'He took a lot of pictures at the dress rehearsal that I haven't seen yet.'

Arthur began pouring the wine for the Pembrokes whose conversation had now become quite animated. I took Melanie's arm and steered her towards the door. From the corner of my eye I saw the landlord lean forward and speak to Roland who made a big show of fumbling for his wallet.

'I'm sure that young man said he was in the chair, didn't he m'dear?' I heard him say as we slipped out.

Melanie sat on my bed flipping though the album until she got to the pages containing the *Waiting On The Bridge* pictures.

'Here's one of everybody,' she said excitedly. I looked over her shoulder. It was a shot of the whole cast including the backstage staff, Mayberry, Dolan and Brian Chambers. I asked who had taken it.

'Oh, Ronnie of course, he has one of those clever timing things on his camera. He just poses everyone leaving a space for himself, sets the clock running and then runs and joins the group. It's easy.'

★ ★ ★

The next picture was of a girl in a gossamer dress engaged in conversation with a rather arrogant-looking young man.

'That's you!' I shouted, jabbing at it with my finger. Without the heavy spectacles and the worried expression Melanie was quite a looker.

'Yes, with Tarquin,' she said coldly.

'You're in the play!'

Behind the thick lenses her eyes lit up and a smile tugged at the corners of her mouth. 'Yes!' she said proudly. 'I'm Melissa.'

'Then I look forward to being your lover!' She blushed and I laughed. 'On stage of course,' I said. 'Look, I'd really like to have a shower and change now, but if your offer to help with the lines is still on, what do you say to making a start after dinner?'

She nodded her head happily. The church photographs had slipped out of the envelope. She helped me to gather them up. One of them caught my eye. Ecclesiastical architecture is not something I know a lot about. The exposed beams and plaster infill of this building said Tudor to me but the rather primitive-looking, squat, castellated stone tower stuck on one end looked much older. I asked Melanie about it.

'That's St Bede's,' she said. 'It's on a little rocky peninsular that juts out into the estuary near Marshbank; just behind the Pilcher's garage . . . The tower was there long before the church. Mr Mayberry says it was built originally, not as a bell tower as it is now, but as a place where people could go for safety in the days when the Vikings raided along the coast . . . I think it makes a lovely picture, don't you?'

'It would look better in colour.'

'Yes. Ronnie thought so, too. He said he was going back to take more pictures of it for a competition in one of his photography magazines.'

'Why was Ronnie so interested in old churches?'

'He had a commission from the *Cannford Clarion* — the local weekly newspaper — to do some photographs for a series of articles on forgotten churches. Not that they are really forgotten of course, but congregations have dwindled so much over the years that it's not unusual nowadays for country vicars to look after four or five of them.'

I turned the envelope over and pointed out the scribbled name.

'Who's this Jim Murray?' I asked.

'Actually it's *Tim* Murray. He's the editor. Ronnie got on well with him. I've met him, he's a nice man.'

I thought it most unlikely that a provincial weekly would send Ronnie jetting off to some remote spot but I had to start somewhere and where better than with Ronnie's newspaper buddy, Tim Murray.

★ ★ ★

I didn't spend long in the shower and arrived at the bar first. Polly was serving so I ordered a half of lager and as I stood waiting for Melanie to join me I watched Arthur's daughter at work, idly wondering what it was that possessed young women to poke bits of metal through their skin. Polly's mannish shoulder line and fuzzy peach complexion suggested she had more than her fair share of male hormones but for all that I suppose she was attractive in a kinky sort of way. She obviously appealed to Ronnie — and to Benny also, by all accounts.

She suddenly turned to me. 'Benny Pilcher's honest and he's kind,' she said.

I was taken completely off guard. Had she read my mind? 'I don't doubt it,' I shot back, defensively.

'Not like that Ronnie. Only after one thing, his sort is. I was taken in by the likes of him once but I was only a kid then and I knew no better. They say he's friend of yours. Well, I have to speak as I find and I'm glad he's gone. Good riddance I say.'

There was no answer to that so I stared

into my beer. She obviously wasn't finished.

'I heard what my dad was telling you about Benny. Well, he may not be clever but he's got a heart of gold, Benny has.' She lifted my glass to wipe an imaginary spillage off the counter top. I looked up and our eyes met. 'I'll tell you the kind of person he is,' she said forcibly. 'They had an old dog up at the garage, had him years they did. The poor thing was stone deaf, almost blind and could hardly walk. Benny's dad told him to take him out on the marshes and shoot him. Said it would make a man of him and do you know what Benny did?'

I shook my head.

'He took him to the old wildfowler's hut out in the estuary and sneaked out there every day with food for the poor creature. That dog lived for months and died peaceful like without Caleb Pilcher knowing a thing about it. That's the sort of person Benny is.'

I avoided further hostile eye contact by reading the blackboard on the wall behind her. This listed the snacks that could be ordered at the bar, sandwiches, salads and the like, but the idea of cold food and frosty looks from Polly didn't appeal. When Melanie eventually turned up I took her through to the dining room which proved to be a large room with tables of various sizes spaced well apart, no doubt to allow for Arthur's ample girth. Melanie and I sat by a window and watched our host at work. He was clearly in his element, clearing and re-setting tables, taking orders and serving food, and all the time keeping up a flow of small talk and good-natured banter with his customers.

We were quickly spotted and he bore down on us grinning broadly. I explained that whilst we were hungry we were limited for time.

'Having a night on the town are we, sir?'

I was busily studying the menu and replied without thinking. 'No, we're rather keen to get back to my room.'

'I see, sir,' he said, pointedly.

Melanie shot him a withering look over her glasses. 'I'm helping Mr Carter to learn his lines.'

'Yes, of course you are, Miss.'

I ordered the roast chicken and a bottle of chilled Chardonnay. They were both delightful, and so was Melanie, once she allowed herself to relax. We skipped dessert and went back to my room for coffee and made a start on the script with Melanie reading the other parts and periodically testing me on what I'd learned.

Taking the genial Arthur at his word, ('If there's anything you want, sir, anything at all, just ask') and to keep us awake, I ordered a

46

pot of coffee to be delivered to my room at hourly intervals. Even so, Melanie had had enough around midnight and retired to her room, but I managed to keep going. It had turned two o'clock in the morning when I finally called it a day.

3

No matter what time I go to bed I always wake up early and when I wake up I get up. So it was no surprise to find that I was the only member of our little troupe at breakfast the following morning. No sooner was I seated than Arthur came bustling in, the customary wide smile on his face. He really was the perfect front of house person. Bonhomie seemed to come naturally to him, even this early in the morning. I wondered what Mrs Arthur was like as I'd never seen her. I imagined her to be fat and jovial like him and possibly smelling of chip fat.

'What'll it be, Mr Carter?' he asked, setting down my tea and toast. 'The 'Full Monty' is it?'

I guessed this was his jokey way of referring to a full English breakfast. His smile was infectious and I returned it with an eager nod of my head. As he was about to go I asked if he had seen Ronnie on the day he left.

'No, I didn't,' he said, 'He rarely showed up for breakfast, always off somewhere on that motorbike of his. He left his key on the bar as usual and it wasn't until our Poll went

48

to do his room that we found he'd cleared all his stuff out.'

After plodding through a mountain of bacon, egg, sausage, mushrooms, tomatoes, black pudding and baked beans I staggered back to my room, grabbed the local telephone directory and dialled the number listed for the *Cannford Clarion*. There was no reply.

My conscience prompted me to call Sam. He was at home and having *his* breakfast, which, knowing Sam, was more likely to be bagels and coffee.

'I was going to ring you from the office,' he said with his mouth full. 'Deejay Associates are casting for a series of TV ads. Just four are planned initially, but if all goes well, who knows? Remember how those great *Oxo* commercials just went on and on? Anyway, Deejay are looking for someone to play the bad guy, the one who doesn't use the product, and would you believe they actually approached *me*? When I said you were available, they flipped.'

'Sorry, Sam, I can't do it.'

There was a choking noise at the other end. 'What d'you mean, you can't do it? I'm talking principle character here, primetime television . . . Listen, I'll call you back when I get to the office. It'll give you time to think

. . . They like your work, Nick, the job's yours, my boy.'

'Did you get a call from a Melanie Naylor?'

A pause. 'Yeah, she's the ASM for the Pembroke Players, right? She called me Monday. Said Ronnie Simmons had walked out on them. Wanted to know if I'd heard from him.'

'And have you?'

'I hadn't then and I haven't now . . . Listen, Nick, I know he's a friend of yours, but when you see him tell him he'd better have a damn good reason or find himself another agent. You can't do that sort of thing in our business, you know that . . . Be back to you in an hour, okay?'

'The answer will still be 'no', Sam. Roland Pembroke has asked me to fill in for Ronnie and I've agreed.'

Another splutter. 'You're kidding me,' he gasped.

'Sorry, Sam. I owe it to Ronnie. There's something fishy about him going awol and I'm going to find out what it is.'

'But you're a television celebrity now, Nick, you've got to keep that ugly mug of yours in front of the viewers . . . '

I interrupted him. 'Got to go, Sam, I'm late for rehearsal,' I said and switched off.

Cannford is not Fleet Street, so it was

turned eight thirty before someone finally answered at the *Clarion*. I asked how soon I could see Mr Murray and after a lengthy wait I was told he would see me at midday.

* * *

When I got to the village hall, Roland Pembroke was already there, as was Eddie Dolan, Brian Chambers and the enigmatic George Mayberry.

I'd spotted Mayberry in dining room at *The Grapes* the previous evening when Melanie and I went in for dinner. He was sitting on his own and I suggested we join him, fellow member of the company and all that, but she steered me away.

'He's a lovely man, a real gentleman,' she said. 'But he doesn't like company. Mr Roland says he was once a top theatrical designer. Now he paints our scenery and does odd jobs. His wife left him and he took to drink, or the other way round. Sad isn't it?'

The rehearsal went reasonably well and although I carried my script with me for security I surprised myself by only having to refer to it a couple of times. Pembroke junior failed to put in an appearance but it wasn't a problem as Brian Chambers was only too pleased to read his part. The boy was good and I was impressed. His performance, although understandably over-enthusiastic, was quite convincing. No one said anything about Tarquin's absence, which led me to suspect that he was in a habit of cutting rehearsals.

'I want you word perfect tonight, dear boy,' Roland shouted to me across the stage 'I don't allow my actors to read from the script in front of an audience . . . You'll have people asking for their money back, and that will never do!'

He couldn't have been all that displeased with his new recruit, as he had no objection to me ducking out of lunch at the sixth-form college.

'We start the class promptly at two,' he said sternly, and as I turned to go, he added with a puzzled frown, 'I did tell you the meal is free of charge, did I not?'

'Nick.' I felt a tug at my sleeve; it was Brian Chambers. 'The college is on the Cannford road out of Marshbank,' he said, with a matey grin. He was another Ronnie for shadowing me. He'd been bombarding me all morning with questions about the TV stars I'd worked with. I was grateful that he was a local lad who lived at home; at least I should get some peace in the evenings.

'Marshbank,' I said, thinking aloud. 'Isn't

that where the Pilcher's have their garage?'

'Yeah, only they don't have nothing to do with cars now. They don't even sell petrol.'

'Arthur at *The Grapes* tells me they're into transport and antiques.'

He chuckled. 'Which is a posh way of saying they shifts flowerpots and cart junk from old houses.'

He was a likeable young rogue who reminded me very much of myself at his age.

'I happen to know there's a lot of money to be made in junk from old houses,' I said.

'So Mr Dolan says. I heard him telling Arthur he got over five hundred for an old cupboard he'd bought for ten quid. He said it hadn't reached its reserve and the owner didn't want to sell but his mate had a quiet word, know what I mean?'

I imagine Eddie Dolan's mates could be quite persuasive.

★ ★ ★

After the chocolate-box quaintness of Chapel Heath, Marshbank was dull and depressing. At some time in its recent history someone in the county planning department must have decided it was the ideal spot to build an overspill housing estate. I drove past row after row of similarly boring, pebble-dashed houses, the only differences in them being the positioning of the satellite dish and the number of cars parked outside. Here and there some of the original village cottages remained but they too seemed to be affected by the overall drabness of the place and looked more rundown than picturesque. The Players had performed here last week at a church hall, so there must be one of those somewhere but I didn't see it. I eventually came to a ramshackle garage at the crossroads with a faded sign over the door, upon which the words, 'Pilcher & Son', could just about be made out. I pulled in on the weed-covered forecourt.

The designation 'garage' was too up-market for what was in fact a solitary, rusty petrol pump and a small, dilapidated, single-storey, wooden hut. The building had a veranda, which gave it the appearance of an old cricket pavilion. Its windows were boarded up and on either side of the door were two outdated enamelled signs screwed to the clapboard wall, one promoting Castrol Motor Oil and the other Firestone Tyres. The whole scene was one of neglect and decay and I felt that if Mr Pilcher or his son should ever decide to sell they'd probably get more for the antique petrol pump and the old signs than they would for the entire lot.

The door of the pavilion was locked. I banged on it for a while without success and then I wandered around the back to see if there was another way in. There wasn't.

The area behind the little wooden building was littered with heaps of worn tyres, old exhaust pipes and other junk left over from the garage's motoring past. A strong wind blew from the open marshland. It whistled through the rusting hulks of several ancient cars bringing with it the smell of rotting seaweed and low-tide mud. In the distance, flocks of gulls filled the air with their raucous cries as they foraged for food on the mudflats, laid bare by the outgoing tide.

The tower looked temptingly close and I felt sure there must be a way to it from the yard but it would have meant crossing the marsh, which I decided was something best left to those who know what they're doing. I went back to the car, and keeping the tower in sight, I drove slowly along the main road looking for a turning. After about half a mile I came to small group of shabby cottages, a rather incongruous Chinese chip shop, a bus shelter and a wide gate with a sign that read, 'St Bede's Church — Private Road.' I let myself in and drove along the single-track road beyond the gate for about half a mile. For a barely used country lane its surface was surprisingly good, which was just as well as my low-slung Mini doesn't take kindly to deep wheel ruts.

St Bede's was just as it appeared in Ronnie's photograph. I parked on an area of gravel by the side of the church. The old boundary wall had crumbled away and in places a chestnut-paling fence was now all that prevented the unwary from wandering over the edge of the plateau. There was one other car standing there, a black Rover that was quite old but well cared for. I stepped out of the Mini and back into the strong wind blowing in from the estuary. From this vantage point the far bank was clearly visible and as the tide was now completely out, all that remained of the river was a narrow strip of water running through the middle of a vast expanse of undulating mud.

Inside the little church it was cool and still, its smell reminding me of the undertakers shop where, as kids, we used to dare each other to put our heads round the door and shout, 'have you got any empty boxes?' I suppose it was all that wood, the pews, the choir stalls and the altar screen. It was actually quite pleasant inside, the sunshine streaming in through the big, stained glass windows and the plain, whitewashed walls making it very light and bright. Cheery bunches of fresh flowers added colour, provided no doubt by the ladies of the parish, as I couldn't imagine the Pilchers doing that sort of thing. A touch of curiosity was a large Stars and Stripes flag standing next to the high altar. (I was to find out later that it was to commemorate the hundreds of American servicemen who were camped nearby in World War Two — and who still come back as tourists.)

The church had been built abutting the tower and behind a big, old, stone font was what appeared to be its original arched entrance. An iron grille now screened it off, a large padlock holding it securely fastened.

'There are postcards if you want, twenty-five pence each. Put the money in the collection box, that ugly metal thing screwed to the back pew. We had a nice wooden one once but it was stolen; can you believe that?'

The voice was female, authoritarian but not unfriendly. I turned towards the speaker and saw an elderly and quite formidable looking woman in a dark blue dress with a white collar, rather like a hospital matron. She carried a large bunch of cut flowers.

'There is also a short history of St Bede's, and that's a pound. It has a chapter on the Second World War if you are interested. General Patton once read the lesson here.'

She looked at me quizzically. 'Are you American?'

I shook my head. How refreshing it was to be unrecognised. I could appreciate the old lady not being a fan of *Brooklands*, and at Marshbank, Ronnie had played Seth Cartwright.

'St Bede's is a lovely old church, isn't it?' she continued. 'It was built in the late fourteenth century you know — the tower is *much* older, of course. We don't have any bell ringers now, in fact we keep the tower locked because it's not safe for visitors.'

'It doesn't look as though it's going to fall down.'

She laughed at that. 'No. That's not likely. It's to stop people going down into the vault.'

'The vault?'

'Oh, yes, a large chamber carved out of the natural rock, some say it was there before the tower. After St Bede's was built it was used as a tomb for the more affluent members of the parish. I believe there are still coffins down there, if you like that sort of thing. Personally I find it rather macabre. Anyway, we don't want visitors falling down the steps do we? I don't have a key, so if you want to go down you must ask Mr Pilcher.'

'It seems strange to build a church in such an isolated place.'

She smiled patronizingly. 'The farms in the

parish were big employers of labour once — of course it's all done by machine now — and there used to be quite a busy little port here until the estuary silted up.'

I felt obliged to purchase a copy of the guidebook and several postcards. I thought I'd send one to Auntie Marjorie; she'd like that. The beauty of a postcard is you can pen a greeting without having to go into a lot of detail.

The flower arranger escorted me off the premises, standing protectively in the doorway and watching me as I walked back to the car park. I caught sight of Caleb Pilcher in the churchyard behind me having, no doubt, used the shortcut across the mudflats that I felt sure existed. As I had no particular desire to meet him I slipped into my car and drove away.

★ ★ ★

The road to Cannford from Marshbank proved to be wider, cleaner, faster and altogether better than the one I'd used the previous day. Young Brian Chambers was right in that it went past the college, which was a large red-brick structure with a classical, columned portico. It looked pre-war, probably built in the thirties as a grammar school but now the graffiti on its walls and the portable classrooms on its playing field proclaimed it a truly twenty-first century educational establishment.

I still had time to kill before I was due at Tim Murray's office so I drove on into Cannford with the idea of finding somewhere to stop for a coffee. I found the police station first so, acting on impulse, I parked the car outside and went in.

Being on television you get used to people giving you a double take and a puzzled, I-know-you-from-somewhere, look. This time it was the police sergeant behind the counter but, unlike the little old ladies in the supermarket, his stare was undeniably hostile. I could almost see the wheels going round in his brain as he mentally flipped through the current wanted posters. I gave him my name, said I was from the Pembroke Players and that I would like to know what they were doing to trace the whereabouts of Ronnie Simmons. He told me to wait.

He was gone a long time. I had just reached the conclusion that he must be outside checking the date on my car's tax disk when he reappeared.

'The inspector wants to see you. This way.'

I was impressed, an inspector no less! I followed his broad uniformed back along a corridor between rows of offices created by steel and glass partitions until eventually he stopped at one of the doors and gave it a respectful tap. 'Come!' said a voice from within. The sergeant opened the door and followed me inside. He closed it behind him and stood in front of it like a sentry. All part of the training, I thought, in case 'chummy' tries to make a bolt for it.

A man in a hairy tweed jacket was sitting behind a desk shuffling papers; the top of his head shone pink through his thinning, grey hair. He looked up. 'Mr Carter?' he said. He spoke loudly and in a high voice, barking out his words out like a drill-sergeant on a parade ground.

'Yes.'

'My name's DI Crabbe.'

I suddenly had a vision of a priest with a tiny babe in his arms saying, 'I baptise thee, 'Dee-eye'.' I smothered a grin; the Detective Inspector didn't look the type who could take a joke. His manner matched his bristly moustache. He was older than I expected with a large, fleshy nose and almost colourless grey eyes that he fixed on me with a penetrating stare.

'You are something to do with the Pembroke Players?' he said, accusingly.

'Yes, I've just joined them . . . I'm here about Ronnie Simmons. He was an actor

61

with the company but he left them almost a week ago without telling anyone where he was going. They contacted the hospitals in case he'd had an accident or something — and the police. I wondered if you'd had any luck tracing him.'

He seemed a bit put out. 'You've not been with the company long then?'

'This is my second day.'

He expelled his breath in one long drawn-out puff. 'Do the Pembroke Players wish to register an official complaint against this person?'

'Of course not!'

The inspector went back to his paperwork. 'Unless your Mr Simmons has gone off with the takings or something like that, it's not a matter for the police,' he said. 'Walking out on one's job is not a crime, Mr Carter, it happens all the time . . . Now, if you'll excuse me I've a lot to do.'

Feeling a touch on my arm, I turned around. My escort had the door open. He jerked his head in the direction of the corridor leaving me in no doubt that the interview was over.

I was determined to get something out of my visit so when we got back to the foyer I asked the sergeant for directions to the offices of the *Cannford Clarion*.

* ★ ★

The headquarters of the local newspaper proved to be a featureless, flat-roofed building wedged between a cardboard-box factory and a lingerie manufacturer on a dreary industrial estate just off the wide, concrete ring road that bypasses the ancient market town.

The tiny entrance lobby was cold and smelled of mildew. It was meagrely furnished with one tubular metal chair and a small Formica-topped table. A few back copies of the *Clarion* lay on its grubby, coffee-ringed surface along with a dirty ashtray and a scattering of brochures and business cards left by a succession of frustrated salesmen who had failed to gain an interview.

In one wall there was a glass-panelled door marked 'private' and a sliding window in another. At the side of the window was a bell push with a notice that read, 'Please ring for attention'. So I did.

The reeded-glass panel slid back with a terrifying crash and I found myself eye-to-eye with a severe looking female of the none-shall-pass variety. Giving her the friendliest smile I could summon up, I told her my name and asked for Mr Murray.

I didn't have long to wait before the door rattled open to reveal a smallish man with silver-grey hair that was cut very close to his head, giving it the appearance of a fuzzy tennis ball. Old-fashioned, steel-framed glasses were balanced on a thread-veined nose. He was his in shirtsleeves with his waistcoat unbuttoned. He held out his hand. 'Tim Murray,' he announced cheerfully. He was a Scot, (from Aberdeen, I was to learn later). 'Something about Ronnie Simmons, is that right?'

I said it was.

'Sorry I couldn't speak to you when you rang this morning,' he said, 'but I was still on my way here. It *was* a bit early.'

I was puzzled. 'But your switchboard operator told me you said you'd see me today at midday?'

'She called me on my mobile.' He chuckled. 'She's the only one I trust with the number. If I gave it to every Tom, Dick and Harry I wouldn't have a moment's peace. I'd left her a message saying I wanted to speak to Ronnie, so when you rang and mentioned his name she used her initiative and called me.'

He stopped, and stared at me, quizzically.

Here it comes, I thought.

'Just a wee minute. Aren't you that chap in *Brooklands?*'

I nodded.

'What are you doing in this part of the

world? Shouldn't you be up in Manchester, in Granadaland?'

'Not any more. Watch the next few episodes and you'll see why.'

His eyes lit up. 'Are you doing something down here then, opening a supermarket or something?'

'As a matter of fact I joined the Pembroke Players yesterday.'

The look on his face was priceless. 'Forgive me for being blunt,' he said, 'but aren't you a bit out of their league?'

'I'm doing it because Ronnie walked out on the Players.' (Well, I was hardly going to say I was conned into it, was I?) 'I don't know how well you knew Ronnie, but it's not like him to do something like that.'

'Indeed it's not,' he said, stroking his chin thoughtfully. 'If you don't mind me asking. What is Ronnie to you?'

'A friend.'

'And you feel responsible for him?'

'No I don't. I came here at the request of his sister; she was worried about him. I arrived to find a theatrical company struggling to keep afloat because Ronnie had left them in the lurch. So, as I'm between engagements, I said I'd stand in for him until they find a permanent replacement.'

He bustled me through the door into a

large office where a dozen or so assorted girls, women and men sat talking into telephones or tapping at computer keyboards, or both, all with their eyes glued to the monitor screens in front of them.

'Ella!' he called.

One of the women looked up. Her jet-black hair was bobbed and cut with a severe fringe. She wore tiny, blue-lensed, John Lennon glasses and long, dangling, pink-plastic earrings. Tim Murray called her over.

'This is Ella Thompson, who writes our showbiz column,' he said. 'Ella, this is Nick Carter.'

'Oh, I *know* who this is,' she said with enthusiasm. 'Mr Carter, there's talk of your ex-wife's show going to Broadway. Do you have a comment?'

'If it happens, I'm pleased for her. She deserves it. She has great talent.' I pulled Tim Murray to one side. 'I came here to talk about Ronnie Simmons not my ex,' I whispered out of the corner of my mouth.

'Yes, yes, of course,' he said with a big smile. 'We'll go to my office . . . You don't mind if Ella comes do you? She's a big fan of yours you know.'

He led the way to a small cubby-hole that was just big enough for two more of those tubular-steel chairs (someone at the *Clarion* must have bought a job lot) and a metal desk — the top of which was almost completely filled with telephones and all the computer apparatus that seems to be obligatory in offices nowadays. The walls of the room were painted in white matt emulsion, the only decoration being an out of date Pirelli calendar, which Murray no doubt kept pinned up for its artistic merit.

He squeezed himself into a swivel chair behind the desk. 'Mr Carter is with the Pembroke Players,' he said to Ella. The columnist's face registered surprise and interest in rapid succession. She made no reply though, seemingly content, for the moment, to take notes.

'Are you staying at *The Grapes* in Chapel Heath?' he asked.

'Yes, as a matter of fact I'm in Ronnie's old room, I've taken his place in the company.'

He stroked his chin and stared at me. 'Tell me, where do *they* think he's gone?'

'One theory is that he's been sent on a job by a newspaper.'

'Well it's not the *Clarion*.'

'I had rather hoped you were going to solve the mystery by telling me you've sent him chasing off to the other side of the world.'

'We once sent a reporter to Colchester,' he replied, winking at Ella. 'But seriously, if

Ronnie's gone somewhere for a newspaper it would more likely be one of the nationals.'

'Is he up to their standard?'

'You'd better believe it!' he said. 'That young man could earn big money with his camera. He took some pictures for a feature we're running at the moment.' Murray scratched his round, grey head. 'I offered to send his cheque to *The Grapes* but he said he'd call and pick it up. Odd that he went off without it . . . Especially after calling to say he had a story for me.'

'You spoke to him? When was that?'

'Friday night, and I didn't actually speak to him. I was out at a lodge meeting and you know how those things go on. He called my home and left a message. He sounded keyed up, you know, speaking in an excited whisper. He said he was on to something really big and couldn't wait to see me.'

'But you didn't?'

'No, I tried phoning him back the following morning but I got no answer from his mobile and the people at the pub said he'd gone out. They said later that he'd left.'

He was lost in thought for a moment and then he slapped the top of his desk. 'I'll tell you what we'll do,' he said. 'We'll use the *Clarion* to track him down . . . Ella, write a piece on Ronnie Simmons. Say he left the touring company in the lurch.' He turned to me and smiled. 'Which is completely out of character.'

I nodded and smiled back.

Murray continued: 'And say his friend and TV star, Nick Carter, *Brooklands*' 'Nasty' Ned, has stepped in to save the day,' Say the *Clarion* is anxious to contact him . . . Like the idea?'

I did and I said so.

'Have you a recent photo of him?'

'Yes, back at the pub.'

He leaned back in his chair. 'There's one condition.'

'What's that?'

'You give Ella an interview.'

I shrugged my shoulders and nodded. The publicity would be good for the Players. 'So long as I get to see the copy before it's printed,' I said. 'You've no idea the problems I've had with reporters in the past.'

'You'll have no trouble with the *Clarion*, laddie. We only print the truth.'

That's what they all say, I thought, but we shook hands on it and they both came to the small entrance lobby to see me off. 'Don't forget that photograph!' Murray called after me as I left the building.

4

Space was obviously at a premium at the sixth-form college. A small, red, two-seater was just going in through the gates. I followed it to an asphalted area, which, judging by the faded lines on its surface had once been a netball court. Roland Pembroke's big old Jaguar was there, as was Eddie Dolan's Volvo. The little red sports car pulled in alongside them.

Hardly had it stopped before a group of young people, who I assumed to be students, descended on it, jostling each other to get to the driver. They were all very tall, as kids are these days. There was obviously no college uniform as such, but all the males in this noisy throng were dressed the same in wide, baggy trousers with woolly hats pulled down over their ears and the females were all bare midriffs and short skirts, their long legs in black tights. Most of the boys had backpacks slung on their shoulders and a few of the girls were carrying hockey sticks.

The driver got out of the car. I recognised the haughty-looking young man from Ronnie's photographs as Tarquin Pembroke. He opened a briefcase and began passing things out to the assembled throng. Publicity handouts, I wondered? He looked the sort.

Leaving him to the adoration of his fans I went into the college, passing George Mayberry who was lolling against the wall writing something in a small red notebook, a curl of smoke from the cigarette in his mouth causing him to screw up one eye. He looked up and nodded a greeting as I passed.

Guided once again by Pembroke senior's honeyed tones I found my way to the hall where there must have been another thirty or so sixth-formers, just like the ones outside, more baggy trousers, more woolly hats, and more long legs in black tights.

Marcia, in a flowing dress that wouldn't have looked out of place at a royal garden party, was in a corner with one group and Melanie, wearing her usual baggy cardigan and tweed skirt, another. Up on the stage I spotted Eddie Dolan doing something in the wings and, standing centre-stage, wearing a white shirt with huge puffy-sleeves (which surely must have come out of a props basket) and a red neckerchief carefully knotted at his throat, stood Roland, loudly holding forth to a group of suitably mesmerised youngsters.

He spotted me. 'Carter! How's your Shakespeare?' he shouted.

The talking stopped and all heads turned in my direction. Was he was trying to make me look foolish? Perhaps he was getting his own back for the incident of the wine last night.

'I can just about remember King Henry's speech at Agincourt,' I said. This seemed to surprise him and he came forward onto the apron to peer at me over the footlights, one eyebrow raised quizzically. Then, stepping back, he drew himself up and let rip with, 'And gentlemen in England now a-bed shall think themselves accursed they were not here, and hold their manhood cheap . . .'

He came forward again and looked down at me, a wicked smile on his handsome face.

My words may not have been so beautifully rounded but they certainly matched his in volume. 'While any speaks, that fought with us on Saint Crispin's day!' I roared.

There was a deathly hush. The kids were staring at me, open-mouthed. Then one of the girls yelled that I was 'Nasty' Ned from *Brooklands* and suddenly I was surrounded by a gaggle of excited youngsters all thrusting pieces of paper at me for my autograph.

Roland forced a thin smile. 'Bravo,' he said reluctantly. Then in a voice that everyone could hear, added, 'But this merry group have chosen the Scottish play. You wouldn't believe how many pretty girls wanted to be one of the witches.'

I heard someone come through the door behind me and I turned expecting to see either Tarquin or Mayberry, but I was wrong.

At first I thought was it was Caleb Pilcher but then I realised I must be looking at his son, Benny.

The younger Pilcher had inherited his father's build and the same tousled, sandy hair, he even wore similar brown overalls but there was none of Caleb's flinty hardness about him. His mouth was weak with a slack, drooling lower lip and he seemed nervous and unsure of himself.

He stood by the door twisting his cap in his hands. 'I've come for the chairs,' he announced to no one in particular.

Eddie Dolan's shaven head appeared around the tabs. 'I've arranged to borrow fifty chairs from the college for a couple of days, boss. Those at Chapel Heath are bloody awful, you said so yourself.'

Roland Pembroke was visibly irritated by this unscheduled interruption. 'Yes, er, well done, Dolan,' he said grudgingly. 'Carter! Get some of these strapping young men here to help you load them on the van. Shouldn't take you long.'

As I've said before, I've done my share of

scene shifting and this wouldn't be the first time I'd moved auditorium chairs.

'I need a few strong lads!' I shouted and I wasn't surprised when there wasn't an immediate rush of volunteers. 'Come on, girls, who are the real tough guys here, who's your favourite hunk?'

That did the trick. The two groups in the hall merged into one, the boys, all feigning reluctance, were surrounded by giggling girls and one by one, candidates were either pushed or dragged forward until I had eight sturdy young males standing before me, all trying to appear nonchalant but obviously delighted to have been selected.

I counted out fifty chairs and began stacking them in threes. My 'volunteers' quickly caught on and mucked in but the younger Pilcher made no effort to help. He hadn't moved from his position just inside the door. He just stood there with a silly smile on his face gazing at something — or someone. Who *was* he looking at? It wasn't one of the college girls. They were all bunched together in one tittering, twittering group, and Marcia Fontaine had gone on the stage to talk to her husband. That only left Melanie.

I brought him back to earth by asking him if he was going to carry some chairs out to his van.

He looked confused. 'I'll open the van up,' he mumbled, pulling on his cap and walking out of the hall empty handed. Quickly grabbing a stack of chairs I went after him, calling to my team of young porters to do the same.

Benny Pilcher was still in the process of lowering the tailgate when I got outside so I left my chairs at the side of the van. When I got back with my second load, Tarquin's noisy group had turned up the volume. What had previously been nothing more than girlish squeals and giggles was now a series of loud shouts followed by screams of laughter. It was as though they were playing a game. Still holding my stack of chairs I peered around the van and saw that they were doing just that.

Tarquin and some of the boys had formed a wide circle around Benny and were playing piggy-in-the-middle with his lunch box. The rest of the group were shouting encouragement from the sidelines.

'Here! Gimme back my sandwiches!' Benny was shouting, ambling uselessly from one player to another.

Tarquin caught the box and waved it teasingly at him only to throw it over his head as he went to grab it. 'You'll have to ask your pretty Polly to make you some more, won't you,' he teased.

This set off more catcalls from the boys and howls of laughter from the girls. For a moment Benny didn't know what to do. He stopped and stood in the middle of the jeering mob wide-eyed and bewildered. I couldn't just stand there while they bullied him. I was about to intervene when he grabbed a hockey stick from one of the girls and with a loud shout rushed at Tarquin. I sprang forward and thrust the chairs in the way of a wild swipe aimed at the head of his tormentor. The force of the blow splintered the hockey stick and knocked the chairs from my grasp. I stepped back with my hands stinging. Tarquin, who had come within an inch of having his head bashed in, didn't look in the least bothered and was still grinning sardonically. Benny stood panting with his head bowed and his arms hanging limply by his side. I snatched the lunchbox and thrust it at him. The big simpleton took it and walked away, totally bemused. There were shouts of 'Hey!' and 'Spoilsport!' but having the appearance of a pugilist does tend to deter people from arguing with you.

'I say, you're Nick Carter aren't you?' Tarquin said in a languid, public school drawl.

I nodded.

'You'd better trot along with your Neanderthal friend. You make a good pair.' With a loud braying laugh he turned to his audience for approbation.

I'm all for giving a chap the benefit of the doubt. In Ronnie's photographs Tarquin Pembroke had looked a spoilt, arrogant prig but now having met him in the flesh I'd say he was all that, and more. I snatched his briefcase and threw it to one of the lads. A new howl went up.

'Let's see how you like being piggy-in-middle,' I said and walked away.

★   ★   ★

'Ah, there you are, Carter,' Roland shouted as I re-entered the hall. 'Come along now, there's work to be done . . . See if you have any budding Scottish noblemen among your furniture removers. We need a MacDuff and a Lennox . . . Melanie! Give Nicholas a script, will you?'

Melanie left her group and hurried over. 'Will you keep an eye on my class for a moment, Nick? There's a kettle backstage, I'll make us all a nice cup of tea.' With that, she thrust her script into my hand and scurried away.

As she ran up the short flight of steps to the stage, I couldn't help noticing that she had very trim ankles. I wasn't the only one gazing at her admiringly. Benny Pilcher was back at the door, standing there with that same daft grin on his face. Eddie Dolan was talking to him but I doubted if he was listening.

When Melanie came back with the tea I looked over to see if Benny was still watching. He was.

'I think that chap fancies you,' I said.

She blushed, 'Who, Benny? What rubbish! He's only got eyes for Polly at *The Grapes*.'

'But his face lights up whenever he sees you.'

'That's because I got him out of a spot of bother last week.'

We sat on the steps to the stage with the tea and she told me all about it.

'We hire everything from a stage supplies company near Victoria Station, our scenery, props, lights, everything,' she said. 'They deliver it to our first location and pick it up from the last, but in between we have someone local to move it from place to place.'

'Benny Pilcher.'

'Right! Last Sunday, when we came here from Marshbank, we set the stage and everything looked fine. Then, just as Mr Dolan was telling Benny he could go, Mr Roland discovered we didn't have the mattress.'

'Mattress?'

'For the sickbed scene when Sir William visits Seth. You know, it's played in front of the curtain.'

'Yes, of course,' I said, although I didn't. We hadn't used any props that morning at rehearsal. I'd played the scene stretched out on the stage.

'And where was it?' I asked.

She struggled not to laugh. 'Benny had dumped it in a skip!'

'He'd done what!'

'Well, he's not the brightest of people is he? And it *is* just a big old sack stuffed with straw, after all. Well, the place was in an uproar. Mr Roland, who was already upset about having to cancel Saturday's show, was telling Mr Dolan to find another removals firm and Mr Dolan was arguing that it was impossible to get someone who would work on Sundays and Benny was pleading with them both to be given another chance. Then, Benny turned to me saying his father would kill him if he lost the contract. He had tears in his eyes and I felt so sorry for him that I took the blame saying I'd forgotten to give him a checklist. I got a roasting from Mr Roland who told me never to let it happen again — and Benny has been my number one fan ever since.'

That evening we played to a packed house, which was quite something considering the weather wasn't all that good and there was a premier league football match on television. I'm surprised people still turn out to see a hoary old piece like *Waiting On The Bridge*. Amateur theatrical groups have done it to death and the film version (always referred to as 'a classic of the cinema') is repeated *ad nauseam* on television. Melanie and Brian had been round the village pasting stickers with, 'NOW STARRING BROOKLANDS' NICK CARTER', on all the playbills but I refuse to believe I've got that much drawing power.

In spite of the play's familiarity, Roland Pembroke maintained theatrical tradition by having a brief synopsis printed in the programme. 'An enthralling story of love and conflict of class' is how he describes the piece in which Seth Cartwright, (originally Ronnie's part and now played by me) a common mill hand, is in love with his employer's daughter Melissa (played by Melanie). Roland is Melissa's father, the cotton baron, Sir William Haslett, and Marcia, his wife, Lady Haslett. Tarquin Pembroke is the preferred suitor, The Honourable Reginald Finchingfield.

I like Seth Cartwright. He's loud and he's coarse. He spits, he swears and he wipes his nose on his cuff. He's about as far removed from Ronnie's rather Byronic persona as you could get and I take my hat off to him for tackling the job. Makeup would help, of course. It's amazing what a dab of Leichner and a shaggy wig can do.

I have to admit that when I arrived at the village hall I did wonder what the hell I was doing there, but once the performance was underway I thoroughly enjoyed playing the rough, tough mill worker and to have an actor of Roland Pembroke's experience as Seth's adversary proved to be sheer delight.

Marcia Fontaine looked elegant, overacted shamelessly and absolutely revelled in her part, whereas her son, although equally elegant, was quite the opposite. Tarquin behaved as if the whole thing was totally beneath him, and in consequence, The Honourable Reggie was surly and wooden — and had to be rescued by Mayberry (the prompter) more often than I did. Afterwards, of course, he claimed that his pauses had been intentional and introduced deliberately for dramatic effect — and we've all heard that one before, haven't we? Eddie Dolan and Brian Chambers, shared the lighting, the curtains and the incidental music between them with consummate skill, but of all those involved in the production it was Melanie who, in my opinion, stole the show. She was utterly captivating as Melissa, the magic of the footlights transforming the drab and nervous ugly duckling into a beautiful and confident swan, which made playing my scenes with her an absolute pleasure. I looked for her after the final curtain to congratulate her but she had disappeared.

It's a tradition in the theatre to have a party on stage on opening night with the actors, still in costume, being joined by friends and VIPs, especially those sponsoring the show, for a glass or two of bubbly. The company's first four performances at Chapel Heath having been cancelled made tonight opening night.

Still on a high after the show, I cheerfully allowed myself to be swept along with Roland and Marcia as they progressed through the guests. As the visiting celebrity I was in great demand and I was trying tactfully to retrieve my hand from the determined grip of a very earnest young woman from the Quentin Minnow Society, when I noticed a fresh-faced young man on the fringe bobbing up and down in an attempt to see over the heads of the people on the crowded stage. He didn't look much older than the sixth-formers we'd been working with that afternoon but this was no skateboarder in baggy pants, this chap was smartly dressed in a sports jacket and neatly pressed trousers. He even wore a tie. He caught my eye and made his way over.

'I enjoyed your performance enormously, sir,' he said. (He called me 'sir': I liked him.) He went on, 'Can you tell me where I can find Miss Melanie Naylor? She doesn't appear to be here.'

'A fan of hers, are you?' I asked.

'Rather!' he replied enthusiastically, adding quickly, 'But I'm not here for her autograph or anything like that.'

'So what *do* you want her for?'

He reached inside his jacket. 'I'm DC Partridge,' he said. 'I've got a message for her.'

I'd never seen a police warrant card before. I was flabbergasted. The lad looked barely old enough to shave.

'The sergeant said it should be delivered personally,' he continued, 'and as I was coming to see the play, I volunteered to be the messenger.'

Melanie had defied tradition and changed back into her cardigan and tweed skirt. She no doubt needed the owlish glasses and thought (quite rightly) that they wouldn't go with Melissa's costume. Detective Constable

Partridge's face fell when I produced a bespectacled and rather dowdy young woman out of the crowd. But he wasn't to be deterred from his duty, and taking out a notebook, he deftly flipped it open. (I'm intrigued by the way they do that. I'm sure it must be part of the curriculum at police training school.)

'Miss Naylor, you reported a missing person, a Ronnie Simmons.' He looked up and Melanie nodded, her knuckles white as she tightened her grip on the clipboard. Why is it we always expect policeman to bring bad news?

'Have you found him?' I asked anxiously.

'No, sir, but his motorcycle has turned up, in Cannford train station car park.'

So Ronnie had gone to London; no doubt chasing that big story he'd been on about. I was sure that once he'd got his pictures he'd be in touch, in fact he could very well be on his way back right at this minute. I couldn't wait to tell Susan . . . but what could I say, I haven't had a chance to talk to him yet because he's walked out on his job? That would only make her worry more. No, I'll give it a little longer; someone's bound to hear from him soon.

I asked the young policeman to pass on my thanks to the grumpy inspector and everyone else involved in looking for Ronnie.

'But we haven't, sir,' Partridge said, 'been looking for him, that is.' He looked boyishly embarrassed. 'The inspector told the sergeant to log Miss Naylor's report in the Occurrence Book and take no further action — and that would have been an end to the matter if it hadn't been for the motorcycle.'

'But if you weren't looking for Ronnie, how come you found his motorbike?' I asked.

'We received a complaint from the railway, sir, they said it had been in their car park for several days.' Partridge scanned his notes again. 'The address on the vehicle's registration turned out to be a bed-sit in Battersea. The police there said the landlady told them Mr Simmons had terminated his lease three months ago to go on tour, she said.'

He turned to Melanie and grinned. 'By rights we should impound the motorcycle, but the sergeant remembered your telephone call, Miss, and knowing the inspector's feelings about the matter, he thought the best thing would be for you to look after it for Mr Simmons until he turns up.'

At that moment Roland Pembroke butted in to remind us firmly but politely (the latter no doubt for Partridge's benefit), that we should be circulating among the guests.

Later, I drove Melanie back to *The Grapes*

and as we said goodnight I asked her, tongue in cheek, if she could ride a motorbike.

'No, of course not,' she said with a coy smile. 'But it's all sorted. Mr Dolan is going to get Benny Pilcher to collect it and store it at his garage.'

★ ★ ★

Eddie Dolan had arranged with Arthur for the Players to have dinner early on show nights, so having spent the afternoon mugging up on my lines, I showered and changed and at about five-thirty I went across to the dining room. George Mayberry was there, sitting alone. This time I asked if I could join him, and contrary to what Melanie had led me to believe, the old man seemed pleased to have company. I asked him if he'd heard the news about Ronnie.

'I haven't seen him lately. I do hope he's all right,' he said, and then he smiled and shook his head. 'You must forgive me but I find I tend to forget things lately. I've taken to jotting things down in a notebook — which is only a good idea if one remembers one's notebook.' Chuckling to himself, he reached into a pocket in his jacket and produced a small, dog-eared, red memo book. 'I must make a note of your name,' he said. He began to flip through the pages before closing the book with a sigh. 'There's no point in burying it amongst all these scribblings, I'll never find it when I want it.'

He turned back the front cover and looked up at me expectantly.

'Nick Carter?' I said.

'Thank you.' He carefully printed my name inside and underneath he wrote *Seth Cartwright*. 'There, now I'll always know where to find you.'

George Mayberry proved to be a most interesting dining companion. Throughout the meal he chatted away, reminiscing about his days as a stage designer and relating some very amusing and fascinating anecdotes about the legendary theatrical figures he had worked with. He told me of his love of nature and wildlife and was quite open about his drinking; saying he now only drank red wine with his evening meal, and then just one glass.

★   ★   ★

That evening we played to a full house again and, if anything, I enjoyed that last show at Chapel Heath more than the first. I now knew my lines backwards and I went out on stage full of confidence and determined to give it all I'd got. I could feel the audience responding, the laughs and gasps came in all the right places, which in turn lifted my performance. There may be glamour in being a TV star but there's nothing to compare with the thrill of working live on stage before an appreciative audience. We took four curtain calls and the punters still didn't want to go home. Some even waited outside the hall for autographs.

The following day was Sunday but it was to be no day of rest for the Players. Roland had called an early start, which was fine by me, and although I was at the village hall by eight I found Brian Chambers already there. He had all the small props already boxed up so I began to strike the set.

I uncleated a flat and let it fall forward onto the stage. Brian's face was a picture. Anyone who hasn't seen it done before is horrified but I knew from experience that it would land gently, cushioned by the air that builds up beneath it on its way down.

'Blimey!' he gasped. 'You had me worried there and no mistake.'

I liked this young eager beaver with the spotty face and spiky hair. I asked him how he had got on with Ronnie.

'We was good mates,' he said. 'He was going to change his name, did you know that?' I shook my head. 'Nah, nobody did 'cept me. He was going to call himself Ronnie Sinclair. Good innit? I'm going to have a stage name. I'm going to be Brent instead of Brian. Brent Chambers, what d'you think?'

'Did he say anything to you about going away?'

The future Brent Chambers frowned. 'Nah! Not a word.'

'Did you talk to him on the Friday night before he left?'

'Course I did.'

'What did you talk about?'

'All sort of things. He was full of this competition he wanted to go in for. He said he didn't have much time before the closing date.'

I felt I already knew the answer but I asked the question anyway. 'What was he going to photograph?'

'The old church at Marshbank. He'd taken it in black and white for the paper but he was itching to go back there with a colour camera.'

'And did he?'

'I don't know. Old Mayberry and me was there that Saturday morning but we didn't see him.'

The staid former stage designer seemed to me an unlikely companion for a young, black-clad, heavy metal fan. He read my expression and smilingly explained: 'He wanted to go and look at birds — the feathered sort,' he added with a wink. 'Mr Roland don't like him going off on his own so I said I'd go with him. I wasn't doing anything special and I like getting the old boy going on about the stage and that. He was as pleased as punch and turned up in walking boots, with a rucksack, binoculars, the lot. I took him to that old church 'cos you can see all round the estuary from there — and you can get there on the bus.'

I let him drop the next flat. 'Wow! That was awesome!' he shouted, grinning broadly.

'And there was no sign of Ronnie?'

'Nah! I even parked old Mayberry in the church so's I could have a good scout round. I wasn't gone long 'cos I didn't like leaving the old boy on his own. I was worried in case he decided to go poking about down in them vaults. Them steps can be very tricky.' He chuckled. 'I needn't have worried though. When I got back he was outside sitting on a gravestone in the churchyard, as good as gold, puffing away at one of his old fags.'

'But the gate to the vaults is kept locked.'

'Not that morning it wasn't. Benny keeps his tools there and he was working in the churchyard cutting some nettles back. I asked him if he'd seen Ronnie. He said he hadn't. He was quite narky about it.'

'Did you go down into the vaults?'

'You've got to be joking! It's real spooky down there!'

★ ★ ★

We had all the scenery down and neatly stacked by the time Benny Pilcher turned up with his van. Eddie Dolan and George Mayberry arrived shortly after, closely followed by Roland, who had waited to give Melanie a lift. There was no sign of Marcia or Tarquin. I mentioned this to Melanie.

'Tarquin is not a team player,' was all she said.

'And I suppose a delicate butterfly like Marcia would have a fit of the vapours at the thought of being asked to do anything physical,' I added cynically.

'Don't you believe it! Miss Fontaine used to be a dancer in a chorus line. You have to be really fit and as strong as a horse to do that, but she's the boss's wife, so why should she hump scenery?'

I wasn't sure I followed Melanie's logic. She went off to take charge of the boxes of props and to his credit our distinguished actor-manager rolled up his sleeves and helped us carry stuff out to the van. We loaded the borrowed chairs first as they would have to stay on the vehicle until the following day when they could be returned to the college. Roland casually detailed George Mayberry and me for this task.

I know that in small touring companies it's quite normal for everyone to muck in, and don't get me wrong, I am quite prepared to do my share, but when all is said and done I *am* an actor, not Roland Pembroke's dogsbody. I was about to voice my objections when Eddie Dolan took the wind out of my sails by volunteering to go in my place.

Roland shrugged his shoulders. 'As you wish, but keep a weather eye on old Mayberry, there's a good chap.' He turned to me and said, 'A remarkable man, George Mayberry, but his mind is going. It's a sad business.'

'Has he seen a doctor?' I asked.

'The very best, dear boy, Harley Street, no less. I took him myself, but there's nothing anyone can do.'

'It's good he's got you for a friend.'

'I wouldn't say we were friends exactly. Don't misunderstand me; I admire George. The theatre is richer for his having been part of it and I'm lucky to have him. He's an extremely talented artist, quite capable of repainting an entire set if need be — *and* he will stack chairs and sweep up after a show if I ask him to. You don't find someone like that every day.'

'He seems content with his lot.'

'Content!' Roland laughed. 'That fellow isn't content, he's grateful, so grateful I find it embarrassing sometimes.' He moved in closer, put a hand on my shoulder and lowered his voice to a conspiratorial whisper. 'George happened to notice that young Pilcher was making a detour to *The Grapes* to see his lady friend instead of going straight to our next venue. He made a note of it in that little book of his and thereafter he kept his eye on the young scamp. When it happened a second time he told me about it and I sent Dolan to have a word with Pilcher senior, we pay by the hour you see.'

'I hope he knocked something off his bill.'

'He couldn't do anything else, dear boy. We had it all, y'see, dates and times, all logged in old George's little red book. I wouldn't have been in young Pilcher's shoes that night for all the tea in China. His father has a reputation for violence, you know.' Roland sighed, smiled grimly and shook his head. 'But I made the mistake of thanking George for keeping his eyes open and now the old love has taken to watching anybody who he thinks is doing something I wouldn't approve of.'

Melanie came out to the van carrying another cardboard box full of bits and pieces. I relieved her of it and was rewarded with a smile.

'I thought we might do something together later on,' I said. 'Go into Cannford perhaps?'

She blushed and lowered her eyes. 'That would have been lovely, Nick, but I've arranged to meet Gavin.'

'Gavin?'

'Gavin Partridge. You remember, that nice young policeman.'

Well, that took me by surprise! I suppose it *was* a bit conceited of me to think Melanie would jump at the chance of going out with me but the last thing I expected was that she would already have a date lined up with someone else. And with Partridge of all people. He was a kid, for goodness sake!

'He's going to take me to the police museum,' she said excitedly, her brown eyes sparkling behind the oversize lenses. 'He says it's full of lots of interesting stuff. Old uniforms and truncheons, even photographs of local murderers.'

'Sounds like a right barrel of laughs.'

She either didn't notice my peevishness or chose to ignore it. 'Gavin enjoys his work and he's so proud to be in the CID. He's about to take his sergeants' exam, he'll be the youngest one sitting it he says. It's good for a young man to have ambition, don't you think?'

If there's one thing I hate it's a smart-arse and DC Partridge had slipped down a few notches in my estimation. I continued loading the van and when we were done I didn't offer Melanie a lift to Hobswood, our next venue, which I thought afterwards was a bit childish of me.

5

Eddie Dolan had done a skilful job in booking halls within easy reach of *The Grapes*. This meant that although we changed the show's venue weekly we didn't have to keep moving to fresh accommodation. This pleased Marcia Fontaine no end; she liked *The Grapes*.

'Compared to some of the dreadful places I've stayed in it's absolutely *marvellous* darling,' I heard her telling Melanie. 'Can you imagine having to *queue* for the bathroom? I mean, actually standing in line holding one's towel and sponge bag. Ugh!'

★   ★   ★

A Union Jack flew proudly over Hobswood Memorial Hall, a fine building that stood four-square and uncompromising on the far side of a large car park, which Brian Chambers told me doubled as a parade ground for the local army cadets. In the bright sunlight its paintwork was dazzlingly white and the glass in its windows sparkled, and waiting for us at the main entrance was a smartly turned out ex-service type in a navy-blue, brass-buttoned blazer that had a large regimental badge embroidered on the breast pocket.

I thought it best to leave the front of the building clear for Benny Pilcher's removals van so I drove onto a paved area at the side, instantly regretting my decision as I had to manoeuvre the Mini round a large, yellow waste-skip that was full to overflowing with strips of roofing felt, broken tiles and scraps of timber. I eventually parked by a flight of concrete steps that lead down to a basement door, which I assumed was the boiler room.

When I got back to the front entrance the old soldier stepped smartly forward and apologised for the builder's debris. 'Roof repairs, sir, completed last Friday. Rubbish should have gone by now, sir. I'll chase 'em up, sir.' I wouldn't have been surprised if he'd saluted me.

He unlocked the door and made a rapid tactical retreat in double-time to the pub across the street.

Our little cavalcade began to arrive. Benny backed the old van up to the entrance, the repeated thump-thump-thump from the over-amplified bass of his cab radio shattering the peace of the neighbourhood. Eddie Dolan's long Volvo came next, closely followed by a taxi, from which Marcia stepped looking cool and ultra-feminine in a flowery summer dress, white, elbow-length cotton gloves and a white, wide-brimmed hat. Just as the taxi was driving away her husband arrived in his Jaguar. She waited until he had switched off its engine before she went forward to greet him.

'*Darling!*' she called out, her arms extended dramatically, overacting as usual. The sight of Melanie in the passenger seat threw her a bit but she rallied quickly. 'I feel I can give of my best here,' she announced grandly as her husband got out of the car. Roland smiled and tilted his head. Marcia gave him a wifely peck on the cheek and carried on. 'Did you know, Roly, they actually have dressing rooms here?' she said, and with her hands clasped to her bosom, added, 'What bliss it will be not having to change in the ladies loo.'

I looked around. Everyone had stopped what they were doing and were watching the performance. I was sorely tempted to clap. Roland did, but for another reason.

'Come on people,' he shouted. 'Let's get on with it . . . Mayberry, fasten the doors back, there's a good chap . . . Brian; make sure the tabs are open, will you? And Pilcher! Will you switch that damned racket off?'

It was very warm inside the hall so by the time all the scenery was moved from the van to the stage I was perspiring freely. I had volunteered to build the set and after cleating up the first two flats so they would stand unsupported I stripped off my shirt. No one was going to see me at the back of the stage, I thought, which just goes to prove how wrong you can be.

A flat is made of painted canvas stretched on a wooden frame, very near the top of which a cord and a cleat are fitted, cord on the right, cleat on the left. To fasten the flats together, and thus build a set, the cord from the top of one flat is looped over the corresponding cleat on the one next to it, pulled tight and fastened off on other cleats lower down. The whole set is then held firm with special braces that are either screwed to the stage or kept in place by weights. Being transitory, we use weights. I enjoy building sets and I'm good at it — I've had lots of practice. I pride myself in being able to loop the cord over the cleat in one. The secret is to crack it like a whip. I slid a third flat alongside the two I'd already erected and neatly flipped the cord over the cleat. Bang! Got it in one.

'Well done!'

I spun around. Marcia was standing behind me looking as though she had just stepped out of *Vogue* magazine. I was suddenly aware of my state of undress.

'*Do* carry on,' she cooed. 'I've never seen our little set put up so efficiently.'

She was staring at me in a way I found quite disturbing. Normally, Marcia floated in a world above us mere mortals, the only time I remember her looking directly at me was at our first meeting in *The Grapes*, and then it was down her nose.

I carried on with my self-imposed task until suddenly I felt the light touch of fingertips on my back, fingertips encased in a thin cotton glove. Well, that was enough of that. There was only the bracing left to do and I could do that with my shirt on.

Fortunately, by the time Roland made an appearance I was properly dressed. 'Right, I'm off,' he said. 'I have to attend a wretched Arts Council 'do' in London this evening that I can't get out of.' He sighed deeply. 'I've no doubt it'll be an overnight job.'

Eddie Dolan was connecting up the lights behind the French windows. 'Would ye listen to that? A Champagne dinner and a night in some plush London hotel! God save us, it's a hard life but someone's got to do it, eh boss?'

Roland ignored him. 'Give the ladies a lift back to *The Grapes* when you're done, will you, Nicholas? By the way, we're doing *The*

Mad Hatter's Tea Party at the local junior school tomorrow afternoon. With your clear enunciation you would make an excellent narrator.' My expression must have said it all because he laughed. 'Don't worry about it, dear boy,' he said. 'There are no lines to learn, you read from a script. Marcia will tell you what's what, won't you m'dear?'

I arranged to meet Marcia later in *The Grapes*. Previously, all I'd had to look forward to that evening was either TV in my room or more of Arthur's garrulousness. But now it looked as though it could be quite interesting.

Arthur may talk a lot but he certainly knows how to run a pub. The smoke-filled taproom was crowded as usual, with all the tables filled and people standing two deep at the bar. Presiding over this popular and prosperous watering hole was its genial host, keeping up a flow of good-natured banter with his customers while all the time watching that people were not served out of turn or kept waiting too long.

I couldn't see Marcia; in fact there was a noticeable absence of Players — with the exception of Eddie Dolan who was closeted with Caleb Pilcher in one of the booths. Now that was a gruesome twosome if ever I saw one. The assiduous Arthur soon had me spotted.

'Miss Fontaine's in the dining room, Mr Carter,' he shouted. 'The lady said she'd wait 'till you arrived before ordering . . . Am I to take it Mr Pembroke won't be joining you, sir?'

Was it my imagination or was his smile a little broader than usual — and surely that wasn't a wink, was it?

★ ★ ★

At first I thought the only occupants of the dining room were an elderly couple who were eating their meal in total silence but then I saw Marcia sitting at a table by the window sipping a glass of red wine. She was dressed in a loose fitting trouser suit in light blue, which, in itself was quite nice, but she wore it with oversized, gold, gypsy earrings and a large, heavily fringed Spanish shawl draped over her shoulders. On seeing me, she called out, 'Nicholas! *Darling!*' in such a piercing voice that the old diners looked up from their plates, the man in bewildered surprise, the woman with a disapproving frown.

I went over to her table. 'Please call me Nick,' I said. 'I always think Nicholas makes me sound like the Tsar of Russia.' She laughed loudly at this and then, closing her eyes, she tilted her head to one side. I assumed she wanted me to kiss her cheek, which I did — and came up gasping for air! Our leading lady was always heavily perfumed, but at close quarters it was knockout!

Arthur bustled in to take our order. An open bottle of Cabernet Sauvignon stood on the table, so I plumped for the roast beef. Then Marcia surprised me by ordering fish — and a bottle of chilled Chardonnay. Well she would wouldn't she?

Also on the table was a slim, dog-eared pad of paper stapled in one corner and folded in half. Marcia slid it across to me. 'I've brought your little script for the *Alice in Wonderland* thing,' she said in her lazy drawl. 'It's such fun and you'll absolutely *adore* doing it. I'm Alice, of course, Tarquin's the March Hare and Roland's the Mad Hatter . . . and this season we've got Melanie playing the Dormouse. Now if that's not typecasting I don't know what is!' She laughed again, a sudden loud bray that caused the old gentleman to drop his dessertspoon with a clatter. I reached for the script and she took my hand. 'I just *know* you and I are going to be good friends,' she whispered, gazing at me from beneath her long false eyelashes.

Fortunately for me, Arthur arrived at that moment with our starters so she had to release her grip.

Eager to change the subject, I asked her when she had seen Ronnie last. It was the first thing that came into my head.

'Friday evening, darling, in his room.'

My Brown Windsor could wait. 'You were in his room?'

'Of course, darling. Ronnie and I were *very* good friends,' she said, biting into a finger of toast, which she had spread liberally with pâté. I waited with increasing frustration until she had finished savouring the mouthful. 'This really is *excellent* pâté,' she said at length. 'Quite the nicest I've tasted in some time. Now, where was I? Oh, yes! When did I last see Ronnie? Well, let me see. After the show we all went to the bar as per usual. When I say 'all' that is everyone except Dolan. Dolan was away somewhere — that's why we have young Brian, of course, to cover for him. Oh, and Tarquin wasn't there. My Tarquin is always in demand, by the young set you know.'

'We were all enjoying a glass of wine when that stupid boy, Benny Pilcher, came in saying Tarquin had knocked him off his bicycle. Have you ever heard anything so ridiculous? Well, that put a dampener on our little party, I can tell you. Roland tried to reason with him but he kept on about his front wheel being buckled and what was he

104

going to tell his father when he got back from Holland. Just to shut him up I said I'd pay for a taxi to take him home, I even offered him my mobile to call one. Well! You would have thought I was holding out a viper. He positively *recoiled*, darling — he has a phobia about them apparently, I didn't know that until I spoke to Polly about it later. But he went on and on, darling. It was so *boring*! Both Melanie and Ronnie left. I stuck it out for as long as I could but in the end I left Roland to it. I intended to have a soak in the bath but I changed my mind and went to Ronnie's room instead.'

'But what about Melanie?' I began and immediately wished I hadn't.

Marcia pushed her plate away and dabbed her lips with her napkin. '*Darling*!' she said with a wicked smile. 'That little mouse was simply *besotted* with the boy. Ronnie and I laughed about it a lot.'

I gulped some wine and attempted to put the conversation back on track by asking her if Ronnie had said anything about going away.

'We didn't talk very much at all.' She fluttered her eyelashes and giggled girlishly. 'The silly boy was taking pictures.'

'Did you, er, stay with Ronnie very long?'

'Oh, no, darling. I *had* to be back in my

room before Roly didn't I? .. And anyway, that girl with the ring through her nose came in and spoilt it all.'

'Polly?'

'Yes, she came to turn down the bed. It gave her quite a shock to find the two of us in it, I can tell you!' Again, Marcia's braying laugh filled the room. 'Poor girl didn't know where to turn. She gave Ronnie such a look, darling — honestly, if looks could kill!'

Ronnie seemed to have been having affairs with every female in the company, and all at the same time. I wondered what Susan would say about that!

I became aware that Marcia was still talking.

'. . . . Ronnie was a dear boy but he was no *actor* you understand, not like Roly. I met him in a travelling production of *Rose Marie*; did I tell you that? He had a lovely singing voice then — and he looked *so* handsome in his Mountie uniform.' She sat dreamy-eyed for a moment sipping her wine and then, suddenly shaking herself out of her reverie, she said, with a degree of finality, 'But that was a long time ago. He spends more time with that old soak, George Mayberry, than he does with me these days.'

Why I should feel the need to come to Roland Pembroke's defence I don't know.

'They do go back a long way,' I suggested.

'Yes, they do but Roly never moved in George Mayberry's circles and nothing pleases him more than to get the old boy talking about all the theatrical greats he's worked with. He enjoys basking in reflected glory I suppose. Me, I think George Mayberry's creepy, always writing things down in that wretched little notebook of his.'

'But your husband's had a most distinguished career.'

She brightened at that, and leaning forward, she whispered confidentially, 'Roly's being knighted in the Queen's New Year's Honours List — for services to children's theatre . . . I'll be Lady Pembroke, now isn't that grand?' She sat back, her face glowing with pleasure and an almost fanatical gleam in her eyes, which I found a little disconcerting. After savouring the thought for a moment she leaned forward and said in a stage whisper, 'But you're not to breathe a word, darling. Otherwise I'll be locked up in the Tower of London or something.'

Our main course arrived and with it so many dishes of vegetables that our host was hard pushed to find room for them all on the table. Arthur had no time for *nouvelle cuisine*. He was a believer in good, plain English food and plenty of it and I, for one, was wholeheartedly with him in that. I put the script in my pocket and Ronnie Simmons on hold for the moment and settled down to enjoy the meal — and the company of the glamorous lady sitting opposite me.

Put two actors together and in no time at all the conversation will turn to theatres and the productions they've appeared in. I discovered that, like me, Marcia loved pantomime. She went into raptures telling me about being in *Mother Goose* at the London Coliseum. I pushed my fork nonchalantly into a piece of beef and said that I too had appeared in pantomime in the West End. So what if it was the Tottenham Court Road YMCA? If that's not in the heart of London's theatreland I don't know what is!

The evening went all too quickly and I was quite sorry when the time came to say goodnight.

Later, in my room, I heard a tap at the door and thinking it was Melanie to tell me about her exciting day at the Black Museum, I opened it only to find Marcia standing there, dramatically backlit by Arthur's emergency corridor lighting. She was wearing a flimsy negligee — and very little else.

'*Darling!*' she whispered, screwing her face into what I suppose she assumed to be a sexy pout. 'I just know we're going to be *very* good friends.' Then she hiccupped noisily and I guessed she'd had a couple of stiffeners before coming to my room.

As the old saying goes, I'm not made of wood and Marcia is a very handsome woman. I was gripping the doorframe and reminding myself of my vow (and this was the boss's wife for goodness sake!) when I was saved by the Old Bill, or perhaps in this instance I should say the 'Young' Bill, for at that moment, DC Gavin Partridge arrived on the scene with Melanie.

'Good evening, Mr Carter!' he called out cheerfully. Melanie said nothing but her look spoke volumes. She hurriedly unlocked her door, briefly shook hands with her escort and disappeared into her room, leaving Partridge standing in the hallway looking somewhat bewildered.

'Miss Fontaine seems to have lost her way, constable,' I said. 'She's in number three; you pass it on the way out. Would you kindly see her to her door?'

'Yes, of course, sir,' the young innocent replied, (he called me 'sir' again. I *do* like him) and taking Marcia gently by the arm he led her away. 'A bit embarrassing for you, madam, I would think, going to the wrong room. Still, it's an easy mistake to make, they all look the same don't they?'

My would-be paramour went off with him quite happily and as they turned the corner I heard her say, 'You're a nice young man. I'm sure you and I could be very good friends.'

6

The show for the primary school kids was great fun. Roland had arranged for them to be bussed over to the sixth-form college, there being no stage in their little assembly hall. As the narrator, I wore my normal street clothes and throughout the performance I stood on the side apron, in front of the curtain. The children were surprisingly well behaved and listened attentively with very little whispering or giggling. When the players appeared in costume there was a deathly hush and the look of wonder on the little faces was really something to behold, but by the time the scene had finished with Roland, the Mad Hatter, trying to dunk Melanie, the Dormouse, in an oversized papier maché teapot, the hall was filled with shrieks of laughter.

I was due to give Melanie a lift back to *The Grapes*, so as I had no makeup or costume to worry about I went straight outside to wait for her in my car (actually, I was ready for a sit down). George Mayberry was also out there, the ever-present cigarette dangling from his lips. He had travelled out with the Pembrokes to do sundry odd jobs backstage and was enjoying a smoke while he stood waiting for them.

Tarquin was the first of the performers to appear. He strolled out to his little open two-seater and hardly had he perched himself up on the folded-back canopy before he was quickly surrounded by a jostling group of sixth-formers. George Mayberry took out his notebook and began to scribble something in it. When Melanie and the Pembrokes eventually stepped out into the sunlight, I leaned across the Mini and opened my passenger door. Mayberry joined Marcia and they stood waiting for Roland to do the same, his old Jaguar not having central locking either. I was surprised to see Marcia snatch Mayberry's notebook out of his hand.

'Let me see what dark secrets you have in your little red book.' She said it teasingly, but there was a hint of malice there, I thought.

George Mayberry looked distressed. 'Please give that back!' he implored. 'I was simply making a note of something I felt Mr Pemberton should know about. I'd rather you didn't read it.'

'Give it back to him m'dear,' Roland said wearily. 'I would like to get back in time for something to eat before tonight's performance.'

Marcia pouted and handed the notebook back. 'I'm determined to know what he keeps writing down in that damned book!' Marcia hissed at her husband, and with a tantalising flash of thigh she flopped into the car.

★ ★ ★

That night we opened at the Memorial Hall. We played to a full house again with the two front rows almost entirely occupied by senior citizens. (Melanie told me later that it was the annual outing of the local over sixties club.) Roland was on top form, and apart from some brief, coquettish smiles, Marcia kept her distance, thank God! Everyone said it was good to work on a proper raked stage again instead of just the curtained proscenium arch found in most village halls. There were flies for suspended lighting, backdrops and quick scene changes, a real lighting board for Eddie Dolan to play with and the curtains were powered so that Brian Chambers could operate both from the same side.

After the show it was opening night, party time again, so we all stayed on stage after the final curtain. Friends and VIP's began to filter in through the wings and I felt a tap on my shoulder.

'My, how tall you've grown.' I wheeled round and stood open-mouthed. It was Susan.

Now, if this were a movie, the string section

of the orchestra would have struck up at that moment. She was older, of course, but there was no mistaking the Nordic good looks that both she and Ronnie had inherited from their grandfather, a U-boat captain in World War II who, when a prisoner of war in England, had fallen in love with a local girl and never went back to Germany. There was that same, almost arrogant, tilt of the head and the crooked smile that dimpled her cheek so attractively. The roguish tomboy who could climb a tree faster and throw a ball further than me had matured into a beautiful woman. Her blonde hair was tied back in a no-nonsense ponytail and she wore little to no makeup. With her athletic figure and healthy outdoor complexion she could have easily passed for the coach of a netball or hockey team at some exclusive private girls' school but the crisp white blouse and the expensively tailored suit ('*Armani, darling*', Marcia was to say later — a tad enviously, I thought) was that of a successful, professional person, a doctor or a lawyer perhaps.

Roland was with her. 'I'll leave you with Nicholas then, m'dear,' he said with a practiced smile. 'I must get back to the County Education Officer.' He gave my arm a squeeze. 'Tell Miss Simmons about the motorcycle.'

For a long moment we gazed at each other

without speaking. Then she said, 'What's going on, Nick. Where's Ronnie? Why are you playing his part? Is he sick or something?'

I steered her to a quiet corner. 'Ronnie left the company in the lurch. He walked out on them; can you believe that? They've had to cancel five performances. It was lucky for them that I turned up otherwise they would probably have had to call off the whole tour.'

'But Ronnie wouldn't let anybody down, it's not in his nature. Where's he gone? And what's this about his motorcycle?'

'The feeling here is that he's gone chasing off on a photographic job and didn't have time to tell anyone. The police found his motorbike at the train station.'

'The police!'

'Oh, they only got involved because the railway people complained about it being left in their car park. Melanie, she's our assistant stage manager, has arranged for it to be stored at a local garage.

'Why the devil didn't you call me?'

'I'm sorry, but what could I tell you? That Ronnie wasn't here and I didn't know where on earth he'd gone? Finding his motorbike at the station, which seems to prove he got a train to London, is the only solid piece of evidence I've had and I only found out about that on Friday.'

I could see she was still worried so I took her hands in mine. 'I'm sure there's a rational explanation for Ronnie's disappearance. I bet we'll all be laughing about it in a day or so.' My smile was reciprocated and that was progress of sorts. 'Tell me, how have you managed to get away? You told me you were tied up for weeks.'

Her smile broadened. 'My Cannford client,' she said. 'And this time I confess I used him as an excuse to pop over this evening and see Ronnie.'

'How did you know where the Players were performing?'

'I took a taxi to *The Grapes*, and the landlord told me. I also booked a room there for the night. It was the last one they had, he said, the place being full of theatricals.' She laughed at that, a short nervous laugh.

After the party I drove her back to *The Grapes* and she came with me to my room to drop off my things. Her eyes widened as she stepped inside.

'So this is how the other half lives,' she said. 'I'm in one of two small attic rooms in the main building. It's all right but I have to share a toilet and bathroom.'

I found myself saying, 'I was only given this room because it was Ronnie's,' like I had to apologise or something, which was silly.

She spotted the portfolio on the dressing table. 'Did he leave his things behind?' she asked, picking it up.

'No, just that — and a couple of photographic magazines in the bedside cabinet.'

'I'd better get back to my room.'

I didn't want her to go. 'Stay and have something,' I said, hurriedly looking through the variety of sachets provided by the management. 'Drinking chocolate?'

'Perfect.'

I went to fill the kettle. 'I'm glad you're here,' I shouted from the bathroom. When I came back she was sitting in the chair looking through the photographs. 'Ronnie told me you were a consultant,' I said. 'I know you're not *Doctor* Simmons so what is it you do, law, finance?'

'I help people, Nick, and by people I mean companies, corporations, even government departments.' She put the portfolio aside and crossed her long, slim legs. 'I did work for a firm of business consultants to begin with, after I left University, so what Ronnie told you was probably right at the time. I learnt a lot while I was with them but more importantly I made many very useful contacts, freelance sales experts and business administrators, yes, and legal and financial people too, all at the top of their professions. I run my own business now and, as I say, if someone needs help — their sales are low, their production's inefficient, or whatever — they contact me because I know just the right person to send in to put things right.'

'For a fee.'

'Of course.'

We finished our chocolate and I walked her back to her room. At her door she said goodnight with a sisterly kiss. I said I'd run her to the station and asked her what time she was planning to leave.

'It rather depends on some phone calls,' she replied cryptically. 'Is the garage that's got Ronnie's motorbike on the way to the station?'

I nodded.

'Then I'd better call in there. I assume someone's going to have to pay for its storage.'

The thought of Melanie getting a bill from the Pilchers hadn't occurred to me.

★ ★ ★

'What made you decide to become an actor?' Susan suddenly fired at me as we were travelling along the road to Marshbank.

So far the journey had been spent with

118

Ronnie's sister lounging in the passenger seat (as well as one can in a 1960's Mini) nonchalantly puffing a long, brown, cigarillo while I concentrated on my driving, praying that I wouldn't meet a tractor at the next blind corner towing one of those lethal-looking, ultra-wide, agricultural implements.

Susan hadn't asked if I minded her smoking in my car. When she lit up I made a big show of opening my window but she didn't get the message.

'I didn't decide, it just sort of ... happened' I said, recalling the day I'd tagged on the end of that long line of kids waiting to be auditioned for *Oliver*.

There was a sudden, welcome draught in the car as Susan opened her window to throw out her small cigar. 'Do we have much further to go?'

'This is it,' I said, turning onto the weed-covered forecourt. I drove past the solitary, ancient, petrol pump and parked in front of the pavilion. 'Hardly a candidate for the Queen's Award for Industry, is it?'

Susan released her seatbelt and opened the car door. 'There's certainly little here to interest any of the petroleum companies, that's for sure but the antiques idea sounds a good one.'

The day was grey and overcast and the

windswept patchwork of spiky grass and mudflats behind the garage looked bleak and desolate but with the car's engine switched off I could hear birds singing and even the sound of sheep in the distance.

We climbed the few wooden steps up to the veranda and knocked on the door. After much rattling of bolts, it creaked open and Pilcher junior peered out from the gloomy depths. He looked as though he'd just got out of bed.

'What d'you want?' he said.

This was very much the sort of welcome I'd expected. 'Good morning,' I said politely. 'This is Ronnie Simmons's sister. She's here to see about his motorcycle.'

'Miss Melanie's in charge o'that.'

'Ah, but Miss Simmons is here to pay you for its storage.'

Susan gave him her card and asked if she could see the machine. Benny looked confused but he stepped back to allow us inside. My eyes quickly got accustomed to the dim light and I saw that the room we were in had once been a shop. There was a big, old-fashioned, National cash register just inside the door and display counters on three sides that were now littered with empty oilcans, lengths of tangled electrical wire and old cardboard boxes. There was junk, muck and cobwebs everywhere. Worn-out tyres leant against the walls and we had to tread carefully to avoid tripping over greasy engine parts that had been on the floor since goodness knows when. The whole place stank of diesel and decay.

Benny moved behind the counter, effectively blocking a doorway, which I assumed led to his living quarters. I hated to think of the state that would be in. He nodded at something behind me. I turned around and there, propped up against the wall was a lightweight, off-road motorcycle, the sort that has deep-tread tyres, a small fuel tank and mudguards set high up over the wheels. Susan went to it and ran her hand around the saddle. I thought this was a show of affection until I realised she was feeling beneath the rim of the seat. She smiled with satisfaction as the whole thing suddenly sprang upwards.

Benny shot out from behind the counter. 'Here, don't you go breaking it,' he shouted.

The roar of an engine cut through the silence. A door slammed and there was the sound of heavy footsteps on the wooden veranda outside. A figure appeared in the doorway blocking out the light. It was Caleb Pilcher. He stood there taking in the scene as Susan rummaged in the compartment under the motorcycle's seat. She produced a pair of leather gloves and shook something out of one of them; it was a mobile phone. For a moment no one spoke, then in a hushed voice Susan said, 'No one leaves their mobile behind, do they?'

'That's mine!' Caleb shouted from the doorway. He moved surprisingly swiftly for someone of his size and before Susan could object, he had snatched the instrument from her.

'But it can't be,' I protested. 'You saw for yourself, it was in Ronnie Simmons' motorbike — in one of his gloves, under the seat.'

Caleb gave me a hard look. 'I took Benny to the station to collect that bike and I lent him my phone in case he had problems on the way back. He's not comfortable having a mobile in his pocket, got a thing about radio waves addling the brain. He probably wrapped it in the gloves to stop it rattling.' He turned and clipped his son hard on the ear. 'Not that you've got much brain to addle, have you, you dozy pillock?'

Benny cowered like a whipped dog, which wasn't pleasant to see. Caleb made a big show of peering at the display to check the phone had come to no harm. I was about to argue but Susan tugged at my sleeve and made for the door. I didn't look back until we were sitting in the car. Caleb was standing in the doorway watching us. There was a hint of a smile on his face and he still held the mobile, which looked ridiculously small in his big leg-of-mutton fist. Quickly grabbing mine, I tapped in a number, it rang for a moment, Caleb turned his back on me and I cursed under my breath. Susan asked who I was calling.

'Ronnie's number . . . I think King Kong just switched it off.'

I got the number for the Cannford police from directory. When I got through I asked for DI Crabbe, saying that my call concerned Pilcher's Garage. The inspector came on the line straight away but he seemed to lose interest when he realised all I wanted to talk about was Ronnie's motorbike

'Mr Simmons' motorcycle is currently being stored at Pilcher's Garage?' he reiterated in a bored voice.

'That's right.'

'And you found a mobile phone with it that you say belongs to Mr Simmons.'

'Well, it was in a compartment under the seat. Ronnie wouldn't go anywhere without his mobile, Inspector. There's something odd about it and I think you should look into it.'

'But you say Caleb Pilcher claims that this mobile phone is his.'

'Yes, but . . . '

'What make is Mr Simmons' mobile phone, Mr Carter?'

I had no idea. I asked Susan who shrugged her shoulders. 'Ronnie was always changing his phone,' she said. 'I couldn't keep up with him.'

'We don't know,' I told the inspector though clenched teeth. I could feel my case collapsing around me.

'It seems to me, Mr Carter, the only ground for thinking this mobile phone belongs to Mr Simmons is that it was found on his motorcycle. How does Mr Pilcher account for that?'

'He says Benny borrowed it from him and wrapped it in the glove to stop it rattling when he collected the motorcycle from the railway station. Now, does that make sense?'

'It does for Benny Pilcher. Now, if you will excuse me, I'm very busy. Goodbye, Mr Carter.'

★   ★   ★

We got to the station in plenty of time for the next train to London. I didn't want Susan to go and I told her so.

She gave me a lovely smile. 'If Ronnie is employed by any of the national dailies, I'll know by lunchtime,' she said. 'I'll call you.'

124

Back at *The Grapes* I collected my key, went to my room and unlocked the door. There was something jammed behind it that prevented me opening it fully. When I eventually managed to squeeze in I saw that the room was a complete shambles. My bed had been stripped (it was the duvet that was stuck in the doorway) all the drawers had been pulled out of the dressing table and the contents of the wardrobe thrown on the floor.

I had just grabbed the telephone to call Arthur when a sudden hard blow on my back sent me stumbling across the room. I tripped on one of the drawers and went sprawling but luckily I landed on the heap of clothing and spare blankets that lay at the base of the wardrobe. Dazed by the suddenness of it all, I sat up and shook my head. I looked around. I was alone. Whoever it was that pushed me had gone. Realizing I was still holding the telephone, I checked it was working and punched the key marked 'Reception'. It seemed to take an age before I heard Arthur's voice answer.

'This is Nick Carter,' I shouted. 'Get here quick, I've been burgled!'

It didn't take long for him to arrive. He was out of breath; he must have run all the way.

'Have you called the police?' he gasped.

I did think about it. Once upon a time, in a small community like this, the village bobby would have known who the most likely culprit would be, but those days are long gone and I didn't see what good a squad car coming all the way out here from Cannford would do. There was no sign of forced entry, or any damage at all for that matter, and there was certainly nothing of value taken. And I could imagine just how interested Detective Inspector Crabbe would be.

'There's no need to involve anyone else, Arthur,' I said. 'When you've lived out of a suitcase for as long as I have, you learn to carry your valuables with you. If there *is* anything missing it won't be worth worrying about.'

He seemed relieved. I could understand him not wanting his establishment to get a bad reputation, particularly if he was trying to sell it.

Melanie appeared.

'I was in my room when I heard a bump and . . . oh, my goodness!'

Her big, owl-like eyes moved around the room taking it all in. Then she spotted me still sitting on the floor by the wardrobe.

'Oh, Nick. Are you all right?' She pushed past Arthur to get to me. 'What on earth's happened?'

I didn't feel very much like smiling but I did to reassure her. 'Don't worry, I haven't had a fit or anything. I interrupted a burglar that's all.'

She was horrified. 'A burglar?'

'Hardly that, Miss.' Arthur had regained his equilibrium and the smile was back on his face. 'Kids more like, having a lark on their way home from school. I've caught 'em in here before, trying the doors. They must have found this one unlocked. I'll ring their necks next time I catch 'em, the little buggers — if you'll excuse my French, Miss.' He reached down and gave me a hand up. 'I'll send our Poll to straighten things up, sir.'

'Polly's got enough to do, Arthur. It won't take me long to sort this lot out.'

'I'll help — if that's all right,' Melanie said.

Arthur went away pleased to leave us to it and Melanie began gathering up the things that had been tipped out of the drawers. 'Has anything been stolen?' she asked.

'No, I don't think so,' I said. 'Although I haven't looked in the bathroom yet. That's where he sprang from. I had a rather nice bottle of aftershave in there. I hope he hasn't pinched that.'

'Did you see who it was?'

'No chance. One minute I was standing looking at the mess, the next I was falling

127

headlong into it. By the time I'd got my bearings he was long gone.' I realised I was saying 'he' but the intruder could just as easily have been female.

It didn't take long to tidy things up. I thanked Melanie and saw her to the door. When she was gone I shut it and turned the key in the lock — *because that is what you did!* The door didn't automatically lock when you closed it; you had to turn a key. I remember Arthur telling me when I first arrived that he'd had special locks fitted so that people couldn't lock themselves out.

'Don't forget to lock your door when you go to bed at night — unless you're expecting a visitor,' he had said with that suggestive wink of his.

I hadn't taken Arthur up on his comment about the room being found unlocked because at the time it seemed likely that Polly had left it that way after changing the towels or something. But thinking about it seriously, I had definitely unlocked the door to get in — and that meant only one thing, *the burglar had a key!* I got changed hurriedly and went across to have a word with the landlord's daughter.

Polly was behind the bar. I asked for a glass of lager.

'I suppose you know about my room being

turned over,' I said conversationally.

'Dad told me about it.'

'He says the room was unlocked.'

'You'd be surprised how many people forget to lock their doors. Some days I hardly need my pass-key.'

'Where do you keep your pass-key?'

'In my apron pocket.'

'But you're not wearing an apron, Polly.'

'No, it's hanging up in my store cupboard.'

'That's in the annexe isn't it, where you keep your Hoover and spare toilet rolls and stuff?'

'Mm.'

'And the key, is it in the pocket now?'

She hesitated. 'Yes,' she said guardedly.

'Where anyone could help themselves to it.'

She took a step back. 'Here!' she said indignantly. 'What are you getting at?'

'Does your father know you leave your pass-key in the store cupboard?'

Her eyes flashed. 'He will if you tell him,' she said truculently.

'Oh, I will, Polly. Whoever ransacked my room had a key. I had mine, so where did the other one come from?' I drank up and as I turned to leave I collided with Roland Pembroke who had come up to the bar without me hearing him. The lovely Marcia was by his side. I had no idea how long they had been standing there waiting for me to stop questioning Arthur's daughter.

'Slow down, young man,' Roland bellowed. 'There's plenty of time yet before we have to set off. Marcia and I are just going to have a small gin. It loosens the larynx, don't you know. Are you in the chair?'

I excused myself saying I had to go back to my room. Roland frowned and Marcia pouted with disappointment.

As I was driving over to Hobswood, Susan called. She'd drawn a blank with the newspapers.

'I've got a bad feeling about all this, Nicky. Call it what you like, a hunch or intuition, but I think something's happened to Ronnie . . . I'm coming back to Cannford.'

I couldn't help feeling a twinge of guilt at the pleasure Susan's announcement gave me. 'What time does your train get in?' I asked. 'I'll be at the station meet you.' (With bells on, I thought.)

'I'm afraid I can't tell you that,' she said. 'I need to spend some time at the office, so I've no idea what time I'll leave . . . I've still got the taxi firm's card so I'll get them to pick me up and I'll call *The Grapes* and re-book my room, so don't worry about that either.'

7

Of all the performing arts, acting is unique. Where else can you slip into an entirely different personality for a couple of hours, leaving your everyday worries in the dressing room along with your everyday clothes?

It was a good house again with young Partridge back in his usual seat, front row centre. The play went well. Roland strutted and bellowed, Marcia overacted outrageously, Melanie was confidence personified and Tarquin needed fewer promptings. (I suppose even the thickest Rupert can't keep repeating the same lines night after night for weeks on end without some of them sticking.) After the show I spotted Partridge standing alone in the wings. Melanie was nowhere to be seen, she was probably still getting changed or doing some assistant stage manager thing. I was still on a high from the performance and I was about to go over to him when a hand gripped my arm.

'Nicky, we've got to talk.' It was Susan. 'God, I need a smoke!'

Reality came flooding back.

As with most village halls these days,

Hobswood's had a strict no smoking rule. 'Wait for me in the car park,' I said. 'I'll get my makeup off and I'll be with you in a few minutes.'

★ ★ ★

It was cold and dark outside. Tortoise-like, I pulled my head down into the collar of my padded coat and set off to fetch the torch from my car. I got to the steps to the boiler room when I heard footsteps.

'Susan, is that you?'

A violent blow to the side of my head brought me to my knees and an agonising thump just below my rib cage sent me tumbling down the concrete steps. As consciousness rapidly slipped away from me, I heard a disembodied voice say:

'You and your bloody questions! Go back where you came from . . .'

The light was so bright it shone through my closed eyelids and a voice I didn't recognise kept repeating, 'Nick. Speak to me, Nick.' There was a roaring in my head and a griping pain in my kidneys. I was vaguely aware of being inside an ambulance and a black girl in a yellow jacket smiling down at me, she had a kind face . . . and then there was nothing until I awoke in a strange, hard

132

bed with someone snoring loudly on the other side of the room.

In the dim light I could just about make out curtains on rails and more beds, instantly recognisable as hospital cots by the clip-boards hanging on their tubular-framed ends. I sat up, setting off a silent scream of protest from a knot of sore and tender muscles in my side. Cautiously I explored the throbbing ache in the left-hand side of my head and my fingers encountering a thick pad over my ear held in place with a turban-like bandage.

'You and your bloody questions! Go back where you came from . . .'

There may have been more but that was all I heard before I blacked out. My questions had obviously pushed someone to the point of violence, but who? I know I'd upset Polly over the keys but she was hardly likely to creep up behind me in the dark and clobber me, was she? Besides, it was a man's voice and somehow familiar, but with my ear ringing like a peal of bells at the time it could have been anyone.

Doctor's rounds put an end to further speculation. The young, smiling Asian shook his head sadly and tut-tutted when the nurse unwrapped my ear. He studied the charts from the end of my bed and then grinned at me.

'You are a very lucky fellow,' he said. 'Your thick coat saved you. Without it your injuries would have been very bad, very bad indeed.'

Having received the all clear to leave hospital, I was almost dressed when the curtains were pulled aside and I was suddenly seized in a fierce bear hug.

'Oh, Nicky!' a voice yelled in my good ear (it was Susan, only Susan calls me 'Nicky'). 'We came last night but they wouldn't let us in to see you . . . are you all right?'

'Whoa, mind the bruises!'

She loosened her grip and I caught sight of Melanie and DC Partridge standing behind her.

'Gavin brought us in his car,' Melanie said. 'He was the one who sent for the ambulance after Susan found you.' She turned and looked up at the young man, her big eyes wide with admiration. 'He covered you with his raincoat until it arrived.'

Susan still held my hands. 'I'm *so* sorry,' she said. 'It's all my fault. If I hadn't gone outside for that damned smoke you wouldn't have fallen down those stairs.'

'If you hadn't found me I could have been there all night,' I said with a smile. 'Anyway, I didn't fall, I was pushed.'

Partridge's notebook was out in a flash. 'A mugger was it, sir? Someone after your money?'

'Let's talk about it later shall we, back at *The Grapes*?'

Partridge's car was a newish Volkswagen, which, in the normal course of events I'm sure is very comfortable, but although I'd been liberally dosed with painkillers before leaving the hospital and given regular sips from a bottle of cognac (that Susan just happened to have in her bag) during the journey, the tender parts of my anatomy felt every vibration and every bump in the road. I was greatly relieved when we eventually drew up outside the pub.

Whether by luck or design, Roland was there, pacing up and down on the tarmac. He peered in at all the car's windows until he saw me sitting in the back.

'My dear Carter! How are you, dear boy?' He yanked my door open and took a pace back. 'Oh dear, that ear *is* a mess,' he said. Then he rallied himself and added in his stentorian voice, 'But it would take more than that to make a seasoned trouper like you miss a performance, am I right, my boy?'

My show-must-go-on smile quickly turned into a grimace as I levered myself painfully off the back seat. 'It will hardly be noticed under my wig,' I said.

'Capital, capital. Take the afternoon off, old chap; put your feet up. The students at the

135

sixth-form college are putting on the Scottish play for their doting relatives. The youngsters are doing everything themselves so it only needs Dolan for the lighting and Marcia to keep a motherly eye on things backstage. I have to be there, of course, for the after-performance speech. Now, I must go if I'm going be there in time for lunch. See you this evening then.'

As Pembroke strode off I was suddenly conscious of Gavin Partridge standing beside me. 'Can I help you to your room, sir?' he asked.

'No thanks. I'm fine really. All I need is a long hot soak in a bath.'

'Will it be all right if I come back, say about three? I'll have to put in a report.'

He was so polite that I agreed without hesitation. He said his goodbyes and drove off. As he was pulling out of the car park, a small, red, sports car roared in, forcing him to brake sharply.

'My God!' Susan exclaimed. 'Who's that idiot?'

'Tarquin,' Melanie said. She spoke his name with such venom that had this been a play she would have spat on the ground.

I wondered what was behind this animosity for the younger Pembroke but I sensed that this was neither the time nor place to ask.

'I'm away for that hot bath,' I said. 'I wonder if Arthur has any Radox?'

The three of us went into the pub together and collected our keys from Polly, who smiled at the girls but ignored me completely.

'I'd like to speak to that local newspaperman, what's his name? Tim something,' Susan said.

'Murray, Tim Murray.'

'I was hoping you'd take me, but I guess it can wait.'

'I could go with you,' Melanie said brightly. 'I've met him. Perhaps we could borrow Nick's car.'

My car! I'd quite forgotten about it. 'Sorry, still at Hobswood, I'm afraid,' I said.

Melanie grinned. 'No it isn't. Gavin found the keys. It's here, in the car park. I drove it over. It was great fun. You can't see it because it's tucked behind Eddie Dolan's big Volvo.' She turned to Susan. 'You'll love it, it's a Mini Cooper S, just like one of those in *The Italian Job*. It's got a roll-bar, bonnet straps, spotlights, everything.'

'Susan's already seen it.' I said. 'And you *will* be careful with it, Melanie, wont you?'

'Of course, silly. It's weeks now since I passed my test.'

I groaned.

I entered my room warily but everything looked normal and there was no one hiding in the bathroom waiting to spring out at me.

'I'll run the bath for you if you like,' Melanie said from the doorway.

'I do like,' I said, collapsing on the bed. There was the sound of running water. 'What is it with you and Tarquin?' I shouted, deciding that this was as good a moment as any.

She came out of the bathroom. 'My glasses are all steamed up.'

'He's hurt you, hasn't he? Tell me what he's done.'

'I don't want to go into that.'

'You'll feel better if you talk about it.'

I eased myself off the bed and got the kettle to make some tea. Melanie stood by the dressing table fretfully clasping and unclasping her hands.

'I joined the company as an assistant stage manager last year,' she said. 'I knew some of the cast were leaving at the end of the season so I asked Mr Roland if I could have a part in his next production. I was over the moon when he said he'd give me a try out as Melissa in *Waiting On The Bridge* . . . But I made a mess of things at the reading, didn't

I? I was so sure I'd ruined my chances that I drank far too much champagne at the last night party and finished up with Tarquin taking me back to my room.'

I didn't like the picture that was beginning to form in my mind. 'And?' I asked.

'Well, it's obvious isn't it? He said he'd use his influence with his father to get me a part in *The Bridge* — if I let him stay the night.'

'The bastard! And did you?'

'I really wanted that part.'

'I can understand now why you dislike him,' I said.

She turned to face me, her eyes blazing. 'Dislike isn't a strong enough word. The next morning, when, not only was I feeling ashamed of myself for what I'd done but I was also suffering from a king-size hangover, Tarquin took great delight in telling me that he'd known all along that his father had decided to give me the part.'

'I'd like to punch him on the nose!'

That made her smile. 'In your condition, Nick Carter, you couldn't punch your way out of a paper bag.'

There was a moment of silence.

'Melanie.'

'Mm?'

'You wear contact lenses when you're on stage. Why don't you wear them all the time?'

'They irritate my eyes, make them water. Now, are you going to get in this bath or not?'

Melanie was very excited with the prospect of driving the Mini into Cannford. Filled with foreboding I watched my pride and joy roar out of the car park before making my way back to Arthur's taproom to await Detective Constable Partridge. The young policeman arrived dead on three o'clock as promised. (Punctual *and* polite, he's got to have a flaw somewhere.) After my long soak, my battered muscles had loosened up a bit so I was able to stand up without too much discomfort and shake his hand when he joined me at my table.

'I took the liberty of ordering afternoon tea,' he said. (This young man is too perfect.) He took out his notebook, opening it with that practiced flip of his. 'Did you see who it was that assaulted you, sir?'

'No, but I heard his voice.'

'Then your assailant was definitely a man?'

'Yes, and the voice was familiar in some way.'

The tea arrived, and with it, some hot buttered crumpets. It made a cheerful sight, which was more than could be said for Polly who brought it to the table.

I declared myself 'mother' and poured. 'I believe this assault has something to do with the disappearance of Ronnie Simmons.'

Young Partridge reached for the sugar bowl and began spooning the fine crystals into his cup. 'What makes you say that, sir?'

'Because the man who attacked me said, 'You and your bloody questions,' and the only questions I've been asking have been about Ronnie — and then there was the bur- glary . . . '

The spoon stopped in mid-air. 'Burglary?'

'Yes. Oh, you wouldn't know about that. It wasn't reported to the police.' I bit into my crumpet; the butter oozed out and trickled down my chin. I dabbed it with my napkin. 'My room was ransacked, nothing was stolen, just messed up. I disturbed the burglar — and no, I didn't see who it was.'

'You're sure nothing was stolen?'

'Positive.'

'Were any of the other rooms disturbed?'

'No.'

'Any idea why your room was chosen?'

'Arthur says it was kids, a target of opportunity. But I think there was more to it than that. The room was definitely locked and the thief had a key. It had been Ronnie's room, I think the burglar was after something he left behind.'

'But I thought Mr Simmons took his things with him when he left?'

'He did. Everything except his portfolio of photographs.'

'But you said nothing was taken?'

'That's right. I'd given that to Ronnie's sister.'

★ ★ ★

It was show time again and I felt like death. It had been a couple of hours since I'd swallowed the last lot of painkillers. The instructions on the box said not to drink alcohol whilst taking them but when I dropped off my key I treated myself to a large whisky. Well, it was for medicinal purposes, and I wasn't actually swallowing the tablets with it, was I?

Arthur seemed a bit distant when he served me. Perhaps Polly had said something but I was pleased in a way because he left me to sip my Scotch in peace.

Melanie drove me to Hobswood. The combination of pills and whisky numbed my aches and pains but I was reminded of them again when I had to climb out of the car.

'Are you going to be okay, Nick?' she asked anxiously.

I grinned at her. 'It would be more painful to watch Mr Roland giving the punters their money back.'

I got through that evening's performance pretty well considering. I remembered to keep my damaged ear upstage and out of sight as much as I could, the odd twinge in my gut helped to add an extra dash of venom to Seth's angry exchanges with Sir William and my feelings for Tarquin spiced up my scenes with him. Roland actually congratulated me after the show.

'Well done, Nicholas!' he bellowed. 'A splendid effort — be a lot easier for you tomorrow.'

Tarquin still spoke his lines as though the whole thing was beneath him, but this actually suited his role in the play. At least he knew them now and I suppose it was because neither of us needed a prompter that I failed to notice that George Mayberry hadn't turned up.

When I got back to *The Grapes* the first person I saw in the taproom was Benny Pilcher talking to Polly. She saw me come in and whispered something to him; he half-turned and squinted at me, mouth agape. Susan was at the other end of the bar perched on a stool smoking a slim brown panatela. I made my way over to her.

'My God, Nicky, you look like shit,' she said. Before I could reply Roland Pembroke's rich voice came from the doorway, 'A bottle of your very best red wine, landlord, if you please.'

The small man with the big personality strode in with the rest of the company following him, including Melanie, who had stayed behind to count the ticket money. She detached herself from the group to join Susan and me.

'Are you feeling all right, Nick?' she asked. 'You look awful.'

'I do wish everyone would stop telling me that,' I said with a smile. 'I'd feel a whole lot better with a large Scotch inside me.'

As Susan turned away to attract Polly's attention, Melanie asked if I'd seen anything of George Mayberry.

'I can't help worrying about him, he's such a sweet old man,' she said.

'Who's George Mayberry?' Susan asked.

I explained that he was the company's odd-job man. 'A nice old chap — very clever with a paintbrush. He was quite a famous artist in his day I'm told, but drink put paid to his career.'

Melanie was up on her tiptoes, peering through the fug of the crowded taproom. 'Well, I can't see him anywhere in the bar,' she said agitatedly.

She was so concerned I found myself

offering to go across to the annexe to see if he was in his room.

'I'll come with you,' she said.

Susan gave up trying to catch Polly's eye and slid down from her stool. 'Well, if you're both going, I'll come too. I've always wanted to meet a drunken artist.'

Mayberry's room was at the front of the annexe between Polly's store cupboard and the room occupied by Eddie Dolan. Receiving no reply after repeated knocking, Melanie tried the door. It opened.

The accommodation was similar to mine only the other way round, the bathroom being on the left-hand side as you go in. The curtains were drawn, the place was in darkness — and it smelled like a brewery. I switched on the light. George Mayberry was there all right, stretched out on the bed fully clothed and completely out for the count. Scattered on the floor were several empty lager cans and on the bedside cabinet was a vodka bottle with barely a mouthful left in it.

The reaction from the ladies varied from Susan's, 'Phew! Let's leave the old soak to sleep it off,' to Melanie's, 'Shouldn't we at least take his shoes off and cover him with a blanket or something?'

I went along with Melanie and while she fiddled with his shoelaces I headed off to the wardrobe where, from experience, I knew the spare blankets were kept.

I suppose all of us at sometime have had flashes of *déjà vu*, for as I tugged at a blanket something fell at my feet, only on this occasion it wasn't a photograph album, but what I took to be an electric razor in a leather case. Why would old Mayberry keep his razor in the wardrobe, I thought? Maybe it was a gift he hadn't got round to using, he did look more a soap and cutthroat man to me.

'Let me see that,' Susan said. I picked it up and gave it to her. 'I bought Ronnie one just like this for his birthday.'

'A razor?'

'No, a digital camera.' She pulled a small silver object from the case. 'Just as I thought. This *is* Ronnie's.'

'There are probably hundreds, if not thousands just like it.'

'Not with this written in the case there isn't,' she said triumphantly.

I looked, and there, neatly printed in ballpoint pen on the canvas backing inside the flap, were the words, 'TO RONNIE, HAPPY SNAPPING. LOVE, SUSAN.'

'Let's see what's in the memory,' she said, switching the camera on and peering at the small monitor screen. 'Damn, the battery's flat.'

She was all for shaking Mayberry to wake him but I managed to dissuade her. No one would get any sense out of him for hours yet.

'We must call the police,' she said firmly.

I had to agree with her but I didn't fancy being lectured by DI Crabbe again. Partridge had given me his mobile number so I called him instead. He said he'd come straight away so all we had to do was wait. Hanging about in Mayberry's smelly room wasn't at all pleasant, particularly for the girls.

'Melanie, why don't you take Susan back to the bar and get her a large brandy?' I said. 'Put it on my tab.'

Gavin Partridge arrived within twenty minutes. 'I was in the area,' he said.

He looked at the still comatose Mayberry (now minus shoes and covered with a blanket) and flipped open his notebook. Taking this as my cue, I explained how I came to be in his room. I handed over the camera, which I had returned to its case.

He carefully lifted the flap with his pencil and read the inscription. ''Ronnie'', he said, 'Would that be Mr Ronnie Simmons, sir?'

'Yes, it's his camera.'

'I wonder out how our Mr Mayberry came to have it? I don't see him as a villain.'

I looked at the grey-haired old man on the bed, his aristocratic features completely relaxed in sound sleep. I tried to imagine this gentle, scholarly person ransacking my room, or worse still, hitting me from behind. 'Me neither,' I said fervently.

'I really should take him in for questioning.'

I was beginning to have second thoughts about involving the police. 'At the moment I doubt if the poor old sod could walk unaided,' I said. 'You'd have to get an ambulance — and call out the police doctor. Why don't we just leave him to sleep it off? Can't we say I called you in the morning?'

Partridge looked uneasy. 'Well, I don't know about that, sir,' he said, a worried frown on his young face.

'I'm as anxious to know how he got hold of that camera as you are. Take it from me, George Mayberry isn't going anywhere tonight.'

Partridge took another look at the man on the bed and I could tell there was a tussle going on between sentiment and duty.

'Right. I'll be back in the morning then, at eight o'clock,' he said. Sentiment had won the day and I was relieved.

I'd only just got back to my room when there was a gentle tap at the door. It was Melanie.

'I did as you said and took Susan back to

the bar,' she whispered.

'Did you get her a brandy?'

'She had several as a matter of fact, and finished off a packet of those little cigars. She's gone to her room now saying she feels tired but if you ask me she's a bit squiffy. How did things go with the police?'

'Your Gavin's coming in the morning.'

Melanie blushed. 'He's not *my* Gavin, silly,' she said.

I ached all over, so after liberally dosing myself with painkillers again I stretched out fully clothed on the bed and immediately fell into a deep sleep — and plummeted slap-bang into the middle of a nightmare.

I was at a party with Sam Abrahams. We were at *The Pineapple*, which is a pub just across the road from the Granada TV studios, only we weren't there at all, we were at the Minack theatre and George Mayberry was hammering at the scenery with Ronnie Simmons' camera, knock, knock, knock.

I woke up sweating. The bedside clock/radio said it was just after seven. There was loud knocking coming from the door

'I know I'm early, sir,' Partridge said as I let him in. 'But I didn't sleep very well last night.'

'Tell me about it!' I grumbled.

I splashed some water on my face and we

went along to Mayberry's room. The door was unlocked. That was all right, I'd left it that way but I got a shock when we went inside. The bed was empty. Oh, my God! I thought, and then I heard the cistern flush and the man himself appeared from the bathroom, peering at us bleary-eyed.

'What's going on?' he asked. 'What are you doing in my room?' Then, catching sight of Partridge, he said, 'I know you. I've seen you at the shows.'

The young policeman put the camera (now shrouded in transparent plastic) on the bed and produced his warrant card.

Mayberry read it aloud. 'Gavin Partridge, Detective Constable.'

'I'm sorry, George,' I said. 'Melanie was worried about you last night so we came to see if you were all right. You didn't answer the door and when we tried it we found it was open. You were sleeping like a baby and from the empties by the bed it was obvious you'd been on a bender. All we could do was make you comfortable and leave you to sleep it off.'

'Was it you who took off my shoes and covered me with a blanket?'

'Melanie did the shoes and I got the blanket from the wardrobe — and that's why DC Partridge and me are here now.'

He sat on the edge of the bed; his

shoulders slumped dejectedly. 'You found Ronnie's camera,' he said.

Partridge had his notebook out in a flash. 'You know the camera belongs to Mr Ronnie Simmons?'

'Yes, of course.'

I couldn't contain myself. 'For crying out loud, George, what the devil was it doing in your wardrobe?'

Mayberry looked up at me, his rheumy eyes pleading. 'I don't know,' he said.

The young detective snapped his notebook shut, shrugged his shoulders at me, and said to Mayberry, 'I'll need you to come to the station, sir.'

I guided Partridge away from the pathetic figure sitting on the bed. 'Look, Gavin,' I said, and for the first time deliberately using his Christian name. 'George Mayberry does have serious lapses in memory and I believe him when he says he doesn't know how he came to have Ronnie's camera. I know he sometimes drinks to excess but perhaps that's because his forgetfulness frightens him — or it could possibly be the cause, I don't know, I'm not a doctor or a psychiatrist.'

'But he knows Mr Simmons has gone missing?'

'Of course he does. I'm not saying he's completely gaga; in fact he's a highly intelligent man — and a very talented artist. Give him a paintbrush and he will amaze you, give him a script and he's the best reader and prompter in the business, get him talking about some of the major London productions he's been involved with and his recall will astound you. Just don't ask him what he did yesterday because the chances are he won't know.'

'Shouldn't he be in a home or something?'

'And what would that give him, a room with all meals provided, care and attention? He's got all that with the Players. He's part of the family here and no one could care more for him than Roland Pembroke; I've seen that for myself — plus he has the pride and satisfaction of doing a useful job.'

'I still need him to make a formal statement.'

'I'll go and see Roland,' I said.

I found the actor-manager sitting alone in the dining room. His face lit up when he spotted me in the doorway. 'Nicholas!' he shouted. 'Have you had breakfast? Pull up a chair, dear boy.'

I went to his table but I remained standing. I told him about George Mayberry's drinking binge and the finding of Ronnie's camera.

He pushed his unfinished 'full English' away with a heavy sigh.

'So, old George has fallen off the wagon has he? Well, I'm not surprised. He got word yesterday that his only daughter got married.'

'So he tied one on to celebrate?'

'No, to drown his sorrows. The wedding was last week and the poor old chap wasn't invited.' He got up. 'I'd better go with him to the police station. I'm sure there's an innocent explanation for him having Ronnie's camera . . . Do something for me, dear boy, tell Marcia where I've gone, will you?'

And that is precisely what I did — before I set out for Cannford to attend to some business of my own.

The previous evening, while I was waiting in George Mayberry's room for DC Partridge to arrive, I slipped out to Polly's store cupboard and there, on top of a large wicker hamper upon which, 'The Pembroke Players', was boldly stencilled, I found just what I wanted, a pair of Marigolds. It took a bit of stretching to get the smallish rubber gloves over my thick fingers but I was able to remove the camera's memory card, safe in the knowledge that I hadn't added my finger-prints to those already there.

8

The entrance lobby at the *Cannford Clarion* offices was still as cold and soulless as it was on my last visit but Tim Murray greeted me warmly enough.

'Nick Carter! Nice to see you again,' he said. 'I had Miss Naylor and a friend of hers here the other day, Ronnie Simmons' sister. Now, there's a bonny lassie for you.' He looked at me enquiringly but with a twinkle in his eye. 'You've been in the wars I hear. What do the police have to say about it all?'

'They've taken a statement about the attack in the car park.'

'But are they taking any action, laddie?'

'I'm going to see DI Crabbe when I leave here.'

He looked at me over his glasses. 'A bitter man is Tom Crabbe. I'd watch out for him if I were you, Mr Carter. He came to us from the Met nearly twenty years ago. Took the move after his promotion to Inspector but that's as far as he's got. He'd be about due for retirement now I should think . . . Now then, what was it you wanted to see me about?'

I took the memory card out of my wallet. 'Can you make me some prints from this?'

He looked puzzled 'Why bring it to me?'

'I can hardly take it to Boots.'

'It's Ronnie's isn't it?' he said, the light dawning.

'Yes.'

'Exclusive rights to any story?'

'Yes, of course.'

'Then leave it with me.'

* * *

I may have failed to convince DI Crabbe that the mobile phone on the motorcycle was Ronnie's but there was no doubting the ownership of that camera. I was sure he would agree now that there was something odd about Ronnie going awol and take some action, but in that I was to be proved wrong.

'Yes, Mr Carter, DC Partridge has reported the discovery of a camera belonging to Mr Simmons,' he said in response to my enquiry.

'But don't you think it bizarre that Ronnie Simmons, a professional photographer, would go on assignment to London without his camera?'

'I'm given to understand that it is not unknown for professional photographers to have more than one camera.'

He was stonewalling me again. 'Okay, but what about the attack on me the night before last? Have you had DC Partridge's report on that?'

'The alleged assault? Yes, I have.'

'There was nothing *alleged* about it! It was a warning, pure and simple, hammered home with the toe of a boot . . . And what about the burglary? Did he mention the burglary?'

'Burglaries take place during the hours of darkness, Mr Carter. He did say something about your room being messed up but, as I understand it, nothing was stolen. The licensee says it was the work of children.'

I saw red and I found myself shouting at him. 'For Christ's sake, Mr Crabbe, can't you see that all these events are connected to Ronnie Simmons' disappearance?'

The dour detective sat back in his chair and folded his arms. 'Calm yourself, Mr Carter,' he said wearily. 'I'm sure there's a very simple explanation for the various articles he left behind. As for the vandalism to your room and the alleged physical attack on your person, there's no evidence to link those events to Mr Simmons, in fact I've a good mind to report the Hobswood Old Comrades to Health and Safety. There should be a gate at the top of those steps — with a lock on it

... Did you have a drink after the show by any chance?'

It was all I could do to hold myself back from punching his silly head.

'No, Mr Carter,' he continued, 'your Ronnie Simmons will turn up again when his photographic assignment is completed, you mark my words; I've seen it all before ... Now, if you'll excuse me, I am working on matters of a more pressing nature.'

I stormed out of his office almost colliding with DC Partridge in the corridor outside. He looked just how I felt.

'Gavin! Where's George Mayberry?'

'Uniform have taken him and Mr Pembroke back to *The Grapes*.'

'That was quick!'

He grimaced. 'The DI gave me a rocket for bringing him in. He said there is no evidence to prove Mr Mayberry intended to keep the camera.'

'That man's always got a reason for doing nothing,' I said angrily.

The young detective drew himself up. 'That's not strictly true, sir. It's just that when Mr Crabbe is working on an important case he becomes very single-minded.'

Young Partridge's loyalty to his senior officer didn't surprise me.

'Blinkered, more like,' I said testily.

'No, sir, more focused. I can't tell you what the job is of course, except that it's big. It could mean promotion for him if he pulls it off.'

'And that wouldn't do his pension any harm, would it?' I said cynically.

★ ★ ★

When I got back to *The Grapes*, I found Roland Pembroke holding court from a bar stool in the taproom. Assembled around him were Susan and Melanie, Marcia and Eddie — even Tarquin. It would seem everybody wanted to hear about George Mayberry — except George Mayberry himself, as of him there was no sign. Arthur was hovering in the background but Polly was maintaining her distance at the far end of the bar where she was having her own private conversation with Benny Pilcher.

The actor-manager saw me. 'Nicholas, my boy!' he bellowed.

It occurred to me that Roland Pembroke appeared taller sitting down. He would look good on a horse I thought. He waved me over.

'Where's George?' I asked.

'Gone to his room.' He drained his glass and replaced it on the bar where it was

158

immediately refilled. There was no affectation in his voice when he spoke again. 'Mayberry has worked alongside all the greats, Gielgud, Olivier, Richardson . . . Surely no one could seriously believe a man like that would steal a paltry camera?'

'That's one thing the police and I seem to agree on,' I said. 'What I want to know is where he found it. It could be a clue to Ronnie's disappearance.'

He flicked a silk handkerchief from his cuff and dabbed his lips. 'You'll just have to wait and see if he remembers, Nicholas.'

'Do you think he will?'

'There's always a chance, dear boy,' he sighed. 'Poor old Mayberry. These bouts of amnesia have been occurring more frequently lately. It's all very worrying. But he does get flashes of recall occasionally. The problem is you can't make it happen, you have to wait until something triggers it off.'

★ ★ ★

I found it easier to perform that night. My injured bits were still sore but I wasn't conscious of them while I was acting. They were either getting better or I was becoming used to the discomfort.

In terms of audience numbers it looked like

being a rather poor house. Later, as we were packing up, Melanie confirmed this by announcing that the night's takings were disappointing.

'We need something to bring the people in,' Marcia said.

Eddie Dolan's voice came from the wings, 'And there was me, thinking Mr-la-di-dah-Carter was the answer, so I was.'

'We have Nick Carter's fans to thank for the full houses we've enjoyed since he joined our merry band,' Roland Pembroke shouted in response. 'But we have drunk that well dry, dear boy. Our catchment area is exceeding small, Dolan, as well you know.' He gave me a sympathetic smile.

'What we need is music!' his wife said dreamily. 'Oh, how I'd *love* to be doing *Oklahoma* or *My Fair Lady*.'

He looked at her tenderly. 'One has to be practical, my sweet. Just think what such a large cast would cost — not to mention an orchestra!'

I pulled on my jacket and checked my mobile. There was a recorded message so I found a quiet spot in the wings to listen to it.

'Nick, this is Tim, Tim Murray,' it began. 'Call me as soon as you get this. Don't worry about the time, just call me.'

He then went on to give me his number. It

was his mobile number, I felt very privileged. I programmed it in and rang him back.

'Nick? Good. Where are you?' He sounded breathless, excited even.

I said I was just about to leave the Hobswood Memorial Hall.

'Going back to *The Grapes*?'

'Yes.'

'What's your room number?'

I told him.

'Right! I'll see you there in half an hour. I've got something to show you ... And Nick!'

'Yes.'

'Just the two of us, understand?'

Melanie drove me back to *The Grapes* where I played on my injuries to excuse myself from the usual get-together at the bar. I'd not been in my room long before there was a knock at the door. It was Tim Murray. He was wearing a brown felt hat with the brim pulled down and an overcoat with the collar turned up. He looked like a fugitive from a late-night gangster movie.

'Are we alone?' he whispered as I shut the door.

'That's what you said.'

'Good, good.' He delved into the inside pocket of his coat and brought out a large manila envelope. 'These are the prints off that

161

digital memory card you left with me. Do you have anything to drink, laddie?'

'I could make you tea or coffee?'

'Nothing stronger?'

I remembered I still had the remains of Susan's bottle of cognac. My only glass was in the bathroom holding my toothbrush. I swilled it under the tap and dried it on a hand towel. 'Brandy all right?' I called to him, pouring out a generous measure.

'Only if you've no Scotch.'

I came back into the room and saw that he'd taken the prints out of the envelope and spread them out on the bed. There were half a dozen in all. I peered at them over his shoulder.

'My God! That's Marcia Fontaine!'

Murray chuckled. 'In the flesh, laddie, in the flesh.'

The photographs were all of the company's leading lady lying naked on a rumpled bed. And, as I've said before, she is a very handsome woman.

'That's Ronnie's room, the one I've got now. I recognise that painting over the bed.'

'Is there a painting? I never noticed,' he said casually, taking the tooth glass from me. 'Anyway, knowing Arthur, the paintings are probably the same in all his rooms.'

'No, no they're not. That's definitely

Ronnie's room and I believe these were taken the evening before he disappeared.'

'How do you know that?'

I touched the side of my nose with my forefinger. 'A gentleman never tells tales about a lady,' I said. 'If there's one thing I've learned it is to be very careful when talking to newspapermen.'

I must admit I was disappointed. I had hoped the film would provide a clue to Ronnie's whereabouts and I said as much to my visitor.

'Whisht, laddie,' he whispered, carefully extracting another print from the envelope which he laid beside the others on the bed.

Talk about from the sublime to the ridiculous! This was a picture of something in the back of a car covered over with a travelling rug. The rug had been pulled back on one corner revealing the object to be a number of cardboard boxes. There was some printing on them but I couldn't make it out.

'It's not a very good shot. Are you sure this is one of Ronnie's?'

'It was on that same card. It's my guess it was taken in a hurry using what light there was.'

'Why didn't he use a flash?'

'Perhaps he didn't want to be seen taking it.'

'Why would he be taking pictures of boxes, any idea what's in them?'

He took another print out of the envelope. 'I knew you'd ask that so I had a blow-up done.' He smiled grimly. 'No pun intended, laddie, this isn't anything to laugh about.'

It was fuzzy and grainy but I was looking at a black and orange diamond with 'SEMTEX H' stencilled alongside it.

I whistled. 'Plastic explosive! Where the hell did Ronnie find that?'

'Do you have any more of that brandy?' he asked.

I went back to the bathroom and drained the last of the cognac into his glass. 'An old photograph already in the memory?' I suggested.

'No, it came after the girlie shots.'

A thought suddenly occurred to me. 'Didn't you say Ronnie called you on the Friday night saying that he'd discovered something he wanted to talk to you about?'

'Aye, if only I'd spoken to him.' He took the glass from me with a nod of thanks. 'I *had* to tell the police,' he said, almost apologetically. 'I can't have the *Clarion* accused of withholding evidence. I spoke to Tom Crabbe. He wanted to send someone to collect the prints straight away but he agreed to let me take them to him in the morning . . . I thought you might want to come with me.'

* * *

The Detective Inspector merely looked up from his desk when we were shown into his office. There was no greeting, just a perfunctory wave of a hand indicating the four bentwood chairs that were lined up along the wall opposite him. They looked more suited to an old-fashioned tearoom than a CID office. I pulled one forward and sat on it. Tim Murray did the same.

Addressing Murray, Crabbe said, 'I wasn't expecting Mr Carter.'

I was ready for him and cut in quickly with, 'It was *Mr Carter* who found the digital memory card.'

He turned to face me, his colourless eyes glinted in triumph and for a moment it looked as if he were actually going to smile.

'And where *was* that exactly?' he purred.

Talk about being hoist with your own petard! Oh well, honesty is the best policy they say. 'I took it out of the camera in George Mayberry's room.'

'Mr Simmons' camera.'

'That's right.'

He'd got me where he wanted me and we

165

both knew it. Content to let me stew for a bit, he turned back to Murray and held out his hand. The newspaperman gave him the envelope from which Crabbe extracted some photographs and placed them on his desk blotter. I was relieved to see there were only two.

Without looking up, he said, 'By rights I should charge you, Mr Carter, with tampering with police evidence.'

I had nothing to lose. 'And what exactly did *you* do with the camera?' I retorted. 'I bet you did nothing, right? You just locked it away with the rest of the lost property.'

A slight tightening of his facial muscles told me I'd scored a bull's-eye.

Murray gave me an admiring look then stood up and moved round behind the policeman. He pointed to the blow-up. 'This is the one I wanted you to see,' he said.

Crabbe looked at it. 'How do I know this hasn't been faked?' he snorted. 'You can do anything with computers these days.'

'You have my word, Inspector, this is nothing more than a straightforward enlargement taken from the other photograph,' Murray replied. 'The *Cannford Clarion* is a responsible newspaper, sir, we don't fake things.'

If he was expecting an apology he was to be disappointed.

'The tailgate's open, you can't see the number plate when it's like that,' Crabbe grumbled. 'And I can't make out what make or model it is. I'll have our experts look at it, of course, but all I can say at the moment is that it's an estate car, dark in colour.' The policeman bent forward, his large nose almost touching the prints. 'I would say whoever took this picture pulled that blanket back. Look how scuffed and battered those boxes are, they must have been kicking around for ages.'

Murray peered over his shoulder. 'They build obsolescence into Semtex now I believe but I'm told the old stuff is good for twenty years.'

Angrily, Crabbe pushed the prints away. 'It's damned frustrating not knowing where or when the photograph was taken.'

I couldn't resist butting in. 'Ronnie took it just before he disappeared,' I said.

'How do you know that?' he asked.

'There were other pictures on the camera's memory that I *can* date,' I said. 'We didn't bother with those. They were, er, overexposed, isn't that right Mr Murray?'

The *Clarion*'s editor winked at me behind the inspector's back.

Crabbe then surprised me by asking if I would wait outside, which I did without hesitation. It would seem I was off the hook for tampering with Ronnie's camera. I breathed a sigh of relief. I really didn't want to waste time briefing lawyers and attending a Magistrate's Court.

When Tim Murray eventually joined me in the car park he wasn't looking particularly pleased.

'And what was all that about?' I asked.

He was fuming. 'I do my civic duty and I'm told, *told* mind you, not to print anything until he's had time to make enquiries. I've got the best local story of the year — the decade even — and I can't print a thing until DI-bloody-Crabbe says so.'

'But you'll have the exclusive?'

'Too right, laddie!' he said determinedly. 'I made him promise me that.'

He pointed his remote at the car, the hazard lights flashed twice and there was loud clunk as the doors unlocked.

'I've still got those nude shots,' he said. 'I'd better send them back to you. There's no embargo on them, of course, but the *Clarion*'s a family newspaper, we don't go in for page three girls . . . By the way, what was that about Ronnie's camera being in George Mayberry's room?'

'Oh, he was looking after it for him,' I said. It was the first thing that came into my head.

★ ★ ★

Murray dropped me at *The Grapes* where Polly grudgingly gave me a message that Sam Abrahams had telephoned. (I'd dutifully switched off my mobile phone at the police station.) I knew what he wanted but I rang him back anyway.

'Hello, Sam.'

There was no preamble. 'Daniel Jacobs of Deejay Associates is a personal friend of my cousin Reuben,' he said. 'They're very close. Their kids go to the same school. Their wives play bridge together. Reuben is embarrassed that I can't give his friend an answer.'

'My answer's still the same.'

For a moment he didn't speak, then he said, 'The other day when I couldn't reach you I called that Miss Naylor and she told me somebody had put you in hospital . . . For pity's sake, Nick, whatever Ronnie Simmons is mixed up in, drop it and get the hell out of there!'

Sam wasn't angry; he was mystified. I'd been badgering him for work ever since I knew I was leaving *Brooklands*, and now that he'd found something for me I was turning it away. I didn't feel sorry for him. Sam is in business to make money and he does that very effectively. He lives in a riverside

169

mansion on the Thames with a villa in Minorca for his holidays, which is a very long way from the two-up-and-two-down terraced house in London's Whitechapel where he grew up. No, I felt sorry for appearing to be so awkward. After all, Sam *had* kept me in work all these years (Although sometimes I did feel I was the one doing the favours.) I promised my nagging conscience that I'd give him a full explanation the very next time we met.

'I'm really sorry, Sam, believe me, but I'm close to finding out what it was that caused Ronnie Simmons to disappear. I've got to see it through.'

'Nick, my boy,' he wailed. 'When will another chance like this come along? I'll tell you when, never!'

There was silence at his end and I could picture him sitting at his big untidy desk puffing away at one of his fat cigars, looking for a way to turn this problem into an opportunity.

Suddenly he said, 'I'll tell Daniel you're sick.' (I knew he'd come up with something.) 'Sympathy is a very powerful emotion, my boy. I'll say you haven't fully recovered from the beating you got from those muggers. I bet you waded in to help some poor little old lady, right? Did it make the newspapers? If it did, send me copies! Remember what I keep telling you about publicity. I may be able to negotiate a better fee for you. Leave it with me, Nick, I'll get back to you.'

I didn't want to prolong the conversation. I had more important things to think about than Deejay Associates and their TV adverts.

9

Susan joined me for the early dinner Arthur provided for us theatricals. Neither of us was very hungry so I suggested we eat in the taproom. I knew she preferred it there because she could smoke. I ordered the tuna fish salad and a glass of Californian Chardonnay for us both.

When the food arrived she sat toying with it idly with her fork. 'One of my consultants has broken her ankle,' she said, gloomily.

I poured the wine.

'I really must sort out a replacement, but that means going back to the office.'

I smiled. 'Then go. There isn't very much you can do here anyway — and we're bound to hear from him soon.'

Pushing the plate to one side she fumbled in her handbag for her slim cigars. 'You don't really believe that. I know what you're thinking. You're thinking the same as me. That Ronnie is here somewhere. He's either gone into hiding or being held somewhere against his will.'

I was actually thinking about the boxes of explosive and whether or not to tell her about the image on Ronnie's digital camera that followed the girlie shots. I finally decided not to mention it until I knew more. It would only add to her worries. It would be bad enough her finding out that her baby brother had a penchant for taking naughty pictures.

Her voice brought me out of my reverie.

'Nicky, we should go to the police.'

'I have.'

'And?'

'They're going to make enquiries.'

'Christ! How long is that going to take?'

I was about to point out that it was a minor miracle in itself to get that proverbial non-action man, Inspector Crabbe, to do anything at all related to Ronnie's disappearance but her eyes were filling with tears so I found myself searching for some crumb of comfort to give her. I took her hand. 'Tim Murray is publishing an appeal for Ronnie to contact his paper.'

'But isn't the *Cannford Clarion* a weekly?'

'Yes, it comes out on Wednesdays. The article appeared yesterday.'

There was a flicker of a smile. 'Will he have any luck do you think?'

'Of course he will!' I said, hoping I sounded more confident than I felt. 'And from now on I'm going to stick to George Mayberry like glue. The moment he remembers where he found Ronnie's camera I'll be the first to know.'

★ ★ ★

We played to a full house that night. I don't know if the good turnout was due to Tim Murray's article or not, but it certainly pleased our leader. I kept my promise to Susan and stayed at George Mayberry's side all evening — when I wasn't on stage that is. When he went for a smoke in the interval I went with him. I even waited outside the Gents while he relieved himself. When the show was over I drove him back to *The Grapes* and without thinking I asked him if he fancied a nightcap. He surprised me by saying he would enjoy a tonic water, as he was quite thirsty. I was really pleased and I took him to join the others at the bar, the 'others' being Roland, Marcia, Melanie and Eddie. Tarquin always seemed to disappear right after the show, even on opening nights. Not that it bothered me because, like Melanie, the less I had to do with him the better. Nevertheless, I was intrigued to know where he shot off to as soon as the curtain came down, so I asked his mother.

'There's a club in town called *The Hang-out*,' she said in her lazy drawl. 'He

174

goes there most nights and stays until the early hours. He took me there once. I didn't like it. Not my scene at all, darling, *far* too noisy. But that's Tarquin for you; the dear boy *has* to be where the action is. This place, he says, is only for oiks and wrinklies.'

'Well it suits this wrinkly,' Roland said and roared with laughter.

George Mayberry took out his cigarettes and asked Marcia if she objected to him smoking.

'No, but *do* try to keep the smoke to yourself, darling. The smell does tend to cling to one's hair.'

In the middle of lighting his cigarette Mayberry froze. 'He said if I wanted to smoke I'd have to go outside.'

Conversation ceased.

'Well, don't look at me!' Arthur protested. 'I never said that! You can smoke anywhere here except in the dining room.'

Roland held up a hand. 'Be quiet! Mayberry is remembering something.'

'Where was this, George,' I asked him gently.

He turned to me and I saw a flicker of fear in his eyes. 'I don't know,' he said desperately.

★　★　★

175

Susan arrived apologising for being so late.

'I've been packing,' she explained. 'I'll take the early train, I can make some telephone calls on the way. I should have it all sorted by Tuesday at the latest.'

I asked if I could give her a lift.

'Thanks, but I'll take a cab. I hate goodbyes at railway stations.'

Marcia fluttered her eyelashes. 'I know just what you mean, darling. They always remind me of Celia Johnson and Trevor Howard in *Brief Encounter* and I feel like weeping.'

The party began to break up. Eddie was the first to leave followed shortly after by George Mayberry who I thought tottered a bit on his way to the door. I put it down to sitting for a long time on a bar stool but Arthur corrected me.

'He'll sleep well tonight,' he chuckled. 'He asked me to slip a large Vodka in his tonic on the q.t.'

Marcia looked at him wide-eyed. 'Really?' she breathed. 'The sly old devil.'

Arthur and Roland became deeply engrossed in a conversation about the possibility of a tour next year. Another bottle of wine appeared and I wasn't surprised when, a few minutes later, Marcia announced she was going leave them to it and go to her room. Susan and I followed shortly after.

I saw Susan to her door. I bent forward to kiss her cheek and she surprised me by turning her head, allowing our lips to meet. They say you never forget your first love but this was no inexperienced, blushing, thirteen-year-old that I now held in my arms.

When I got my breath back, I daringly asked if she was going to invite me in.

She stepped back. 'Certainly not!' she said.

Thinking I'd blown my chances, I hung my head. She touched my cheek.

'You're the one with the king-size bed and the en-suite. Why don't you invite me?' she whispered.

* * *

We sneaked in to breakfast like embarrassed newlyweds at about eight-thirty the following morning. So much for me getting up when I wake up! Arthur came to take our order but I don't remember what I asked for, I just sat there, gazing at Susan across the table. Fate had brought her back into my life and I was completely and utterly smitten — I wondered if people still use that old-fashioned word — anyway, it described perfectly the way I felt about her. Just having her around made me feel good. I didn't want her to leave me and I told her so. She smiled understandingly.

'I have to go, people are relying on me,' she said. I was about to speak when she reached across the table and placed a finger on my lips. 'It's been wonderful, Nicky, but it wouldn't work, you and me. I have strong feelings for you too but I could never live a nomadic life as you do, I need to put down roots.'

Arthur chose that moment to arrive with our breakfast and conversation ceased for a while as he set the plates down in front of us.

When he had gone she said, 'At least I can go knowing you are here for Ronnie. You will find him won't you, Nicky?'

I stared down at my 'full English' wondering how I was going to swallow it with a big lump in my throat.

'I'll find him all right,' I said hoarsely.

★ ★ ★

George Mayberry didn't turn up for breakfast, so after an emotional farewell to Susan, I ordered a pot of coffee and stationed myself at a table at the end of the taproom bar near the main entrance to wait for him to appear.

Arthur's 'Reception' consisted of nothing more than a brass bell at the end of the bar and an oblong piece of peg-board screwed to the wall behind it upon which to hang the room keys. From where I was sitting I could see the hook underneath George Mayberry's room number was empty so I comfortably assumed him to be still in his room.

My coffee arrived and with it a copy of the latest *Cannford Clarion* and a large manila envelope, which Arthur informed me, had been delivered to *The Grapes* by hand that morning. It bore the Clarion's logo and above the typewritten name and address, 'Private and Confidential', had been scrawled. I guessed it to be copies of the photographs and left it unopened on the table and picked up the newspaper.

On the front page, under a two-column headline: 'WAS FORMER *BROOKLANDS* STAR VICTIM OF MUGGER?' there was an account of an ambulance being called to the Hobswood Memorial Hall followed by a description of my injuries. It didn't surprise me that a wily newspaperman like Tim Murray would have a source at the local hospital but I wondered how the Clarion had got hold of the photograph which was a publicity shot I'd had taken some years ago. I made a mental note to cut the article out and send it to Sam Abrahams. At least he'd be pleased.

I found Ella Thompson's piece on Ronnie which I enjoyed reading, she had done a good job on him although to call him acting's David Bailey was, I thought, a bit over the top. It concluded with an appeal for him or anyone knowing of his whereabouts 'to contact this newspaper, a reward will be paid for all useful information!' The photograph of Ronnie was the one I'd provided. I was thinking how ridiculously young he looked in it when the outer doors burst open with a crash.

'Quick! Quick! Where's the landlord? Where's the phone? We must get an ambulance!'

A young black woman carrying two large shopping bags and a child's scooter dumped her burden by the bar and began hammering on the bell. I got to my feet and went over to her.

'Can I help?' I asked. 'Has your child had an accident?'

She stared at me blankly. She was in a state of shock. 'My Cherie's in school,' she said. Then, suddenly remembering her purpose, she began hammering on the bell again. 'We must get an ambulance — for him!'

'Him?'

'In the pond! The man in the pond!'

Arthur arrived wiping his hands on a bar towel. 'What's all the commotion?' he said, frowning at the young woman.

'She said something about a man in the pond.'

'Our pond?'

'Yes,' the woman said breathlessly. 'I was on my way back from taking my Cherie to school when I saw him. We always feed the ducks on the way to school but we were a bit late this morning so I stopped on the way back. I still had the bread you see?' She shuddered involuntarily. 'At first I thought it was some old clothes floating on the water but I'm sure it's a man . . . We must get an ambulance!'

'More likely some rubbish the kids have thrown in,' Arthur grumbled. 'They tossed my Pensioner's Lunch sign in there once, the little buggers.'

I dialled the emergency services on my mobile. When the call was answered I handed it to the woman.

'I think you'd better ask for the police as well,' I said.

Arthur left us while she was on the phone. He now returned carrying a large steaming mug and with Polly close on his heels.

'Here you are, love,' he said. 'A nice cup of tea. I've put two sugars in it, and a little drop of something stronger . . . Poll, you stay with the lady while Mr Carter and me go and have a look at what's out there in the pond.'

With no wind to chill the air it felt pleasantly warm outside. Everything appeared quite normal. On the far side of the green someone was throwing a ball for a dog, a Royal Mail van was waiting with its engine running for a tractor to rumble past before it could pull away from the general store and in the opposite direction a milk float with empty bottles rattling, hummed along the road on its way back to the depot. At the pond a flock of pigeons were competing with the resident ducks for the scraps of bread thrown there by Cherie's mother.

'Look at that!' Arthur said. 'There's my bloody luggage trolley in the water. I tell you if I catch those little buggers I'll swing for 'em I will!'

'Over here!' I shouted and began pulling off my shoes and socks.

With my trousers rolled up like some Bank Holiday seaside paddler, I waded out into the water. It was cold and I could feel slimy mud oozing between my toes. A body was lying face down, spread-eagled in the water, the head draped with pondweed. She said it was a man and I had no reason to argue with her on that score. I know a lot of women these days wear their hair short like men, Polly being a prime example, but this fellow was well over six feet tall and was wearing a man's, military style trench coat and very masculine striped pyjamas. I grabbed hold of his coat and towed him to the bank.

The fat publican was busily engaged in cleaning the muck off his trolley but my shout of, 'I'd appreciate a hand, thank you!' secured his attention. He took in the situation in an instant and without a second thought waded into the pond. With one combined heave we had the sodden mass out of the water and onto the grass verge. I knew it was a forlorn hope, but nevertheless I felt for a pulse, then together we rolled the body over and I found myself looking into the sightless eyes of George Mayberry.

Arthur volunteered to go back to *The Grapes* and get a towel for my wet feet. I was grateful for this solicitude, which, from Arthur, was not unexpected. He went off, his wet trousers flapping around his ankles, dragging the retrieved luggage trolley behind him. When the paramedics arrived I had my socks and shoes back on. The police got there as Arthur and me were standing in respectful silence as the ambulance crew were loading poor old George Mayberry's body into their vehicle. The flashing blue lights and the smell of antiseptic took me back to my own recent experience, my hand automatically going to my ear which was still sore to the touch.

Both policemen obviously knew Arthur and seemed more interested in his account of the affair than mine. You would have thought he'd waded in and brought the body out of the duck pond single-handed. I didn't hear either of them ask if George Mayberry was in the habit of going for an early morning stroll in his bare feet and pyjamas but with Arthur stressing the old man's drink problem they probably didn't think it necessary. I followed them back to the pub where they began interviewing the woman with the shopping bags and scooter. I retrieved the envelope, which was still as I'd left it on the table with my now cold pot of coffee and the newspaper, and went to my room quite unnoticed.

★ ★ ★

Feeling better for a shower and a change of clothes, I got in my car and drove to the police station. Inspector Crabbe knew all about George Mayberry and Ronnie's camera. I wondered what he was thinking now that the old scenery painter was dead.

The officer on desk duty on this occasion was a rather attractive WPC. As I approached the counter she looked up and did the old double take. I smiled and said she'd probably

184

seen me on television in *Brooklands*. She blushed and said she hadn't, but she had seen *Waiting On The Bridge* at the Hobswood Memorial Hall. Oh well, such is fame! She put a call through to Crabbe who agreed to see me. He must have told her I wasn't a violent criminal as I was allowed to make my way to his office unaccompanied.

He was wearing the same hairy jacket, the same look of exasperation and if anything, there was more paper littering his desk. I knew the drill. He didn't rise, we nodded at each other and I sat on one of the bentwood chairs.

'Mr Carter,' he said, fixing me with his penetrating stare. 'I understand you are here about Mr Mayberry's unfortunate accident.'

'Are you sure it was an accident?'

'There's nothing suspicious about a known inebriate falling in some water and drowning, regrettably it happens quite often, in canals, lakes, rivers, even duck ponds.'

How does a man get to be so pig-headed? 'What if the same person who tried to stop me asking questions also tried to stop poor old George from giving answers — only this time he tried a bit too hard?' I found I was shouting. I didn't care. 'You must do something!'

Crabbe sat back in his chair and placed his

hands flat on the desk in front of him. 'This is not one of your television soap operas, Mr Carter. There will be a post-mortem examination of the body and what I do rather depends on the findings.'

He stood up and came round to the front of his desk. He was a small man. Not as small as Roland Pembroke but small for a policeman. Perhaps that was why he was in the CID.

'I'm not trying to be obstructive but my department is currently undertaking an investigation of major importance in which all my officers are fully engaged. I really don't have the manpower to look into unsubstantiated suspicions.'

I could see I wasn't going to get anywhere with him so I left to seek solace and a cup of coffee at the offices of the *Clarion*.

Tim Murray bustled me through to his little den in the corner of the busy general office. He saw me seated and shut the door, the shouted one-way conversations and the incessant ringing of telephones being instantly muted.

'Where have you been, Nick? I've been trying to reach you all morning.'

I shrugged my shoulders. 'I obey the rules and switch my mobile off in the police station. I've been to see Inspector Crabbe.'

'About George Mayberry?'

'You know about him being found in the pond?'

Murray nodded. 'Of course,' he said.

'Crabbe says he can't do anything until after the post-mortem.'

'Why should he do anything at all? The way I heard it, the old boy had a few too many, went walkabout and fell in the pond. Unfortunate accident, end of story . . . Talking of stories, you waded in to get him out, right? Would you mind answering a question or two?'

With my name in it, Murray would no doubt sell the story to one of the nationals as: '*BROOKLANDS STAR IN DROWNING TRAGEDY*'. Well, it would please Sam, that's for sure.

I was treated to a passable lasagne followed by a surprisingly good steamed sponge pudding in the *Clarion's* canteen while Murray plied me with questions about this morning's incident at the pond. As I was about to leave I asked if he wanted a picture.

'Don't worry about that, laddie,' he said, grinning. 'Ella got a dozen publicity photos from your agent as soon as we knew you were here.'

When I got back to *The Grapes* I found a note under my door announcing that a meeting of the company had been called that afternoon in the taproom at three o'clock. I assembled with the others at the appointed time. No one seemed to want to talk; there was none of the usual jokey chitchat, bellowed directives from our actor-manager or the drawn-out, drawling interjections from his wife. Only Tarquin, who was standing at the back of the group casually smoking a cigarette, seemed unaffected by recent events. Roland Pembroke cleared his throat. He spoke quietly for effect, his voice like velvet.

'If you were expecting me to announce that there will be no performance this evening you would be wrong.'

Melanie gasped audibly, Marcia gave a little sob, Eddie Dolan sniffed and Tarquin's handsome face twisted into a cynical smile.

'In recent years I have come to understand George Mayberry, perhaps better than anyone,' Roland continued. 'He was a true professional and although he has taken his own final curtain I know he would want the show to go on. So, company, that is precisely what we are going to do — and we will dedicate tonight's performance to his memory. Has everyone got a glass?'

There was a general reaching for the drinks that had been acquired out of habit on entering the bar but barely touched.

Roland held a glass of red wine aloft and

thundered, 'I give you, George Mayberry!'

'George Mayberry!' we echoed emotionally.

Well and truly fired up by the actor-manager's little speech we all went on stage that evening determined to do our very best for the old scenery painter. The audience that Friday evening didn't realise it but they witnessed possibly the best performance of *Waiting On The Bridge* by the Pembroke Players, or anyone else for that matter. After the show Tarquin sat next to me at the makeup mirror.

'The old boy certainly knows how to motivate people,' he said, helping himself to a generous scoop of cold cream from my jar.

I felt drained of emotion and certainly in no mood for conversation, particularly with him. 'Yes, he does,' I replied tersely. 'I found his words quite inspiring.'

'It was all crap of course.'

I stared at him in the mirror. 'What do you mean?' I asked.

'Well, if he'd cancelled he'd have lost tonight's takings and he would have had to return all the advanced bookings.'

★   ★   ★

When I got back to *The Grapes* I didn't bother to go to the bar. I was in no mood for socialising and I doubted if any of the others would be there anyway. Back in my room I made myself a coffee and sat staring at my mobile. I wanted to talk to Susan — I needed to hear her voice — but if I were to call her she'd be bound to ask if George Mayberry had regained his memory. How could I tell her he was dead? The phone rang and I nearly jumped out of my skin.

'Nick? It's Tim Murray. Good news, laddie. We've had a response to the appeal. A postman says he saw Ronnie the morning he disappeared. I've arranged to meet him at my office lunchtime tomorrow. He'll be there at 12.30. Is that okay for you?'

They say that when one door closes another opens.

10

Because of road works on the bypass I only just managed to get to the *Clarion* offices on time. In fact I was still talking to Tim Murray in the little entrance lobby when the door opened and a dark, sinewy man wearing a white baseball cap, light blue shirt, dark blue shorts and white trainers squeezed his way in. He had a wrinkled walnut of a face and big brown eyes that constantly flitted back and forth. They finally settled on me.

'Mr Murray?' he asked.

I gave the editor a nudge and he stepped forward holding out his hand. The visitor didn't notice, his eyes were still fixed on me.

'I seen you somewhere before, man.'

'My photograph was in the *Cannford Clarion* this week,' I said. 'I'm Nick Carter.'

The crumpled face grinned, exposing a mouthful of gleaming, white teeth. 'That's it! You're what's-his-name, Ned Tucker, in *Brooklands* . . . Hey, man! Can I have your autograph for my wife? She'll be thrilled to bits!'

Tim Murray pointedly cleared his throat. 'Mr Cole?' he said loudly, gaining our visitor's full attention for the first time since he arrived. 'You told me on the phone that you saw Ronnie Simmons on the morning of Saturday the twenty-fifth of June.'

'That other fella whose picture was in the paper?'

'That's right.' Murray said and waited.

Andy Cole cleared his throat. 'I'm a postman,' he began.

'I guessed that by the uniform,' I said.

There was no mistaking the look Tim Murray shot at me, it said, 'Shut up and let me handle this interview'. I raised my hands and looked skywards, resolved to keep quiet in future.

'This is my own hat,' Cole said proudly.

Murray was losing patience. 'Aye, and very smart it is too. Now, what can you tell us about Ronnie Simmons?'

'The paper said there'd be a reward, man.'

'The paper said a reward would be paid for any useful information. So far, Mr Cole, you've told us nothing.'

'All right, all right. I was getting to it.' He rolled his eyes at me. He obviously regarded me as some sort of ally. 'I saw this Mr Simmons coming out of *The Grapes* when I was delivering there that Saturday morning. Is that good enough for you?'

'Saturday the twenty-fifth?'

'That's right, man, Saturday the twenty-fifth, like it says in the paper. Do I get my reward now?'

'How can you be sure it was Mr Simmons?'

'I seen him before, man! I'd know him anywhere with that long blond hair of his. I see him most mornings at that time getting on that motorbike of his and zooming off somewheres.'

I couldn't keep quiet any longer. 'And is that what he did on the twenty-fifth?'

'Sure thing, man. He came out, helmet on, got on his motorbike and rode off, same as always.'

'Are you sure?' Murray asked.

He thought for a moment. 'Yeah. He did all that, man. He had a big backpack on — and he was in a hurry.'

'In a hurry?'

'Yeah, head down, man, like a rugby player going for the line. I had to do a bit of quick sidestepping, I don't mind telling you, or I'd still be picking letters up today.' He chuckled at that.

Murray was carefully extracting some banknotes from his wallet. 'And is that all you have to tell us, Mr Cole?'

The postman nodded, eyeing the money eagerly. Murray wrote something in his notebook, which he asked Cole to sign.

'I may be the *Clarion*'s editor,' he said, 'but I'd never get my money back without a receipt.'

The postman pocketed the cash and then looked at me expectantly.

Of course, the autograph! I asked Tim Murray for a page from his notebook.

'I'll do better than that,' he said.

He slipped into the main office and was back a few moments later brandishing one of my publicity photographs.

I asked Cole for his wife's name, to which I added, 'with love', and signed it with a flourish. He went away a happy man — and so did I.

His testimony of Ronnie dashing off on his motorcycle supported Melanie's theory that he'd gone chasing after a scoop. I was prepared to go along with that, I only hoped Susan would be.

When I got back to *The Grapes* I found the place in turmoil. Marcia was weeping and wailing and shrugging off Melanie's attempts to comfort her and Roland was shouting and waving his arms at Arthur. The little actor-manager turned as I came in.

'Ah, Nicholas, just the man! Find young Chambers, there's a good fellow. Tell him he's playing the Honourable Reggie tonight.'

'He's standing in for Tarquin?'

'That's right, my son has been, er, unavoidably detained.' He made for the door. 'I've got to go now — but don't worry, I'll be back in time for the show.'

Before I could ask what was going on he'd left so I appealed to Melanie.

'Tarquin's been arrested!' she said, and Marcia started bawling again.

'He's *what*?'

'He's been arrested, something to do with drugs. Gavin came with two uniformed officers and they took him away.'

I remembered passing a police car as I drove into *The Grapes* but I'd thought nothing of it. When they're going in the opposite direction they don't bother me; it's those coming up behind that worry me and have me driving with one eye on the road and the other on the speedometer.

Tarquin arrested? My first impulse was to shout, 'hooray!' But Marcia was so obviously upset I contented myself by quietly asking why.

'You'll have to ask Gavin. He's still around somewhere. I heard him say he's been watching Tarquin for some time.' She moved away from Marcia and lowered her voice. 'Nick, you don't think that's the only reason we've been seeing so much of him do you?'

In her relationship with men, Melanie had

received two nasty knocks in a relatively short time. Tarquin had taken wicked advantage of her naivety and she was of the opinion that Ronnie had dumped her in favour of his photographic career. I fervently hoped the young detective had not simply been using her as means to stay close to Tarquin.

'I should think he's been combining business with pleasure,' I said, which was probably true.

I found DC Partridge sitting in his car writing up some notes. The Volkswagen must have been in the car park when I drove in but I hadn't noticed it. He saw me and wound the window down.

'You've heard we've arrested Tarquin Pembroke?' he said, looking very pleased with himself.

'On what charge?'

'Possession to begin with. You wouldn't believe the amount of amphetamine tablets he had stashed in his room.'

And there was me thinking it was publicity handouts Pembroke junior was distributing to that eager bunch of sixth-formers.

'Mr Crabbe's on his way to Harwich right now to meet the afternoon ferry,' Partridge continued excitedly. 'Although Tarquin's not saying, the DI feels sure he knows who his supplier is. There's nothing like a good drugs bust for promotion, Mr Crabbe says.'

'So we won't be seeing you at the show anymore then?'

The young policeman looked puzzled. 'Why do you say that, sir?'

'Well, I thought with Tarquin banged up, duty done and all that.'

Realization dawned. 'Oh, no, sir. I always began my surveillance *after* the show. I may have to miss tonight's performance but I'll definitely be at the next.'

'Just you be sure to tell Melanie that,' I said and walked away, feeling relieved for her sake.

I suddenly remembered Brian Chambers. Melanie had given me his address as Rose Cottage, Chapel Heath. This proved to one of four small terraced houses just off the main road by the church.

The lady who opened the door was big bosomed and rosy cheeked, the typical countrywoman straight out of central casting, right down to her floral wraparound pinafore and a grubby-faced infant clinging to her skirts. Her jaw dropped when she saw me standing on her doorstep.

'Good afternoon. Is Brian at home?'

'You *are* him,' she said.

'I'm Nick Carter,' I said politely. 'I'm with the Pembroke Players.'

'Brian said you was him but I said it

couldn't be. 'Nasty' Ned's still on the telly, I said.'

'Not for much longer I'm afraid. I take it you haven't seen *Waiting On The Bridge?*'

'I don't go out much, what with the twins to look after.' She bundled the little one inside and stepped back. 'Here, I'm forgetting my manners. Come in, Mr Carter, come in.'

The cottage was small, the ceiling low with exposed beams that I had to duck under. A brick fireplace took up the whole of one wall, a large vase of cut hydrangeas stood in front of the empty grate. A small child, a mirror image of the one clinging to her skirts, was playing on the floor with colourful wooden bricks. She ushered me over to a big, over-stuffed sofa, gesturing that I should sit down. I sank into its depths wondering how the devil I was ever going to get up again. She brushed away the clinging child who immediately sat on the floor with its sibling and took over the building bricks game.

'A cup of tea!' she announced, going through into what I took to be the kitchen. This was confirmed by the sound of a kettle being filled from a tap followed by the rattle of china.

'Yes, please,' I said.

The children stopped playing and stared at me. They were both a bit grubby, but like their mother they had glowing red cheeks and looked the picture of health. I made a face at them. They made a face back and they both chinked with laughter.

'Can you get someone to look after these two tonight, Mrs Chambers?' I called.

A tray loaded with teacups, plates and a homemade fruitcake appeared. 'I could always ask my neighbour,' she said with a puzzled frown. 'And I'm not Mrs Chambers anymore, Brian's father is dead. He was a soldier.'

I struggled to get to my feet and failed. 'I'm terribly sorry,' I said.

She went back in the kitchen to reappear almost immediately with a teapot. 'It was a long time ago, Mr Carter. I'm Mrs Turner now and these two keep me busy, I can tell you. I don't get time to brood.' The tea was poured and I was handed a plate with a large slice of cake on it. 'Now, why should I ask someone to look after the twins tonight?' she asked.

'Because Brian will be in the play.'

'What, on the stage?'

'Yes, on the stage and in front of a live audience. He doesn't know yet, I came here to tell him.'

'Oh, I'd love to see that,' she said, brushing away a tear.

The cake tasted good but it took a lot of eating. Politely declining a second slice, I finished my tea and successfully got to my feet. 'I really must be going Mrs, er, Turner.' We both laughed. 'Ask Brian to meet me at Hobswood Memorial Hall at six, will you? There will be two tickets waiting for you there tonight with my compliments. The curtain goes up at seven-thirty. There are no reserved seats so get there early. It's usually a good house on a Saturday.'

As I drove the short distance back to *The Grapes*, my thoughts were not of the play, but of Ronnie. I go to bed at night thinking about Ronnie and I wake up in the morning thinking about Ronnie. Here we are, another Saturday. Even if he'd gone to Timbuktu, surely someone would have heard from him by now. He'd been missing for almost two weeks and I was no nearer to discovering his whereabouts now than when I first got here.

When I got to the pub, I went to my room resolved to go though all the evidence again logically. Arthur had thoughtfully provided each of his rooms with writing materials, so using the dressing table as a desk and one of Ronnie's old photographic magazines to rest the notepaper on I sat down to make a list of what I'd discovered so far.

At the top of my blank sheet I wrote:
                     What are the facts?

And under that:
*Ronnie walked out on his job with no
explanation.*

*He phones Tim Murray Friday night
saying he'd discovered something.*

*The postman sees him leave The Grapes
on Saturday morning with a large backpack
(presumably containing the things from his
room) and in a hurry, 'head down like a
rugby player going for the line'.*

*He rides off on his motorbike, which is
later recovered from the train station.*

I sat and stared at what I'd written. So?
I said to myself. Ronnie was a wannabe
photojournalist wasn't he? Everything thus
far points to him chasing off after a big story.
Which is what Melanie believes.

I then wrote another heading:
                     The Unexplained.

Followed by:
*Why did Ronnie behave completely out of
character?*

*Why did he leave without telling his
girlfriends, Polly or Marcia — he was with
Marcia the night before he left — or Melanie,*

who was only in the next room?

Because the picture of the explosive was on the digital memory card after the nude shots of Marcia, he must have taken it on Friday night.

Caleb Pilcher was lying about that mobile — why did Ronnie leave it in his motorbike?

Where did George Mayberry find the camera?

Who searched my room — and why?

Who tried to scare me off — and why?

I sat staring at the paper then I pushed it away and went across to the bar for a sandwich and a beer.

★ ★ ★

Brian Chambers was at the Memorial Hall waiting for me when I got there. He was beaming.

'You're not pulling my leg are you Nick? Am I really going on tonight?'

'You've not heard about Tarquin then?'

'Blimey! Don't tell me he's done a bunk as well!'

'No, he's been arrested. It's to do with drugs.'

He took the news very calmly. 'It was only a matter of time,' he said philosophically.

202

'He's been a pusher as long as I've known him. He offered me some once. I told him it was a mug's game and said I'd tell his dad if he tried it on again.'

The Pembroke Player's Wardrobe Department consisted of large wicker hampers containing an assortment of costumes, wigs and other sundry properties, the origins of which were lost in time. I remember seeing one at *The Grapes*, which I think Roland regarded as an extension of his wardrobe. Fortunately there were several others at the theatre. I guided young Chambers over to them and began sorting through their contents. I felt we would get away with the top half of The Honourable Reggie's costume but with Tarquin being a lot taller than Brian we needed to find some suitable trousers.

'Here, go and try these on,' I shouted, flinging a pair at him. 'How are you with his lines?'

'I'll be all right. It's not what you would call a big part is it? And I've stood in for Tarquin that many times at rehearsals.'

I suddenly thought of poor old George Mayberry. 'There'll be no prompter.'

'Nah! I'll be all right.'

He had the trousers on; they looked okay. 'We'll have to do something with your hair,' I said.

*   ⋆ ⋆ ⋆

As things so often do when you least expect them to, the performance that evening went off well. The people of Hobswood packed the hall. The Players had been the subject of much gossip recently and I hoped the house was full for the right reasons. I spotted two people who undoubtedly were there simply to see the show. Young Brian's mother and a man who I assumed was Mr Turner were in the front row. I was surprised but pleased to see Gavin Partridge in the audience as well. The Pembrokes demonstrated their professionalism by becoming Sir William and Lady Haslett immediately they put on costume and makeup. Our apprentice (with his hair slicked down, a small stuck-on moustache to add age and plenty of Leichner flesh tone to cover the pimples) did a good job as The Honourable Reggie and only once faltered with his lines. I was in the wings at the time (we took it in turns to be the prompter with whoever wasn't on stage picking up the prompt book) and I fed Brian the line which he picked up like a seasoned professional.

DC Partridge and the Turners were waiting outside when I left the hall. Brian's mother came over, pulling her partner with her.

'This is my Jim, Mr Carter,' she said.

Jim Turner was a large man and I wondered how he managed with the low beams in Rose Cottage. 'How do?' he said, demonstrating that he was also a man of few words.

Mrs Turner was bubbling. 'Wasn't our Brian wonderful!' she gushed. 'He's always loved acting. He was in every play they did at his school. I can't thank you enough for giving him this opportunity, Mr Carter.'

I was about to explain that her son being in tonight's production had nothing to do with me when the boy himself appeared and I was forgotten as Mrs Turner rushed off to gather her son to her capacious bosom.

'A good show tonight, sir,' Partridge said.

'I didn't expect to see you here. What happened to the big drugs bust?'

He looked at his feet. 'We had everyone there, Drugs Squad, Customs Officers, Sniffer Dogs, the lot — and it was a complete washout! It was Caleb Pilcher we were waiting for, there's no harm in me telling you that, it'll be the talk of all the pubs in the county by now anyway.'

'Tarquin said Pilcher was his supplier?'

DC Partridge stiffened. 'I never said that, sir. Let's say we had reason to search Mr Pilcher's van when he arrived at Harwich.'

'And found nothing?'

'Oh, we found something all right. Six cases of Beaujolais and two thousand cigarettes.'

'Not enough to arrest him for?'

'No, he claimed they were for his own use.'

So much for Crabbe's investigation of major importance, I thought. 'The Inspector is not going to get much promotion out of that, is he?' I said, trying not to grin.

Partridge was silent for a moment. 'We've had the result of the autopsy on Mr Mayberry.'

That took the smile off my face.

'He didn't drown,' he continued. 'There was no water found in his lungs.'

'So he *was* murdered?'

'Too early to say, sir. The DI's asked for a full forensic examination.'

11

With Melanie having gone on somewhere with Partridge, it was a rather gloomy group of four who arrived back at *The Grapes*. Marcia, who still had the sniffles, went straight to her room, and Dolan made a beeline for Benny who was in his usual Polly ogling corner at the far end of the bar. Finding myself left with Roland, I asked him if he would like to stay for a nightcap.

'Why not, my boy?' he said. 'I could do with a large Scotch.' I called for two. 'Tarquin is up before the Magistrates on Monday,' he said grimly. 'My lawyer believes he will be released on bail, but until then he remains in police custody.'

'It's a bad business,' I mumbled, which was all I could think of to say.

He then took me quite by surprise. 'A couple of nights in a cell will probably do him a power of good!' he growled. 'His mother spoils him you know, only child and all that. She knew what he was up to. I found some pills in his dressing room once and showed them to her. She laughed, telling me they were only ecstasy tablets and no stronger than my night-time brandy. All the bright young things use them nowadays, she said.'

Arthur brought the drinks over. 'On the house,' he said. 'I'll have one with you if you don't mind.'

'She had such ambitions for him,' Roland continued. 'She had visions of him at Stratford with the Royal Shakespeare — but Tarquin isn't interested in the theatre. He isn't interested in anything really, except having a good time.' He took a gulp of the neat whisky and grimaced. 'Marcia bought him that car,' he said huskily. Arthur pushed a jug of water within his reach and he dribbled some into his glass with a mumbled thanks. 'It was a bribe to get him to come on this tour, and what does he do? He goes out damned clubbing night after night!'

Without his usual bluff and bluster Roland Pembroke seemed smaller somehow, shrunken, and older.

'Perhaps he just needs to be taught a lesson,' I said, and Roland nodded his head sadly.

'The police thought Caleb Pilcher was involved,' Arthur volunteered. 'They pounced on his van when he got off the ferry but all they found was booze and fags.'

'Which was for his personal use,' I put in, remembering my conversation with DC Partridge.

Arthur grinned and winked. 'Of course.'

Roland declined my offer of another drink and left the bar. 'Full company meeting tomorrow morning at ten,' he called over his shoulder. 'Spread the word, my boy, spread the word.'

Bidding Arthur goodnight, I followed the little actor-manager's example and made my way to my room.

Roland had sounded more his old self as he left and I was pleased about that. He was right, a night or two in the cells is just what Tarquin needed.

It was late but I took a chance and rang Tim Murray on his mobile.

'Nick! You certainly pick your times. I was just about to get into bed.'

'George Mayberry didn't drown.'

'I know. He was suffocated. Crabbe has ordered a forensic examination.' (I should have known that the *Clarion*'s editor would have a contact in the coroner's office as well!) 'He's pulling all the stops out on this one,' he continued. 'He desperately needs to save face after that fiasco at Harwich. I know how Tom Crabbe's mind works, laddie, if he thinks a drugs case could get him his Chief Inspector, then a murder's got to be worth Superintendent at least!'

'It's a pity someone had to die to spur

Crabbe into action,' I said bitterly.

Murray was silent for a moment and then he said, 'This has something to do with Ronnie's camera. Am I right?'

'There was a good chance George Mayberry was silenced because of it. I said as much to Crabbe but he scoffed at the idea.'

'Why should Mayberry be silenced?'

'To prevent him remembering where he found it.'

'He found it? You said he was looking after it.'

It was time to own up. The truth couldn't hurt George Mayberry now. 'The girls and I came across it in his room. He said he couldn't remember how it came to be there and I believed him. Ronnie had gone missing and there he was with his camera in his wardrobe. He would have died of shame if it had got in the papers.'

'You could have trusted me, laddie,' Murray said, sounding somewhat aggrieved.

'The poor old chap suffered from short-term memory loss, at least that's what Roland Pembroke called it. Anything from the past he could recall in the smallest detail, but yesterday? Forget it!'

'Then why bother to silence him?'

'According to Roland, old George had flashes of recall and sooner or later something would trigger off the memory of finding the camera.'

'Who else was aware of that?'

'Everyone. Roland talked quite openly about it.'

'But you never witnessed Mr Mayberry have one of these, er, flashbacks?'

I was suddenly transported back to the taproom at *The Grapes*. It was late evening, after the show. There was Roland and Marcia, Melanie and Eddie — and Arthur pouring George Mayberry a tonic water. 'I was there on one occasion when he did start to remember something,' I said.

'Yes, yes?' Murray sounded excited. 'What was it?'

'It was something about going outside to have a smoke.'

There was an exasperated puff from Murray. 'That could be anything, laddie,' he said.

'Mm.'

'And nothing to do with the camera.'

'Right! But it proved he did have flashes of recall and someone wasn't taking any chances because the next day he was dead.'

There was another pause and then Murray said, 'You know what you've done now, don't you?'

'No?'

'You've ruined any chance I had of getting some sleep tonight. Perhaps you can understand now why I keep my mobile number confidential.'

I couldn't help thinking how different things might have been had he given it to Ronnie. I said goodnight and rang off.

Like Murray, I didn't feel much like sleep so I decided to experiment with a sachet labelled 'cappuccino' from the tray. The photographic magazine was still lying where I'd left it on the dressing table and while I was waiting for the kettle to boil I flipped though its glossy pages. Apart from a lengthy article headed, *Digital versus Thirty-five millimetre*, it seemed to be nothing more than a collection of whole-page advertisements. The kettle boiled and I was about to give up on it when a picture of a place I knew well caught my eye. It was St Michael's Mount just off the Cornish coast. I don't think a year went past without Uncle Stan walking us kids out to it at low tide along the causeway from Marazion beach. The photograph had been taken at sunset, the rocky island topped by its castle a dramatic silhouette against a backdrop of blood red clouds. The heading was, *This Month's Competition*, and it went on to urge readers to send in their shots of coastal sunsets. I could see why Ronnie was so anxious to get back to St Bede's with a colour film in his camera. The old church with its stubby tower would look well with the sun setting over the estuary behind it.

★ ★ ★

As usual, there was no one else in the dining room when I went across for breakfast. Arthur was very subdued, which was out of character but understandable in the circumstances I suppose. I was grateful, as I certainly wasn't in the mood for jolly banter. I wasn't in the mood for a full English either and settled for just tea and toast.

'I suppose the tour could still go ahead, sir?' he asked, a tad hopefully I thought.

Business was obviously in the forefront of Arthur's mind this morning. Next week we were due to play Oxlow Ferry, which again was easily reachable from our base at *The Grapes*. There was another month to go yet before the group was due to split up and begin rehearsals for pantomime or whatever. He'd be left with a lot of empty rooms to fill if they were to pull out now.

'Roland has called a meeting at ten, but I wouldn't build your hopes up.'

'But the show went off all right last night?'

'Thanks to young Brian Chambers,' I said, buttering some toast. 'He took over Tarquin's part. But we can't go on like that.'

'I see what you mean, sir. If the lad's acting on the stage, how's he going to cover for Eddie Dolan when he's off on one of his little trips?'

That really hadn't occurred to me. I'd been thinking more of what would happen should one of the principals, Marcia, or Roland himself perhaps, succumb to a dose of flu or whatever.

★ ★ ★

Young Brian joined the little group in the taproom at ten, as bright-eyed and bushy-tailed as ever. My compliance with the actor-manager's request to 'spread the word' was to slip a note under Melanie's door. It was she who had telephoned both him and Benny.

We sat at the small but immovably heavy iron tables, each of us looking expectantly at Roland who stood at the bar waiting patiently until the scraping of chair legs on the stone floor subsided and Arthur had finished flitting around ensuring everyone had a cup of coffee (everyone that is except the tragic looking Marcia who, I noticed, had her own personal pot of tea (*Earl Grey, darling, I drink nothing else*).

'Last night's performance was saved by young Chambers here boldly stepping into the breach,' Roland began.

The pimply-faced hero acknowledged this accolade by bobbing up and down in his seat and grinning at everyone.

'There were some who said this young man was too immature to be taken seriously as Melissa's suitor but it's amazing what a little makeup and a lot of enthusiasm can achieve.'

'Don't forget talent, guv.'

The little actor-manager smiled grimly at this cheeky response. Although back to full voice, he did not appear to be at ease, directing his gaze over the heads of his audience rather than looking them in the eye.

'Since Nicholas joined us we have not cancelled one performance — and, yes, Nicholas, I know you agreed to stand-in for Ronnie only until a permanent replacement could be found.' He paused for a laugh that didn't come. He did turn his head in my direction as he said it but still he didn't make eye contact. It was all an act. 'We have not cancelled one performance,' he repeated. 'Not even following the recent sad and tragic death of an old and dear friend.' He walked over to the table where his wife sat and took her hand tenderly. 'But as you all know, legal matters concerning my son will demand a great deal of my time and that of Miss Fontaine in the coming weeks.' Marcia dabbed an eye. 'This, and only this, has forced me to a decision which, I am sure will come as no surprise to you.' He stuck out his chin defiantly. 'I'm ringing down the curtain on this present tour of the Pembroke Players.'

There was a gasp from Melanie, a rattle of glass from behind the bar and a long, drawn out, 'Coor!' from Brian. Eddie was impassive. I guess he'd been briefed beforehand.

Benny was on his feet. 'But you can't, Mr Pembroke. My dad will play hell with me,' he wailed.

'Sit down, Benny,' Eddie growled. 'You leave your da to me.'

Roland then went on to deal with the mundane items like pay and accommodation at *The Grapes*. It would seem that everyone would be paid until the end of the month and we could keep our rooms for another week — which pleased me as I was expecting Susan back in a day or so. When he had finished speaking, both Benny Pilcher and Brian Chambers got up to leave. Benny hurried away but Brian walked dejectedly out of the taproom, his narrow shoulders hunched and his hands deep in the pockets of his black jeans. I caught up with him in the car park.

'Cheer up, Brian. Nothing is ever quite as bad as it seems.'

'It's all right for you, you've got that advertising job your agent's been pestering you about. What have I got to look forward to? Bloody A-levels that's what!'

'Everything will have to stay at Hobswood until Eddie Dolan arranges collection by the company in London, so we haven't got the job of moving it to Oxlow Ferry . . . We've got the day off old son. Fancy going for a spin?'

His face lit up. 'In your little red Italian Job? Not 'arf!'

'There's a short stretch of private road I know. I thought you might like to drive it.'

'Blimey!'

★ ★ ★

I stopped at the bus stop on the Cannford road and Brian scrambled eagerly out of the car to open the gate. On the way over he could hardly contain his excitement. He told me he'd been driving big Jim's Escort in and out of his lockup garage for ages and he'd even had some sessions with him on a nearby abandoned airfield so he wasn't completely without experience. Nevertheless, as I sat in the passenger seat waiting for him to buckle up I began to regret offering him the inducement of driving my pride and joy. Why didn't I simply ask him to come with me to St Bede's?

I suppose I was expecting a grating of gears and a lot of wheel spin but although his getaway was fast it was surprisingly smooth.

'I can't believe this car was built in the sixties,' he shouted as we roared along.

'Nineteen sixty-seven actually.'

'But it looks so new, the seats, the chrome and the paint job. It all looks like it was done yesterday.'

'Not quite yesterday but it wasn't all that long ago. I got it from a firm of classic Mini specialists in Putney. The chap who sold it to me said they'd replaced just about everything and the only original part left was the boot lid. Mind you, he was smiling when he said it so he may well have been pulling my leg.'

The little church looked just as quaint and picturesque and just as lonely as the last time I saw it. I indicated the gravel patch at the side and Brian pulled onto it. There were no other cars there and I couldn't help feeling a little sad that this lovely old building that once would have been bustling with people at this time on a Sunday morning was visited now only by the occasional curious tourist. I could hear a motor mower on the far side of the graveyard and as the door of the church was open I assumed Benny was attending to his duties as groundsman, probably keeping out of the way of his father until Eddie Dolan had spoken to him.

Brian was still grinning as he got out of the car. 'That was awesome! Can I drive back?'

He'd actually driven the little car well, I only hoped he wouldn't be tempted to be more adventurous on the way back. 'Oh, all right,' I said resignedly. 'But I didn't bring you here just so you could drive my car. I want you to show me exactly where you found George Mayberry when you came back from looking for Ronnie.'

'Over here,' he said, indicating a large stone angel at the back of the parking area. 'Mind your step. It's a bit dodgy here in places, really crumbly at the edges. They found some old skulls and bones on Easton beach not so long ago that they reckon came from the graves here what the water had washed away . . . I looked in the church first 'cos that's where I'd left him. He was looking at that old stone font but I told him he'd have to go outside if he wanted to have a smoke, so he came out here.'

'*He said if I wanted to smoke I'd have to go outside.*' That was what George Mayberry

219

had said that night at the bar. The fateful flash of recall that had probably got him killed.

The angel was the sort of thing loved by the Victorians. It was sculpted in marble, all of six feet tall and at least three feet wide across its partially opened wings.

'I was getting real panicky when I couldn't see him,' Brian was saying. 'And then I saw the smoke.'

'Smoke?'

'Yeah, from his fag! He was sitting on this old tomb thing puffing away like a good 'un. I was that relieved!'

Behind the angel was a brick sarcophagus about two feet high topped with a large slab of stone upon which the names of its occupants were inscribed. I looked around, there were no benches in the churchyard and the tomb was just the right height to sit on. I sat down on it myself to mull things over. The scenario that was taking shape in my mind was of Ronnie dashing over here on his motorbike to photograph St Bede's in the sunset only to find a car parked outside the church spoiling the shot. He looks for the driver. The tailgate is open so he looks inside. Pulling away a corner of the rug he discovers the boxes of explosive. What to do? He's always wanted to be a photojournalist and here's one hell of a story! He snatches a quick, flashless shot with his digital camera and then takes a quick peek in the church. That's where he phones Tim Murray. He is disturbed, possibly by the driver coming back and in his haste to get away he leaves the camera by the font, where it remains until the following morning when George Mayberry finds it. The old chap probably put it in his rucksack meaning to return it to its owner and then forgot all about it. It all seemed to tie in but it doesn't explain Ronnie dashing off in such a hurry the following morning or why he left his mobile in his motorbike at the train station . . . And what was a car full of explosives doing parked outside an out-of-the-way house of worship in the first place?

'Wake up, Nick, I was talking to you.'

'I'm sorry, Brian, I was miles away. What were you saying?'

'I asked if you'd like to have a look inside the church?'

Well, that was why I was here, I thought, to try and find answers to the questions that were bugging me. I slid off the tomb. 'Sure, let's go,' I said.

Inside it was just the same, cool, quiet and smelling of flowers and furniture polish.

'The last full-time vicar here was a footballer,' Brian whispered. (Why is it one always whispers in churches?)

'Took holy orders after giving up the game?' I asked, equally reverently.

'Nah! He played Sunday league. Their matches fitted in nicely between his morning and evening services. I had an old auntie what lived here and used to go to this church. She said football was more a religion with him than the one what paid his wages . . . His boots are over there.'

I hadn't noticed it before but there they were, like holy relics in a small glass case fixed to the right-hand wall halfway down the church. I wondered idly if Arthur knew the story.

The tower gate was unlocked and standing open.

'I think I heard Benny mowing the grass as we came in, go and find him, will you? And keep him talking for at least ten minutes. I want to have a look in the tower.'

'All right, but what do I talk about? It isn't as though me and Benny have a lot in common.'

'I don't know! Ask him how he's making out with Polly? You think of something.'

Brian went away shaking his head and I slipped through the gate. Immediately in front of me was the set of bell ropes tied neatly together. They hung down through holes in a wooden floor that was obviously reached by a wide ladder attached to the right-hand wall. Behind me and out of sight to casual visitors to the church were Benny's tools. Various handheld implements such as trowels, shears and pruners lay on the floor and larger items like rakes and brushes leant against the wall. There was also a petrol can, evidence that the lawn mower was also stored there when he wasn't using it. Beyond the gardening implements was a stone archway with a flight of steps that led down, presumably to the burial chamber. An old-fashioned metal light switch was on the wall by the arch. Flicking the switch illuminated a grotto-like passageway and I cautiously made my way down the flight of narrow sandstone steps, which were quite dry although the walls on each side felt cold and damp. Electric light bulbs were strung across the roof of the vault that was, as the flower arranger said, cut out of the living rock, the pick marks being clearly visible in the walls and roof. The chamber was about twenty feet square by about eight feet high. Wooden coffins lay on shelves around the walls and there were a few on trestles in the centre. They all looked to be in an excellent state of preservation. Dates and names of the occupants were etched into brass plates on the lids. I was just thinking how easy it was to read the inscriptions when the lights went out.

They came back on almost immediately but in those few short seconds I came close to panic. I'd never suffered from claustrophobia but suddenly I was conscious of being all alone with only the remains of dead people for company in a man-made cave under I don't know how many tons of rock. It had been cool down in the vault but when I got back to the surface I was sweating. Brian was waiting at the top of the steps. He didn't know how close he came to having the cheeky grin knocked off his face.

'Why the hell did you turn the lights off?' I asked angrily.

'To let you know I was here. You didn't want me to shout did you? Blimey, Nick. I couldn't do with that Benny any longer. He likes having someone to talk to but all he does is stand there with a silly smile on his face. I had to keep thinking of things to say, and when I did, all I got was a one-word answer and he'd be back to his smiling again. I tell you, Nick, he is hard work. Did I give you long enough? Did you see anything interesting?'

What had I expected to see? A crypt full of old coffins. Well, I'd certainly seen that — and

I hadn't much liked being surrounded by the dead at such close quarters either — but there was something else that niggled me about that subterranean chamber. Then I suddenly realised what it was.

'It was what I didn't see that was interesting,' I said.

12

I tried phoning Inspector Crabbe, but I was told he was off duty. Well, it *was* Sunday lunchtime. I had better luck with the local constabulary when I got back to *The Grapes*.

After dropping Brian off at his house and declining his mother's invitation to stay for lunch (I really wasn't in the mood for polite conversation over roast meat and two veg) I drove back to the pub and found the star-crossed lovers, Gavin and Melanie sitting in the taproom holding hands and gazing into each other's eyes over a pair of empty wine glasses. I bought them each a refill as an excuse to join them.

'Cheer up, you've got a whole week before you have to say your goodbyes,' I suggested helpfully.

Melanie sniffed and brushed away a tear. 'No matter where I finish up, Gavin has promised to keep in touch.'

'And I'll come and see you as often as I can,' the young man said earnestly, his eyes still fixed on his beloved's woebegone face.

Suddenly, Melanie got up from the table and with a sob excused herself, saying something about going to the ladies room. Finding myself conveniently alone with the detective constable, I told him I'd discovered the place where George Mayberry had found Ronnie's camera. His expression immediately changed from that of a lovesick swain to being the professional policeman. I went on to impress him further by saying I believed it to be where Ronnie took the picture of the carload of explosives. Although visibly interested, he denied any knowledge of the photograph, which didn't surprise me. Crabbe was obviously playing his cards close to his chest. It wouldn't surprise me if the inspector were afraid of sharing the glory.

'What did you expect to find in the vault, sir, the explosives?'

'Perhaps, I don't know.'

'And there was nothing there except some old coffins?'

'Yes, but the floor was clean and there was no dust. At least on the row of coffins down the middle of the chamber there wasn't, I didn't have time to look at those around the walls.'

Partridge looked puzzled. 'It's not against the law to keep a place clean, sir?' he ventured.

The lad had obviously been too long under Crabbe's influence.

'Visitors are not allowed and it's been almost four hundred years since anyone was interred down there!' I retorted. 'So why does someone suddenly feel the need to sweep the floor and dust the coffins?'

'Leave it with me,' he said with the sort of sympathetic frown that people usually reserve for dotty relatives. 'I'll make some enquiries.'

Melanie returned and the steely-eyed sleuth became the tongue-tied suitor once more. I left them to it and went outside intending to call Sam, but on second thoughts I called Susan instead, ostensibly to see if she had heard from Ronnie (although if she had I'm sure I'd be the first to know) but really because I missed her like crazy and I just wanted to hear her voice.

'Nicky, hi! Good news,' she began. She sounded happy. Perhaps she *had* heard from her missing brother. 'I made some calls on the way here and I got lucky. I found the perfect replacement for my consultant. You know, the one with the broken ankle? I saw him yesterday and he can start tomorrow. Isn't that marvellous?'

I said I was pleased for her.

'But Nicky, that means I can come back to Chapel Heath tomorrow! There's a train at three-twenty that arrives at Cannford just after four. I'll call you.'

Now *that* was marvellous! I was actually humming to myself as I tapped in Sam's number.

'Sam, I'll be free at the end of the week,' I announced cheerfully.

Now, I didn't expect to hear him shout hooray, but I did think it likely that there would be some expression of pleasure, relief, or something. All I got was a grunt.

'Sam, did you hear what I said?'

'Nick, my boy.' (Oh, dear! Sam was being fatherly.) 'How can I tell you this?'

'Tell me what, Sam?' I said warily.

'Deejay couldn't wait. Their TV advert job has gone to someone else.'

Surprisingly I found I wasn't really bothered. 'Who got it, Sam? Do I know him?'

'Jason Carp, the cocky chap from that hospital series on Central, you know, the doctor with the phoney Liverpool accent . . . But don't worry, Nick, something will turn up.'

In this business you bump into just about everyone eventually. I did know Jason Carp. I'd met him some months ago at a test for a new BBC TV police series, *Blues And Twos*, and I had taken an instant dislike to him. We were both auditioning for the same role, that of a tough, case-hardened cop who was one of the principal characters in the drama, but instead of being friendly, as most actors finding themselves in that situation are, he was deliberately rude to me and spent the whole day strutting about the studio as if he'd already got the job, flirting with the makeup girls and cracking jokes at my expense with the production crew. I wanted that part more that I've ever wanted anything, so in a way I was pleased when I heard the project had been shelved. At least it meant Jason Carp wouldn't get it.

Sam seemed in a hurry to get rid of me but I did manage to ask if he had heard from Ronnie. All this produced was another grunt and then he was gone.

I went back inside. The lovebirds were still canoodling so I went over to the bar. Arthur was serving. I ordered a half of lager and a beef and horseradish sandwich.

'It's a lovely day,' he grinned. 'I'll get our Poll to bring it to you outside, shall I, sir? There are still one or two tables free out there.'

'No, I'll stay in here.'

I looked around for a spare bar stool. There was only one but it had someone's cap on it.

'Here, let me shift that for you.' He quickly came from behind the bar and snatched up the greasy looking object. He regarded it with distaste and stuffed it in the corner of the bar counter behind a lifeboat donation box. 'That's Benny's that is. He's outside. Likes to watch our Poll attending to the tables. Sit's for hours ogling her, he does.'

'I didn't see his van in the car park.'

'No. He came on his bike. His dad took the van, said if it wasn't being used by the theatricals he'd take the opportunity to do a few deliveries.'

'Isn't Sunday an odd day to do that?'

'Not if you're delivering furniture it isn't. More likely to find people at home on a Sunday.'

Arthur left me sipping my lager while he went off for my sandwich. I glanced idly at Benny's cap. It really was a disgusting object, black and shiny with oil and grease. There was something inside it, some bicycle clips — and yes, a bunch of keys! Benny must have come here straight from Marshbank church!

As far as I could see, all the evidence pointed to the car full of explosives being parked in front of the church on the night before Ronnie disappeared, but I still had to find out why. I looked at the keys. Benny spends hours ogling Polly, Arthur said. I was slipping them in my pocket when Arthur came back with my lunch.

'Another drink, sir?'

'No thank you.' I took the plate from him.

'And I'll take this to my room if that's all right.'

I didn't though; I took it out to my car. The rare beef and horseradish sandwich with its crisp salad garnish went down a treat on my way to St Bede's.

The old Rover was parked outside on the gravel. Damn it! I had hoped to have the place to myself. I was relieved when, just as I was about to enter the church the matronly flower arranger came out carrying a large bunch of wilted marguerites. She shot me an enquiring look.

'You've been here before,' she said accusingly.

I gave her what I hoped was a disarming smile. 'Hello! Yes, we met last week . . . I, er, just popped back for some more postcards.'

I watched her dump the dead flowers on a little heap in the corner of the churchyard and go to her car. She glanced back and I gave her a cheery wave. The air was still inside the church and I could hear the crunch of her tyres on the gravel quite clearly as she reversed off the parking area. I looked around. Everything was very much the same as when I'd been there before. Altar, choir stalls, pulpit, lectern, organ, pews, font, all the things you expect to see in a small country church, nothing unusual — unless you count the football boots! Fetching Benny's keys out of my pocket I made for the wrought iron gate to the tower. As I switched on the cellar light I wished Brian Chambers or Gavin Partridge were with me, anybody for that matter!

My trainers made no noise on the stone steps. As I entered the vault I mentally kicked myself for not bringing the torch from the car. What if the lights were to go off again? I willed myself not to think about that. The floor had most certainly been swept and the coffins down the middle of the chamber had recently been dusted. I moved forward peering upward at those on the racks. Yes, there were cobwebs and the accumulation of centuries of dust still on those. I found myself grinning, thinking that whoever did the spring clean didn't do a thorough job. I was doing fine, I didn't need anyone to hold my hand. Just then I stubbed my toe on a trestle. The damn thing folded and the coffin it supported crashed down. Its end struck the ground and the lid fell off. I remember thinking, 'aren't those things meant to be screwed on?' as its contents spilled out at my feet.

I expected to see a lot of old bones and stuff but what fell onto the floor was made of non-reflective steel and set up a cacophony of ear-splitting clanging that echoed around the chamber.

'Armed police! Stay where you are.'

A fresh-faced Asian youngster wearing a yellow jacket appeared at the foot of the steps wielding a baton. Another officer, similarly dressed but older, stood immediately behind him. Neither wore a hat and were obviously ready for trouble. I stayed where I was on the cold stone floor. I guess I looked suspicious surrounded as I was by automatic rifles. The first policeman's jaw dropped when he saw the weapons.

'If you let me up the stairs to use my mobile. I'll call DC Partridge and he will clear this up very quickly.' I said, trying to sound 'official'.

The first policeman relaxed a little. 'I know you don't I? Are you one of us?' he asked.

'Not exactly.'

He looked at his colleague who nodded.

'All right, but keep your hands where I can see them,' he said and stood to one side.

Holding my hands at shoulder height and with a nervous policeman fore and aft, I slowly mounted the steps. I was not surprised to see the flower arranger standing near the font.

'My mobile's in my left-hand pocket,' I said.

The older policeman reached in for it.

'You'll find DC Partridge listed.' That impressed him. He keyed the number and I thanked my lucky stars when Partridge answered.

'Gavin, is that you? Colin Patterson here. Yeah, that's right. I've got someone who wants to talk to you.' He handed me the phone.

'Gavin, this is Nick Carter.'

The younger policeman snapped his fingers. 'I knew I'd seen him before,' he said. His partner told him to be quiet.

'Remember those explosives I told you about. Well, I couldn't wait. I'm here now at St Bede's church with two of your colleagues — and a lot of guns. Yes, guns.' I held the mobile out to the older policeman with a smile. 'He asked for you.'

PC Patterson listened for a moment without speaking and then gave me the phone back. Turning to his partner, he said, 'Stay with him, Raj, while I call this in.'

I was shepherded into the church, my escort stopping for a quiet word with the flower arranger on the way. She looked a bit put out but she nodded her grey head, flashed a reproving look at me and flounced out, leaving a strong smell of lavender water behind her.

The pews stretched from a centre aisle to the walls on either side of the church. I sat down in the rearmost with the one called Raj and waited.

'What was with all that 'armed police' nonsense?' I asked.

The young policeman continued to stare at me. 'You can't be too careful,' he mumbled. Then the penny dropped, and looking at me smugly as though he'd just unmasked Jack the Ripper, he added, accusingly, 'You're 'Nasty' Ned Tucker, aren't you?'

As I've said before, the trouble with playing a villain on TV is that people really think you are one.

★ ★ ★

It wasn't long before more policemen arrived, followed shortly after by DI Crabbe and DC Partridge. Crabbe was wearing a Pringle golf sweater. He looked even more disagreeable than usual, if that were possible. I wondered if perhaps he'd been called away from a game he was winning and the thought cheered me up. Our eyes met briefly as he came in but he went straight to the vault without so much as a nod of acknowledgement. Young Partridge however, did stop.

'You said it was explosives you suspected of

being hidden in the vault,' he whispered.

'I didn't have time to look in all the coffins.'

Crabbe came back up from the vault. 'Russian AK 47's, all in tip-top condition from what I could see from the steps,' he said. 'Get the place sealed off, Partridge. Forensics are on their way to give it a good going over — and I'm informing Scotland Yard. The anti-terrorist people will want to know about this . . . Who looks after this church, is there a verger?'

'Caleb Pilcher is the keyholder,' Partridge said, reading from his notebook.

'But his son, Benny, does all the work,' I added. 'Like opening the place up and keeping the churchyard tidy.'

Crabbe stopped and glowered at me. 'You seem to know an awful lot, Mr Carter?'

'I've made it my business to find out as much as I can about the places and events connected with Ronnie Simmons' disappearance,' I said, holding myself back from adding, 'because you have consistently refused to do so.'

He gave me a withering look before turning back to his young detective constable. 'Get a couple of uniforms over to Pilcher's garage straight away. I'll see both father and son down at Cannford nick. They can arrest them if they have to, unlawful possession of firearms.'

I didn't volunteer the information that Caleb was most probably away doing his deliveries. If he were, Crabbe would find out soon enough.

'And get hold of the old lady that does the flowers here, the one that blew the whistle on Carter. That PC had no right telling her she could go home without asking me. I want statements from everyone involved and I want them today, understand!'

I have to admit I was impressed. Here was the proverbial non-action man proving to be a veritable whirlwind.

He spun back to me. 'Right, Mr Carter, we'll get back to Cannford. Partridge tells me that's your Mini outside.' I nodded. 'You lead the way then and we'll follow.'

The journey was uneventful. I guessed Crabbe chose to be in the car behind just in case I made a bolt for it. The classic Mini's manoeuvrability in traffic is legendary and I could easily have given them the slip if I'd wanted to but I had no intention of doing so. I was pleased to be going to his office; I wanted to know the outcome of the second autopsy on George Mayberry.

At the police station I was shown to an interview room. Gavin stayed with me until the inspector joined us. I got the impression that he'd been warned not to discuss anything with me but he did keep me supplied with coffee. Crabbe eventually arrived wearing his old tweed jacket over the sweater and carrying a manila folder.

'Forensics are on the scene,' he announced, pulling out a chair and sitting at the table next to Partridge. 'They report finding explosives, ammunition and a variety of small arms in the other coffins. That vault's a regular arsenal.' He stared at me with his cold, grey eyes. 'We'll have to have your fingerprints, Mr Carter, for elimination purposes you understand?'

'Of course.'

'I thought we'd just have a chat,' he continued. 'Off the record. No need for cautions or tapes if that's all right with you?'

'Perfectly.'

He fished a well-chewed pipe and a tobacco pouch out of his jacket pocket and proceeded to fill the bowl with tobacco. Why such an action should surprise me I don't know. I suppose it was because I've always associated pipe smoking with pleasant, easy-going people. He became aware of me watching him.

'You don't mind if I smoke, do you?' he growled.

I shook my head. It was his nick after all.

With the tobacco lit and burning to his satisfaction, he opened the folder and extracted a photograph. It was the one taken by Ronnie of the boxes of explosives.

'What made you think this was taken at the church?' he asked, his pipe clenched between his teeth.

Partridge craned his neck to see the picture, Crabbe grunted and pushed it nearer to him.

I said it had been taken at sunset the evening before Ronnie disappeared. I was sure about the time because of the photographic competition and of the day because there were other images on the camera's memory that were taken that same evening. Crabbe glowered at me and looked to be about to say something but I quickly went on to explain that they were of a lady and somewhat indelicate so we, Tim Murray and I, decided for her sake not to reveal them. I then told him about the visit to St Bede's the following morning by Brian Chambers and George Mayberry and how it seemed reasonable to assume that the latter had found Ronnie's camera then.

'So I went back again to have a good look round. The gate to the vault was open and I went down. It wasn't until later that it

240

dawned on me that someone had recently cleaned the place. I wondered why when no one is supposed to be allowed down there. I mentioned it to DC Partridge . . . '

Crabbe shot his subordinate a reproving look. The young detective blushed and lowered his eyes. I leapt to his defence.

'But before he even had a chance to report the matter I was presented with the opportunity to have another look — and here we are.'

Crabbe took the pipe out of his mouth, looked at it disapprovingly and tamped the smouldering tobacco down with his thumb. 'I've got Benny Pilcher in the next room. He says you stole his keys.'

'Borrowed them, Inspector, borrowed them. They were there in his hat on the bar. I thought I could have another quick look in the vault and be back at *The Grapes* before Benny started for home, with no one the wiser — and I would have if I hadn't tripped over a trestle.'

'If a public spirited citizen hadn't reported you to the police, you mean.' He fixed me with his cold eyes. 'You sail very close to the wind at times, Mr Carter, be careful or one day you'll come a cropper.'

'Can I have some more coffee?' I asked with a smile.

With a nod of his head, Crabbe sent Partridge to fetch some. I think the young detective was pleased to escape for a while.

The inspector leaned forward, his forearms resting on the table and his hands clasped together. 'I was wrong to ignore Mr Mayberry's possession of the camera,' he said quietly. 'But at the time I had, what *I* thought, were more important things to deal with.'

Was this an apology? He suddenly looked so old and tired that I almost felt sorry for the man.

'The results of the second autopsy are in here.' He tapped the folder. 'They found minute fibres in his lungs consistent with him being smothered by a pillow. I propose to interview everyone who was on the premises the night he died. It is quite possible he was silenced to protect the location of these weapons.' He stood up to leave. 'Give DC Partridge a statement on today's little escapade and you're free to go . . . Oh, and by the way, you're not on your own any more in your search for Mr Simmons. As he's now an important witness in this matter all the police forces in Britain will be on the look out for him, and possibly Scotland Yard's anti-terrorist unit as well.'

13

The following morning the county constabulary turned up at *The Grapes* in force, skilfully blocking the exit from the car park with their vehicles and commandeering the reception end of the taproom. Tables were hurriedly rearranged and Crabbe, looking very officious, sat at one (with DC Partridge as his clerk) and two other plainclothes officers, one male and one female, at another. Uniformed constables, brought along for the purpose, were then dispatched to collect the interviewees. It struck me as bizarre that Crabbe should be conducting his investigation into George Mayberry's death from the very same table I'd been sitting at when the hysterical young mother had burst into the taproom shouting that he was floating facedown in the pond.

I passed the Pembrokes on their way to be interrogated. No doubt they had been summoned first because of their appointment at the Magistrates court. Roland strode along with his head high and a noble expression on his handsome face like some elderly Sydney Carton marching to the guillotine. Rather surprisingly, Marcia, her eyes still red from weeping, seemed content on this occasion to follow meekly in his wake. The policewoman accompanying them asked politely for my name and room number.

'If you wouldn't mind waiting in your room, sir. I'll be along for you shortly.' She looked at her notes. 'You haven't seen a Mr Dolan, have you, sir?'

Roland stopped. 'Dolan isn't here!' he said irritably. 'He went off somewhere with Caleb Pilcher and they're not back yet.' The girl looked puzzled. 'They have an antiques business,' he added by way of explanation. 'A shop in the High Street.' He then turned to me. 'It's damned inconvenient, Nicholas. As if I haven't got enough on my plate today. The caretaker of the Memorial Hall has been on the telephone twice already this morning wanting to know when we're going to remove our scenery — they've got a Boy Scout Gang Show on this week apparently. I've tried the stage supplies people but there's no answer from them yet. With Dolan not here I'll have to leave it to Melanie to organise things. Be a good chap and give her a hand will you?'

The little actor-manager was still giving orders but I didn't mind helping out, so long as it didn't interfere with collecting Susan from the station. I could hardly wait for her call. There was such a lot to tell her and, what the hell, I just wanted to be with her again.

* * *

Even though I'd made a statement to the police about finding George Mayberry's body in the pond, Crabbe took me through it all again, in detail.

'The landlord of *The Grapes* was with you,' he said, reading from his notes.

'Yes, he helped me drag him out.'

'The police report at the time says it was you that helped him.'

It was petty and I shouldn't have been annoyed but Crabbe said it in such a sneering way that I bristled. 'Arthur was more concerned about his luggage trolley than anything else,' I retorted.

'Was he indeed?'

Immediately regretting my outburst, I tried to put it right by adding, 'He didn't believe there was a body. He felt sure it was only some rubbish that children had thrown in . . . But when I called on him for help he didn't hesitate.'

'And you both dragged Mr Mayberry's body from the duck pond?'

'Yes.'

'Then I see no need to add anything to the

officer's report, do you?'

'Not at all,' I said, which I thought was very accommodating of me.

Melanie was guided to where the other team of detectives were sitting. Marcia had also been sitting at their table so I assumed it was the job of the lady detective to question all females. Partridge took time out from scribbling notes for his chief to follow his darling's progress across the taproom.

My interview seemed to be over and I was about to rise from my chair when Crabbe produced a transparent plastic bag and placed it in front of me, a supercilious smile on his face. 'I believe this belongs to you, sir,' he said tapping an object in the bag with a stubby finger. 'Can you tell me how it came to be found in Mr Mayberry's room?'

The bag contained a small, red notebook.

'It was no doubt in George Mayberry's room because it's his book. If you don't believe me ask Roland Pembroke, ask any of the Players.'

Crabbe looked as though he was about to explode. 'But it has your name inside the front cover!'

I took a deep breath and told him about my dinner with George Mayberry, of the old man's memory lapses and the need to carry a notebook as an *aide-memoire*. 'He put my name in the front of his book because he said that way he'd always know where to find me.'

Crabbe stared at me for a long moment without speaking. Finally he said, 'I must ask you to give me a sample of your handwriting, Mr Carter.' Partridge was making notes on an A4 pad. Crabbe snatched it from him, turned to a clean page and pushed it in front of me. 'Print your name in block capitals and write *Seth Cartwright* underneath it,' he barked. 'Then sign it and date it.'

'Then can I go?'

'For now,' he said.

Melanie caught up with me as I was on my way back to my room.

'I managed to get through to the stage supplies company,' she announced breathlessly. 'And what do you think?'

I had a good idea but she seemed so pleased with herself I let her tell me.

'They are going to pick up our stuff from Hobswood today! Yes, today! Isn't that good? I'm just about to call the caretaker.'

'I'll drive you over there if you like . . . There's a props basket here isn't there?'

'Yes, in Polly's cupboard. We should take that with us. Although I'm not sure if we will get it in the Mini.'

My suggestion of a quick drink and a sandwich before setting out for Hobswood was also eagerly accepted.

Arthur seemed unusually preoccupied as he poured my lager. He set the glass down on the bar and nodded his head towards the tables still occupied by the police. 'Our Poll's being questioned now,' he said glumly.

Polly was seated at Crabbe's table, which made a nonsense of my theory that the plainclothes policewoman was there to interview the ladies.

I tried to cheer him up. 'Her evidence will be very important to the enquiry,' I volunteered. 'Being the housekeeper and all.'

He looked embarrassed and he was noticeably avoiding eye contact, which wasn't at all like the Arthur I had come to know.

'I've made my statement,' he mumbled, fidgeting with his polishing cloth. He then leaned forward across the bar and whispered, 'Could I have a word with you in private, Mr Carter?'

Melanie seemed quite happy sitting on a bar stool sipping cola and gazing at her Gavin. I doubted if she even noticed as I excused myself and moved farther down the bar. Arthur, keeping to his side, moved along with me.

'I've a confession to make,' he announced gravely, once we were out of earshot. 'It was me what searched your room.'

I was flabbergasted. 'You were the burglar?'

He looked wretched and downcast. 'I'm sorry I pushed you over. I didn't mean to. I panicked.' He took a deep breath, straightened up and looked me straight in the eye. 'If you was a father you'd understand. You said Ronnie Simmons had left his photographs behind and I *had* to see if there was any of our Poll in, well, you know.'

He was so contrite I forgave him immediately. 'There's no harm done,' I said magnanimously and it was a joy to see his expression change; he positively beamed.

'You're a gentleman, Mr Carter. If there's anything I can do for you . . . Wait a minute, what about a slap up dinner? You and a friend, he nodded at Melanie and winked suggestively. Anything you want, on the house. How would that be?'

'That would be very nice, Arthur,' I said. Then suddenly remembering the props basket, I added, 'and I could do with borrowing your van for an hour.'

Melanie and I had finished our sandwiches and were in the process of loading the basket into the van when Susan called. She was phoning from the train which, she told me, was due to arrive at Cannford at three twenty-five. I had a brainwave. Taking a chance on him being at home — and being free for the afternoon — I drove round to Brian's house. As luck would have it I was right on both counts. Brian had proved to be a very capable young man and he was also a cheerful person to have around so, after depositing him and Melanie — and the basket — at the Memorial Hall to await the arrival of the scenery people, I went off with an easy conscience to Cannford station, promising I would return later to take them back to Chapel Heath.

I eagerly scanned the passengers coming out of the station, then I saw her and my spirits rose. She was lovely. Her hair shone like gold in the sunlight and she was wearing a diaphanous short-sleeved summer dress that showed off her trim figure and long legs to perfection. She saw me and waved. I hurried forward expecting a hug at least but I was to be disappointed, receiving nothing more than her suitcase and a rather staid kiss on the cheek.

'Right, Nicky,' she said brusquely, as we walked back to the car park. 'What's been happening?'

There was so much to tell. Where do I start? 'There's no news of Ronnie,' I began, 'but the tour is over. Tarquin Pembroke has been arrested.'

She gasped. 'Wow! What for?'

'Drugs. He's been arrested for possession but I think the police have enough evidence to charge him with dealing.'

'But that will mean a prison sentence . . . His poor mother.'

'And George Mayberry is dead.'

'My God! What happened?'

'The police are calling it a suspicious death. They'll want to interview you I'm afraid. They're talking to everyone who was at *The Grapes* the night he died.'

She looked surprised when I stopped at Arthur's van so I quickly explained about the props basket. Once we were on our way I told her about finding George Mayberry in the duck pond and that the subsequent post-mortem revealed he was dead before he went in the water. I then brought her up to speed with Arthur's confession and Ronnie's picture of the explosives leading to the finding of the stash of armaments in the vaults of St Bede's tower. I didn't mention the nude photographs of Marcia. I thought she had quite enough information to digest for the moment.

She sat slumped in the passenger seat, deep in thought. Eventually she said, 'Do you think Ronnie has gone after the gunrunners?'

'It certainly looks that way. There *was* a response to Tim Murray's appeal. It was a postman who swears he saw him go dashing off that Saturday morning on his motorbike.'

'But what about his mobile phone and the digital camera?'

'Whoever was stashing those explosives in the church vault wouldn't take kindly to someone taking pictures of them would they? He was probably spotted and ran away, leaving his stuff behind.'

'But his mobile? Wouldn't he be holding that in his hand?'

I had no answer to that and I was saved from replying as we had arrived at *The Grapes'* car park and for the next few moments I was busy looking for a place to park near the hotel's entrance. I had arranged with Arthur for Susan to have the attic room she had occupied before. There was now a vacancy in the annexe of course, but somehow I didn't think she would relish sleeping in Mayberry's old room.

The fat licensee greeted her like an old friend and insisted on escorting her personally to her room. He even carried her bag.

'Being an attractive woman has its advantages.'

I knew that voice. I turned around; it was Tim Murray. With the police gone, Arthur's reception area was restored to its usual layout. Murray was sitting at one of the tables having afternoon tea; I noticed he had an extra cup.

'Come, laddie, join me and tell me about this big arms cache you discovered.'

His smug expression told me he knew all about it already.

'Has Crabbe lifted his embargo?' I asked, pulling out a chair and sitting down at his table.

He sighed. 'There are now more powerful agencies than the local police telling me to keep shtum.'

'Scotland Yard?'

'To name but one,' he said ruefully, pouring tea into the spare cup. Then he brightened. 'But I've got some big guns of my own, laddie, I've got friends on the nationals. I've been a newspaperman far too long to be muzzled by bureaucracy.' He pushed the cup towards me grinning broadly. 'Come on, tell me all about it.'

And so I did, from Brian Chambers and his Saturday morning bird watching expedition to me lifting the church keys from Benny Pilcher's cap.

'This man, Eddie Dolan,' he said when I'd finished. 'Did you know he had a police record?'

Tim Murray's sources of information never ceased to amaze me. 'Roland Pembroke told me he'd been in prison.'

Behind the steel-framed glasses his eyes twinkled. 'But did you know it was the Maze prison in Belfast?'

'Isn't that where they put terrorists?'

'Correct. Your man was an active member of an illegal organisation, laddie, although from what I'm told he was never anything more than a messenger. He's always been a bit of a chancer you see and not wholly trusted. There are some who say he turned police informer but I don't know if there's any truth in that. What I *do* know is that there's a lot of valuable weapons out there that no one's got any use for any more and I believe he's turning them into money.'

'By using his antiques business as a cover he gets the arms out of Ireland . . . '

'With Caleb Pilcher doing the collecting. Let's face it, who's going to be interested in a few old worm-eaten wardrobes and chests of drawers in a broken-down removals van on the ferry to Holyhead, eh? They put the antique furniture in their showroom in the High Street and hide the weapons in the vault under St Bede's tower until they've got a buyer.'

'And then they use Pilcher's van again to get them out of the country.' I couldn't resist a wry smile. 'No wonder Inspector Crabbe found nothing illegal in it when it arrived at Tilbury, he should have checked it on the way out.'

'It's my guess it was Eddie Dolan's car those boxes of Semtex were in. He was probably looking for Caleb Pilcher when Ronnie took his picture and telephoned me.'

'And when they came back . . . '

'He legged it. Leaving his camera behind for George Mayberry to find the following morning.'

A strong female voice came from behind. 'That still doesn't explain why his mobile phone was under the seat of his motorbike!'

I swung round. Susan had changed her clothes and stood there looking positively striking in dark blue slacks and a matching sleeveless fleece over a wide necked, horizontally striped, T-shirt. Murray pulled out a chair and asked her to join us.

'I can send for more tea?' he suggested.

My mobile rang; it was Melanie. My God, I'd completely forgotten about her! I was annoyed with myself but I could do no more than apologise and say I was on my way.

'Where to?' Susan asked.

'Hobswood. I promised I'd give Melanie and Brian a lift back.'

'I'll come with you,' she said positively.

'Great,' I said. 'We'll go in the Mini.'

Tim Murray shrugged and waved me away with a smile. 'Keep in touch,' he shouted after us as we made for the door.

* * *

There was one solitary car in the car park at the Memorial Hall, a Volkswagen that I recognised as belonging to Gavin Partridge. Inside the hall Brian was half-heartedly sweeping the empty stage.

'Yes, he's here,' he said with a wink and a nod towards the dressing rooms. 'He saw the scenery van outside and knowing Eddie was away guessed his lady friend would be here supervising the move.'

'He could have saved me a trip,' I grumbled.

'Nah! Melanie thought of that but he said he's got to go straight to Cannford nick from here. Mind you, he's been here long enough to have driven to Chapel Heath and back a couple of times if you ask me.'

Melanie appeared from the green room looking a little flushed, followed by a rather sheepish-looking Gavin Partridge.

'I thought I heard voices,' she said. Catching sight of my companion, Melanie ran towards her, arms outstretched, leaving Partridge standing alone at the rear of the stage. 'Susan! I'm so glad you're back, I've got such a lot to tell you.'

I wandered over to the young detective. 'What happened with Tarquin Pembroke?' I asked.

'He's to appear at the Crown Court,' he said, any lingering embarrassment rapidly evaporating. 'I think he was lucky not to be remanded in custody. But for a QC arguing on his behalf he would have been. That silk his parents have engaged is a highflier; she must be costing them a fortune.'

'Any news of Eddie Dolan and Caleb Pilcher?'

He grinned broadly. 'They've been detained by the Dutch police in Rotterdam. DI Crabbe is on his way there now.'

★ ★ ★

I drove back to Chapel Heath with a full car and a comfortable feeling that everything was falling neatly into place. It was easy to believe that Eddie Dolan or Caleb Pilcher, or both, had silenced George Mayberry in order to safeguard their secret hoard of weapons and I felt sure that one or the other was responsible for pushing me down the steps at the Memorial Hall. As far as the other mysteries were concerned, Arthur had confessed to being my burglar and if Ronnie was hot on the trail of a super scoop then I suppose not hearing from him was understandable if not forgivable.

After depositing young Brian at his door (and making a rapid exit before the voluble Mrs Turner appeared to press us into staying to supper) I drove on to *The Grapes* where Melanie left to go for a shower and a change of clothes. Suddenly I was alone with Susan. I thought about Arthur's offer of a meal on the house. It was still quite early but having established that she'd had nothing to eat that day other than a slice of toast for breakfast, I steered her into the dining room. Arthur was still setting the tables, jiggling his fat body around them and humming a little tune to himself. His chubby face lit up when he saw us. I asked if we were too early for dinner.

'Of course not,' he said. 'I got some lovely eight ounce steaks today. How would one o'them suit you?'

We both agreed that a steak would suit us admirably. I asked him why he was in such a good mood.

Arthur grinned broadly. 'I've had two bits of good news today,' he said. 'I've got someone interested in the pub and Benny's gone home to his mother.'

I quickly explained to Susan that Arthur

disapproved of the younger Pilcher constantly hanging around his daughter.

'Well he won't be doing that no more,' the fat landlord said gleefully. 'He's had the wind up since that arms stash was discovered. He says his dad will blame him and give him a good hiding. So off he went on the afternoon train.'

'I can't see Caleb Pilcher being in a position to harm anyone for a very long time,' I said.

'We know that, sir, don't we, but Benny's not very bright, is he? And I certainly wasn't going to talk him out of going.' He stopped and snapped his fingers as though just remembering something. 'Hang about! He left something for you, sir.'

I was surprised. 'For me?' I said, incredulously.

'Yes, sir, it's got your name on it. I put it behind the bar. I'll go and get it . . . I won't be a minute, perhaps you'd like to have a look at the menu for a starter while I'm gone?'

I had hardly handed Susan the list of options before Arthur returned bearing a grubby Jiffy envelope securely fastened with a generous amount of wide, brown, sticky tape.

'Here you are, sir,' he said, placing the package on the table in front of me. The greasy envelope looked completely alien on the spotless, white linen tablecloth so I stuffed it in my pocket.

'Aren't you going to open it?' Susan asked.

'Later,' I said, giving her hand a squeeze. (I still had hopes) 'Let's enjoy our dinner first.'

The steaks were first-rate, the wine flowed and our host, with a wink and a whispered, 'and don't forget, sir, this is on the house,' was most attentive throughout. The meal was an absolute winner but it went all downhill after coffee. Susan, complaining of fatigue, took herself off to her tiny room in the pub's attic leaving me to toss and turn restlessly, alone in my king-size bed in the annexe.

The following morning, I remembered Benny's package and being in no hurry to face Susan at breakfast, I decided to open it. I was sawing my way through the brown sticky tape when Polly came in to make up the bed. On seeing me still in the room, she apologised and said she'd come back later. I told her to ignore me and carry on.

The dirty, finger-marked package was addressed to me in a childish hand with the words 'very urgent' written in capital letters underneath and underlined several times. I had the dickens of a job with the many layers of tape that had been wound around it but I was eventually able to open it and shake out the contents. All it contained was a key. No note or anything else, just a key, which clattered out onto the dressing table, an old-fashioned, long-shafted, mortise lock key. Attached to it by a ring was a small, brass pulley that I recognised from my Cornish holidays as the sort of thing usually found on sailing dinghies.

There was a sharp intake of breath behind me. 'Oh, my God!' It was Polly.

I swung round in my chair. 'Do you know something about this?' I demanded. 'Do you know why Benny would send me a key?'

She took a step back. I thought she was about to faint but she quickly rallied herself. 'No, sir,' she said hoarsely. 'But I know that key — and I know Benny.' She tugged at my sleeve. 'We've got to go, sir, now. We haven't a moment to lose.'

14

Polly ran outside and across the car park to where my Mini was parked, and stood rubbing her hands together and hopping from one foot to the other with impatience, urging me to hurry up and unlock the doors. I opened mine and slipped inside, reaching over to open the passenger door.

'Right. Where to?' I asked.

She scrambled into the car. 'The Pilchers' garage, where else? You've brought the key, haven't you?' I nodded. 'Well come on! What are you waiting for?'

I stamped on the accelerator and the back wheels spun with tyres smoking like a drag racer. We flashed through Chapel Heath a red blur. I drove in silence, concentrating on the road ahead and keeping a watchful eye out for speed cameras. Polly sat in the passenger seat wrapped in her own thoughts for some time but as we neared Marshbank she began to talk, shouting over the engine noise and the whistling of the wind. She told me that after discovering Ronnie with Marcia, she had taken the pub's van and followed him out to St Bede's church.

'I just knew the two-timing bastard was meeting another woman,' she said. 'I left the van well back on the drive so he wouldn't hear the engine and walked up to the church. Sure enough there *was* another car there and I heard Ronnie's voice coming from inside. I crept in and there he was, in that tower bit behind the font.'

'Was the gate to the tower open?' I yelled.

'It must have been mustn't it? Anyway, he was excited and I heard him say, all sexy like, 'I can't wait to see you.' Well, I saw red didn't I? I grabbed the first thing I got hold of and I hit him, I hit him hard, Mr Carter, and he tumbled all the way down those steps. I just knew I'd killed him.'

'What did you hit him with?'

'Oh, one of Benny's tools, a thing with a long handle — a spade. The sort they use for digging graves.'

'And you didn't go down to see how badly he was hurt?'

'I would have done, sir, honest I would, but I heard someone coming so I went and hid in the pews.'

'Who was it?'

'I expected it to be his new lady friend, didn't I? But it was Benny and Eddie Dolan and they was both carrying boxes. I heard the Irish feller say, 'Funny that, I could have sworn I heard a motorbike.' They went down the steps to the vault and a couple of minutes later Benny came up carrying Ronnie. Limp as a rag doll he was and I just knew he was dead.' She sniffed and wiped her nose on the back of her hand. I took one hand off the wheel and offered her my handkerchief but she shook her head. 'I suppose it was Benny what took Ronnie's motorbike to the train station and cleared out his room. I've asked him more than once to tell me what he done with Ronnie's body but the silly fool just smiles at me and says it's best I don't know, tells me not to worry and that everything will be all right.'

I skidded to a halt on the weed-covered forecourt of the deserted garage feeling that something was wrong. Andy Cole, the postman, who swore he would know Ronnie anywhere, 'with that long blond hair of his,' said he'd seen him leave *The Grapes* on his motorbike the next morning. Benny was a good head and shoulders taller than Ronnie and probably weighed twice as much. Cole could have been lying to get the reward, but I didn't think so at the time and for some inexplicable reason I still didn't.

Polly was out of the car almost before we stopped. She turned to me, her cheeks wet with tears but her eyes were bright and shining. 'This way, Mr Carter. I know what Benny meant now. Everything *is* all right, you'll see!'

I followed her to the rear of the garage where she rushed headlong into the dense thicket of brambles and reeds that surrounded the hardstanding. I hesitated.

'Keep with me!' she shouted.

I crossed my fingers and plunged in, following her along a narrow, winding path that seemed to be endless. Then the track branched off in two directions.

'Polly, where are you?' I called.

'Over here!'

The church tower, clearly visible above the reeds, was to my right but Polly's voice had come from the left. I dashed off in that direction and caught up with her in front of a small wooden hut, rather like those you find on the beach at a seaside resort. A length of narrow duckboard led up to the door.

'Come on, where's the key?' she said excitedly.

I pulled it out of my pocket and stuck it in the lock. It turned easily. I opened the door and stepped inside. The smell that hit me was worse than the most unpleasant public lavatory I'd ever had the misfortune to visit.

From within the dim interior came a dry, rasping voice. 'Listen, Benny, I've been thinking. The best way out of this for all of us is for you to take me up to the main road and leave me there. I'll swear I was a hit-and-run victim and I promise I won't mention you or Polly.'

'Ronnie?'

A pause, then a cautious, 'Who's that?'

'It's Nick, you young idiot! And Polly's here with me.'

My eyes quickly became accustomed to the gloom. The hut was very small, no more than six feet wide and only a couple of feet more than that in length. There was a window but it was boarded up. There was no furniture. I could make out a figure lying on a thin mattress surrounded by screwed up wrapping paper, empty polystyrene food trays and two-litre plastic bottles. One leg appeared to be sandwiched from hip to foot between two rough wooden boards bound tightly together with the same brown sticky tape that had been wrapped around the Jiffy bag. I moved in closer. It was Ronnie all right, albeit bearded, frighteningly thin and disgustingly filthy.

I called the emergency services on my mobile.

'It took you long enough to find me,' he said jokingly after a physically awkward and an exceedingly self-conscious hug. I noticed there were tears in his eyes as we broke apart. I quickly brushed mine away.

Polly shuffled her feet awkwardly in the doorway. 'Nick, you don't need me here. I'll go back and wait for the paramedics. They'll need someone to guide them here when they arrive.'

After she had gone, I said, 'She thought she'd killed you.'

'What the devil did she wallop me with, has she told you that?'

'A gravedigger's spade.'

We then both giggled hysterically like a couple of schoolboys.

'My God, Ronnie,' I said, catching my breath. 'You look bloody awful — and you stink to high heaven!'

'So would you if you'd been cooped up here for a couple of weeks on a diet of curry and chips. I've given up asking that big idiot to let me see a doctor. Perhaps I shouldn't have told him it was his precious Polly that hit me.'

'That leg looks scary, is there anything else wrong with you?'

'No, but its well and truly busted I'm afraid. Benny pulled it straight and put these splints on it. Made me sweat a bit when he did that, I can tell you. If this weren't such an out-of-the-way place my shouts would have brought any amount of people to see what was going on. It doesn't hurt much now though and I can feel my toes, which is a good sign, isn't it? I must have been out cold when he brought me here and my recollection of the first few days is a bit hazy but I'm a lot stronger now. He makes me do exercises before he lets me have my food. Bending and stretching my arms to begin with, then sit-ups, and now I can roll over and do press-ups as well, even with the gammy leg.'

Having always been a very practical person I couldn't help asking the obvious question. 'How do you manage to . . .?'

Ronnie chuckled. 'When a hut is on stilts, old boy, a hole in the floor is all you need, it's that simple. I shuffle over to it whenever necessary and the tide does the rest.'

'Judging by the pong, I would say the water doesn't reach this far very often,' I said, and we both dissolved into another fit of the giggles.

★ ★ ★

By a strange twist of fate the policeman who responded to my call was PC Colin Patterson. He already had my details in his notebook and from the way he exchanged glances with Polly I got the feeling she was known to him also, a little more intimately perhaps. He just had time to take a brief statement from Ronnie before the ambulance team carried him away. We followed them out. PC Patterson relieved me of the key to the hut and locked it behind us with a stern warning not to leave town, as no doubt DI Crabbe would want to interview us in the very near future, he said.

I took Polly back to *The Grapes* and went straight up to Susan's room. From the corridor outside I could hear her tapping away at her laptop. I knocked and she opened the door.

'Ronnie's here, in Cannford,' I said gently.

She stared at me, open-mouthed, without speaking.

'He's all right. He's had a bit of an accident and he's in hospital, but he's all right.'

For a few moments she didn't move. Then her lips tightened and she said, 'Okay, let's go!'

For the second time that morning I found myself following a determined woman out to my car, and me with no breakfast yet!

Cannford Infirmary, which incidentally, was the hospital I was taken to after my own argument with a flight of stone steps, is a pre-NHS hospital of the old school with tiled floors and walls made of white, shiny-faced bricks. It's the sort of place where you expect to bump into a stern-faced matron with starched apron, cap and cuffs. You don't of course. These days I find it hard to tell a qualified nurse from a tea lady.

It was well before visiting time but Susan bullied her way into the small side ward where Ronnie lay propped up in bed. He looked a lot more presentable than the last time I'd seen him and for Susan's sake I was grateful for that. Although he was emaciated, at least he was clean and his hair and beard had been cut. Susan let out a sob and ran to him and I moved back outside to give them some time together alone.

'And I thought the age of chivalry was dead,' said Tim Murray from the coffee machine at the end of the hallway.

Strangely, I wasn't surprised to see him. 'I just thought they needed to catch up, brother and sister and all that.'

'Very commendable I'm sure, but I didn't mean you, Nick, I meant him, our Ronnie. He's been trying to tell me his mind is a complete blank from the time he phoned me until he woke up in that smelly little hut. I know it was Polly from *The Grapes* who took you to him so I'd be grateful if you'd tell me where she fits in to all this?' He looked at me eagerly. 'Come on, laddie, what's the story?'

He was a likeable man, which, from my experiences, made him a rarity in the newspaper business. In my hunt for Ronnie he'd been a valuable ally, but regardless of my promise to give him exclusive rights to whatever my searches may reveal, if Ronnie wanted to keep Polly out of it I certainly wasn't going to go against his wishes, so all I said was, 'She guided me through the marsh to the wildfowler's hut that's all — and for that I'm very grateful.'

He nodded stoically. 'Polly's a strange girl, I can't see her mixed up in arms smuggling but I'll bet my pension she's more involved in this business with Ronnie Simmons than either of you are letting on.'

(Have I already said Tim Murray was wasted on a provincial weekly?)

'I really can't tell you any more, Tim, you'll have to talk to Inspector Crabbe.'

He finished his coffee and threw the paper cup in the waste bin. 'That's just what I had in mind, laddie,' he said with a grin. 'He's on his way back from Holland just now, with Eddie Dolan and Caleb Pilcher in handcuffs. He'll be feeling pleased with himself so I should catch him in a good mood — if that's possible.'

He left and I went back into Ronnie's room.

'The orthopaedic surgeon has seen x-rays of Ronnie's leg and he's very positive,' Susan announced as I entered, she looked relieved.

'He's a Welshman, from Bangor,' Ronnie added with a grin, 'Mr Jones, would you believe? 'Jones the bones' they call him here — he's very well thought of.'

He sat in his hospital cot looking roguishly handsome with his long, flaxen hair and neatly trimmed beard. I could imagine the nurses fighting to attend to him.

His smile faded. 'I really can't believe that George Mayberry, that nice, harmless old man, was suffocated in his bed and then taken outside and dumped in the pond,' he said incredulously. 'Do you think Eddie Dolan did it? I've just been talking to Tim about his arms smuggling business.'

'He had motive and opportunity. His room was next to Mayberry's in the annexe.'

'But what motive would he have to kill a harmless old man?'

It was a while before I answered him. This was something that had been haunting me since I dragged George Mayberry's body from the pond. 'I can't help feeling I was responsible,' I said miserably. 'The poor old chap found your camera the next day. He tucked it in his knapsack, probably fully intending to hand it in, but once back in his

272

room he promptly forgot all about it . . . Cutting a long and painful story short, I found it and Tim Murray had prints made from the memory card.'

Ronnie shot a horrified glance at his sister. 'You didn't, I mean, you haven't?'

I was standing with my back to Susan so I thought it safe to give Ronnie a wink. 'There was only one picture of interest to the police, and don't worry, that carload of Semtex came out fine.'

'That's a relief,' Ronnie said, and it was obvious he meant it.

I carried on. 'There was no clue in the photograph as to where it had been taken. We assumed you'd abandoned your camera at the scene having had to make a quick exit for one reason or another. Poor old George couldn't remember where he'd found it but Roland said he would, sooner or later, so we were all waiting for the penny to drop, and that included Eddie Dolan of course, who, for obvious reasons, wouldn't want the police to go poking around at St Bede's.'

A visit by Mr Jones' registrar, a tall, serious-looking young man with a receding hairline, cut our visit short. After tactfully pointing out that it *was* outside visiting hours he went on to say he had come to inform the patient of the surgery required to reset his leg and he would prefer to do this without an audience. Grateful to be spared the gory details, we fled, promising to return the following day — at the permitted time of course.

Although the car park was still quite full, lunch was almost over when we got back to *The Grapes* so we didn't bother with the dining room. The taproom bar was surprisingly busy but as we went in a couple got up to leave at the far end of the bar so we made a beeline for their still warm stools and ordered a sandwich apiece.

Susan rummaged in her handbag and brought out a mobile phone. 'I'll have to let Auntie Marjorie know that Ronnie's all right,' she said. 'I know it was silly of me but I was so desperate to find out where he'd disappeared to I phoned her to see if she had heard from him.' There was a loud burst of raucous laughter from group of smartly dressed young men standing behind her. She made a face. 'I think I'd better go outside.'

I guessed the high-spirited drinkers to be salesmen attending a seminar somewhere nearby; they looked the type.

'Good idea,' I said. 'And don't rush it. With this lot in here our order will probably take some time anyway . . . Give Auntie Marjorie my love.'

No sooner had Susan gone through the door than Melanie and Gavin Partridge appeared from the dining room. They saw me at the bar and came over, the ever-gallant young Partridge allowing Melanie to reach me first. She appeared worried and on edge.

'Oh, Nick. Gavin told me Ronnie's in hospital. Is he all right?' She chewed her lip anxiously as she waited for my answer.

I smiled to reassure her. 'He's got a broken leg which will take some time to heal, but otherwise he's okay.'

'We're on our way to see him. Is there anything he needs?'

'You could take him some fruit. He's been on a diet of curry and chips for the past fortnight.' Melanie shuddered at the thought. 'Have your lot found Benny yet, by the way?' I asked Partridge.

'I understand he has been detained somewhere in the West Country, sir. Mr Crabbe has asked for him to be sent back here.'

Melanie looked at her watch and said they'd better be going. They got as far as the door and bumped into Susan on her way in. The two girls immediately became locked in an animated conversation. Partridge looked back at me and shrugged his shoulders. I nodded my head knowingly.

'Two beef sandwiches. Did you both want horseradish sauce? I wasn't sure so I brought the jar.'

I swung round. It was Polly with our order. She was wearing hipster jeans with a top that finished well above her navel (which, I noticed, was sporting yet another piece of body jewellery). It was a fashion that on the young and sylphlike may be attractive but on a thirty-something with a sagging belly it looked rather sad. She seemed in no hurry to go.

'I'm that relieved Ronnie's all right,' she said.

'He's hardly all right, Polly. His leg is going to take some time to mend.'

'I know, and I feel terrible about that — but he's not dead, is he.' She fiddled with the hem of her top. 'D'you think it would be all right if I went to see him?'

'You once told me his sort were only after one thing and you were glad he was gone. You even said, 'Good riddance'.'

She immediately went on the defensive. Her chin lifted defiantly but I noticed that her bottom lip was quivering ever so slightly. She quickly glanced around and then leaned across the bar. 'I thought I'd killed him,' she said in a stage whisper. 'You try having something like that on your conscience. The only way I could cope with it was to think of him as a bad lot.'

I will never understand the workings of a woman's mind, and Polly's was more complex than most. For all her outward show of bravado, the hard look, the butch haircut, the body piercing and the tattoos, she was really an insecure and a rather pathetic person. She hadn't had things easy and no doubt Ronnie was as much to blame for leading her on.

'I think you *should* visit him,' I said gently. 'It will be good for both of you.'

Melanie and Partridge left and Susan came back for her sandwich.

'How was Auntie Marjorie,' I asked.

'Very concerned about Ronnie. She's talking about coming up to see him, especially as for once the three of us are all together in one place.'

'Yes, that doesn't happen very often.'

Susan gave me a melting look. 'Not often enough,' she said with a depth of feeling that rather surprised me.

Arthur appeared behind the bar. 'I've got Inspector Crabbe on the phone,' he wheezed breathlessly.

'He'll want Gavin Partridge,' I said, opening my sandwich and spreading the pungent sauce over the meat. 'Pity that. He's just missed him.'

'No, he was asking if you was here, sir, and I said if he'd hold on I'd have a look.'

I put my sandwich back together and slid down off my stool. 'He's a blasted nuisance,' I said.

I was prepared to follow Arthur to the telephone at the 'reception' end of the bar but he didn't budge. 'No, no. He doesn't want to *speak* to you, Mr Carter. He said if you was here I was to ask if it would be convenient for him to come over to see you.'

That didn't sound like the Inspector Crabbe I had come to know. It didn't sound like Arthur either. 'Are you sure he said, 'would it be convenient'?'

'Oh, yes, sir. Those was his very words.'

Well I never! 'Then tell him it would be most convenient for me to see him at four, Arthur,' I said. 'And he can buy me afternoon tea.'

15

I was about to set off for my meeting with the inspector when I got a call from Tim Murray.

'You'll never guess in a million years what happened,' he said excitedly.

'Okay, so tell me.'

'Eddie Dolan was shot getting off the ferry!'

I was stunned. 'Is he dead?' I asked.

'No, but he was at death's door for a while, I believe.'

'I'm due to see Inspector Crabbe in a few minutes.'

'I know, laddie. Try and find out as much as you can, will you? All I know is there was just the one shot fired — long-range from a high-powered rifle. It was a professional job and my money's on the one of the Irish paramilitaries . . . By the way, it's George Mayberry's funeral on Friday.'

'Do you know the details?' I asked.

'Aye. Ten o'clock at Cannford Crematorium. It'll be in Wednesday's *Clarion*.'

Old George had a wife and a daughter somewhere but as far as I knew he hadn't seen either in years so I wondered who was handling the arrangements. I asked Tim.

'Roland Pembroke volunteered. He's the one who placed the announcement in the paper. You'd have thought he'd have enough on his plate with his son's trial coming up, wouldn't you?'

'Will I see you there?'

'Aye, maybe,' he said.

★ ★ ★

Inspector Crabbe was sitting at one of the tables at the reception end of the taproom going through his notes. He actually stood up when I arrived and even held out his hand. I took it in mine. It was moist and clammy, which was par for the course.

'I owe you an apology, Mr Carter,' he began.

An apology even! He's after something, I thought.

He sat down, waving me to a seat. 'I didn't believe you about that notebook but I had it checked by our experts against Mr Pembroke's employment forms and all the handwriting in it *was* Mr Mayberry's.'

'Thank you for that,' I said.

He rummaged through his papers. I was about to ask about Eddie Dolan when he pulled out the book in question, still in its plastic bag.

'The boffins have finished with it so I suppose it's all right to handle it,' he said, sliding it out. 'I thought you may be able to throw some light on something in it that puzzles me.'

I was right! The crafty devil *was* after something! 'Why ask me?' I said. 'You should be talking to Roland, he knew George Mayberry better than anyone.'

'Mr Pembroke is too wrapped up in his son's predicament at the moment to give his mind to anything else.' He opened the book. 'Most of the entries are simply random jottings, such as: *Collect shirts from laundry, Repair and touch-in stage-right return* and *Paint over graffiti on garden scene.*' (I remembered that one) 'All these have been ticked off, presumably as having been done. There are other notes he made about things that interested him: *St Bede's Tower — twenty feet square with walls four feet thick and about sixty feet high from ground level, Estuary birds — mostly Gulls, Herring and Yellow Legged, some Redshanks.*' He looked up. 'What are Redshanks, are they a sort of gull as well?'

'I wouldn't know,' I said with a shrug.

'But it's these other pages that intrigue me.' He flicked through the book and held it open for me to see. 'Look, covered with dates and times. There are several like this but there's nothing that gives a clue what they're about.'

'Mayberry was Roland's self-appointed watchdog,' I said. 'It began when he discovered Benny Pilcher spending time with Polly at *The Grapes* when he should have been on the road with the Players' scenery.'

'I see,' he said and began gathering his papers together. I waited. 'There *is* one other thing — Eddie Dolan was shot at Holyhead this morning.'

I had planned to be surprised when he gave me this news but although I'm an actor by profession, when it came to it I didn't know what to do, so I just said nothing.

'He's in hospital and he's asking for you.'

There was no sham about my surprise now. 'Why on earth would he want to see me?' I gasped.

'When a man has looked death in the face, Mr Carter, who knows what's going on in his mind . . . If it's all right with you, I'll have DC Partridge pick you up tomorrow morning at seven o'clock.'

★ ★ ★

'Eddie Dolan is not being particularly co-operative,' Gavin Partridge said as we sped north. 'Mr Crabbe is hoping that when he's got whatever it is he wants to say to you off his chest he may feel like answering some of our questions.'

A large stolid-looking uniformed policeman stood guarding the entrance to the side ward where the Players' stage manager was ensconced. Crabbe was also waiting for us there.

'DC Partridge and I will come in with you,' he said. 'But we'll keep in the background. Let him do the talking.'

Dolan was lying in bed, propped up by pillows and festooned with pipes and wires that were connected in some way to every exposed part of his body — plus some that disappeared under his bedclothes to parts of his body I didn't want to think about. His face was gaunt and pale.

'If that's you Nick Carter, come in close. I can't shout.'

'I'm sorry to see you like this, Mr Dolan,' I said, and I meant it.

He took me by surprise by grabbing hold of my arm. 'We got off to a bad start, you and me,' he said. 'I wanted you to know it wasn't me that put you in hospital, it was that stupid big lummox, Caleb Pilcher . . . '

Desperately, I looked behind me. Both policemen had their notebooks out. Inspector Crabbe nodded, as if to say, 'It's okay, let him carry on.'

' . . . and your friend Ronnie Simmons was in a heap at the bottom of the tower steps as dead as mutton when I found him — and that's the truth, so it is. I didn't see any point in calling an ambulance. The last thing I wanted was a lot of inquisitive people snooping about in that vault, now did I? Caleb was away so I had young Benny with me and Benny knows the marsh better than anyone — even better than his da — so I left it to him to get rid of the body.

'I hold my hands up to clearing out Ronnie's room and to taking his motorbike to the train station — but I had nothing to do with his death. Honest to God I didn't, you've got to believe that.'

'I do,' I said. 'Ronnie is very much alive.'

The Irishman's mouth dropped open in amazement. I looked at Crabbe's impassive face. He said nothing so I carried on.

'So if it was you who took his motorbike to the station, how come the postman swears it was Ronnie? He claims he would know him anywhere by his long blond hair.'

Dolan smiled for the first time. 'Sure, I got a wig out of the props box . . . As a matter of fact I thought I looked rather good in it.'

Crabbe was busily writing something in his notebook so I took a chance and said, 'What do you know about George Mayberry's death?'

'Just hold on a minute, Mr Carter!' the inspector shouted, but he was too late, the question had been asked.

Dolan lay back on his pillow and closed his eyes. 'And am I in the frame for that as well?'

I pressed on. 'Mayberry found Ronnie's camera at St Bede's church. Fortunately for you the old man couldn't remember where he picked it up. But you were there when Roland said his memory could come back at any time and that must have worried you. If your arms cache was to remain a secret, he had to be silenced.'

Eddie Dolan struggled to sit up, sending his drips and other suspended paraphernalia rattling and jangling. 'I swear to God I had nothing to do with George's death,' he said. 'I liked the old fella, so I did!'

Crabbe stepped forward giving me a withering look. 'I told you to let him do the talking,' he growled. He stared down at the man in the bed. 'Yes, you are in the frame, as you put it, for George Mayberry's murder — and for the attempted murder of Ronnie Simmons . . . Now, if you were to co-operate and tell us where you've been selling these weapons we may be able to help you.' He gestured frantically to Partridge who quickly ushered me out of the room.

'I don't think he did it either,' he said when we were outside.

'How did you know what I was thinking?'

'I saw it in your face, sir, when the inspector was talking.'

I nodded gravely. 'Just don't ask me why, that's all,' I said.

It was evening by the time the young detective and I got back to *The Grapes*. Susan must have been looking out for us because she came running out to the car park as we drew in.

She was beside herself with excitement and could hardly wait for me to get out of the car. 'What do you think?' she asked eagerly.

'So tell me,' I said. It had been a long drive and I was tired.

'Auntie Marjorie's here! She arrived this afternoon.'

'You're kidding me.'

'No, honestly. As soon as she put the phone down from talking to me she dialled Martin Tregannon and he drove her here. I didn't call you. I wanted it to be a surprise. She's staying here, at *The Grapes*. Arthur's given her the other attic room next to mine.

'And Martin?'

'Gone back to Cornwall. He's got his garage to run.'

Well, that was a surprise right enough. I

couldn't wait to see Auntie Marjorie again. I felt very guilty that I hadn't seen her since Uncle Stan's funeral. Was it really three years ago? I asked Susan if she and Auntie Marjorie had eaten yet.

'No we were waiting for you.'

I looked at my watch. 'Let's all meet up for dinner at eight,' I said. 'Can you arrange it? I really must have a shower and change my clothes.'

★　★　★

But I didn't hang about and I was in the taproom bar well before eight. Susan and Auntie Marjorie were at a table just inside the door with a glass of red wine apiece. There was a spare glass so I helped myself from the carafe that was standing on the table.

Marjorie Earnshaw is a small woman, just a couple of inches over five feet. She's tough and sinewy with not an ounce of fat anywhere and must be eighty if she's a day. She is fiercely independent and back in Cornwall she still bombs around the county in Uncle Stan's old Dodge pick-up truck, which I know she wouldn't part with for the world. To be honest, I was surprised she had Martin Tregannon bring her here in his taxi.

She told me later that having made up her

mind to come, she wanted to get here quickly. If she'd made the journey on her own she would have had to stop somewhere halfway. 'I get a nasty headache if I'm behind the wheel too long these days,' she said.

Her naturally wavy hair, completely white for many years now, she wore in the same casual, boyish style that always looked as though she has just run her fingers through it, but her face seemed more wrinkled than the last time I saw her, particularly around the eyes. The light is very bright in Cornwall (a principal reason for artists flocking to St Ives) but Auntie Marjorie simply refuses to wear sunglasses, or spectacles of any sort come to that, which I put down to obstinacy rather than vanity.

She has always been more concerned with others than with her own well-being, so I wasn't surprised when, on seeing me, she said, 'You look tired, Nick. Are you doing too much?'

'It's lovely to see you too, Auntie Marjorie,' I said, and it was. She was the nearest I'd got to having a mother.

Susan joined in. 'We were in time to see Ronnie this afternoon. He was in good spirits.'

'When do they operate?' I asked.

'Tomorrow. We actually met Mr Jones. He says Ronnie stands a good chance of making a complete recovery.'

'But he said it's going to take time,' Auntie Marjorie put in. 'And that's something I want to talk to you about, Nick.'

Arthur signalled that our table was ready so we adjourned to the dining room. At one of the other tables a youngish couple were having a romantic, candle-lit dinner. The man's face was vaguely familiar but I couldn't place where I'd seen him before.

'So let's have it,' I said when we were seated and Arthur had poured us all another a glass of the house red.

Auntie Marjorie put her menu down and cleared her throat. 'We all know it's going to be a long time before Ronnie is properly back on his feet.' I nodded in agreement. She then turned to focus her full attention on me. 'And I hear you are out of work, Nick!' she said accusingly.

'Yes, but that's only temporary,' I replied hastily, feeling like a naughty little boy caught playing truant from school.

'I've had a long talk with Susan this afternoon,' she said firmly. 'And she agrees that I could have the answer to both yours and Ronnie's problem.'

'I'm not sure I have a problem, Auntie Marjorie, but what's on your mind?' I asked warily.

Arthur came back at that moment so we busied ourselves scanning the menu and placing our orders. When he left us she carried on.

'As you know, I've been running the family business since your Uncle Stanley died — actually with having Dennis as General Manager there has been very little for me to do apart from keeping my eye open for any suitable properties that may come on the market.' She shook open her napkin and placed it carefully on her lap. 'Something came up the other week which I think you may find interesting.' She looked at me expectantly.

I smiled. 'Go on,' I said.

'It's an old cinema in Truro and I thought, with a little bit of work, we could open it as a theatre.' She reached across the table and grasped my hand. 'Just think, Nick, *The Pirates of Penzance, HMS Pinafore*, we could do them all, live theatre, the holidaymakers would love it. Ronnie could look after the front of the house until his leg is better — and you've got a lovely singing voice, I remember coming to see you in *Oliver*.'

'That was almost twenty years ago, Auntie Marjorie.'

The old lady sat back and picked up her wine glass and Susan took over. I wondered if they had been rehearsing. 'It would be such fun, Nicky,' she said. Her eyes were shining and she looked so happy. 'I don't need to be in London all the time. I've got a wonderful PA who I know is craving more responsibility so I'll put her to the test. Who knows I may even make her my partner, then you and I could run the theatre together, with me taking care of the business side and you concentrating on the stage productions.'

It was Auntie Marjorie's turn. 'You'll need capital to pay for the restoration work and to tide you over until you get started,' she said. 'I'll provide that as an interest free loan. Your Uncle Stanley would have wanted me to.'

The picture they were painting was certainly attractive. There is something magic about live theatre. Every performance is a new adventure and the buzz you get taking a bow before an appreciative audience, knowing you've put on a good show, is like a drug. And my short time with the players had reawakened my craving for it.

'But you said you couldn't live my kind of life?'

It was Susan's turn to reach across the table and take my hand. 'You're a rolling stone, Nicky darling, you go where the work is. I couldn't live like that. But this would keep you in one place and that would suit me just fine.'

'And you'd never be short of audiences,' Auntie Marjorie added. 'Holidaymakers are always looking for somewhere to go in the evening. We used to pack 'em in during the season and we were amateurs.'

The young man I'd noticed when we entered the dining room left his table and came over. After a brief nod to the ladies he bent down to whisper in my ear. 'I'm sorry to intrude,' he said. 'But could I ask you to autograph our menu? It's for Doris, her over there.' He looked back and smiled at the lady at his table.

It never ceases to amaze me that the person asking for an autograph rarely owns up to be the one who really wants it. I actually had someone tell me once that he didn't much care for me but wanted my autograph for his mother, who was a dedicated fan.

'I've seen you somewhere before,' I said.

He grinned. 'You have. I'm a paramedic — on the ambulances, Dave Nuttall's the name but everyone calls me, 'Nutty'.' He held out his hand. 'I met you here, well, outside actually. You'd just dragged that old man out of the pond.'

I shook hands with him and accepted his menu card. 'A sad business,' I said.

'The poor old sod must have had a right skinful, eh?' He laughed, and that annoyed me.

'That 'poor old sod' as you call him, was a gentleman, Mr Nuttall,' I said firmly. 'And a friend of mine.'

'No offence, I'm sure,' he said hastily. 'But he would have to be drunk or daft to go out in his bare feet with a just a raincoat on over his jim-jams, wouldn't he? And that was done up the wrong way!'

'The wrong way?'

'Yeah. I didn't notice it at first but, Doris — she's my partner on the ambulance — she pointed it out. A trench coat is double-breasted with buttonholes on the inside and he'd buttoned it the girl's way, you know, right over left instead of left over right.'

I prefaced my signature on his menu with the words, 'In memory of George Mayberry' and sent Mr 'Nutty' Nuttall on his way. But he'd set me thinking. What he didn't know, of course, was that George Mayberry was dead before he went into the pond.

Someone had dressed him in that raincoat. Could that someone have been a woman?

16

On my way to breakfast next morning, I knocked on Melanie's door. She opened it wearing a bathrobe and with a towel wrapped round her head.

'What's the matter, Nick?' she said, peering at me myopically. She wasn't wearing her glasses.

'I wondered if you knew about George Mayberry's funeral.'

'Oh yes, Gavin told me.'

'Well someone could have told me,' I said tetchily.

'I'm sorry. With Mr Roland gone, I didn't find out myself until yesterday and it *was* rather late when Gavin brought me back last night.'

Roland Pembroke had moved his family to a rented cottage in the village to escape from all the gawping and whispering that went on whenever one of them was seen in the vicinity of the taproom bar or restaurant. Tim Murray was right I suppose, he did have a lot on his mind so perhaps it was a bit much of me to expect a personal invitation.

Melanie pulled the towel from her head

and began rubbing her hair with it. 'It's Ronnie's big day today, isn't it?' she said.

'The operation on his leg? Yes, it is. It should be okay to visit him this evening.'

'I'll probably see you there then,' she said and withdrew back into her room.

★ ★ ★

After breakfast, Susan borrowed my car to take Auntie Marjorie into Cannford for a spot of retail therapy and I went for a walk to weigh up the pros and cons of provincial theatre management. The strongest argument in favour of Auntie Marjorie's idea was that I could be with the girl I loved — but I would have to get Susan to agree from the outset that it is the artistic director and not the business manager who has the final say on what shows are put on and which actors are hired.

I grabbed a beer and a sandwich at the bar for my lunch and while I sat chewing the ham on brown, I watched Polly restocking the bar with bottles of mixers, swinging the heavy wooden crates up to the counter top as if there was no weight in them at all. She was wearing a knitted sleeveless top. Her strong, sinewy arms fascinated me and I found myself visualising them holding a pillow down on George Mayberry's face.

I tore my eyes away and telephoned the hospital. My conversation with the ward nurse was brief. 'He is comfortable,' was all I could get out of her. While I had my mobile in my hand I decided to check in with Sam.

'Nick, my boy!' He shouted down the line. 'I was just about to call.' (Yeah, yeah. I believe you, Sam, thousands wouldn't.)

'Is that right?' I said.

'I've got you four weeks at the Floral Pavilion, New Brighton. How does that sound, good eh?'

'What about TV work?'

There was a pause before he answered. When he did his voice had lost its exuberance. 'You shouldn't have turned Deejay down, Nick. Word gets around you know.'

'But I found Ronnie Simmons.'

Sam grunted. 'Yes, I read about it in the papers . . . Now what about New Brighton? It's an all-star variety show and they need a really good compère. I thought of you straight away, my boy.'

'Isn't that a job for a stand-up comedian?'

'So, tell a few jokes!'

I was going to sound him out on the Truro project but I could see myself being talked into a month on the banks of the Mersey.

'Sam, I've lost the signal,' I shouted. 'I'll call you back.' And with that I snapped my mobile shut.

We arrived at the hospital at the designated time. Ronnie was back in the same room looking absolutely washed out. His eyes appeared to have sunk deeper into a face that was drawn and white and his hair hung across his damp forehead in straggly tendrils. The offending leg was suspended in a cradle from a frame over the bed and beside it was a drip stand, the end of the tube disappearing under a plaster on the back of his hand.

'My God, Ronnie, you look bloody awful,' I said.

'So would you if you'd spent half the morning with the butcher of Bangor,' he croaked in reply.

'Behave yourselves, you two!' Auntie Marjorie said, smothering a grin. 'The nurse says we can only stay for a few minutes.' She turned her attention to the invalid. 'Now Ronnie. You do as you're told now and concentrate on getting better. You're coming home with me as soon as the hospital says you're strong enough.' It looked as though he was about to speak but she carried on. 'I'll hear no arguments,' she said with mock severity. Then she smiled. 'Nick is coming too, isn't that nice?'

'Get some sleep,' Susan added. 'We'll be back to see you tomorrow. We've got some exciting plans for the future to talk about.'

I was the last to leave the room. On my way out I bent over him and whispered, 'When the police question Benny, will he tell the truth and get Dolan off the hook — or lie to protect Polly? If I'm asked, I'll have to tell them what she told me, you know that don't you?'

He smiled grimly and nodded.

★   ★   ★

The change in Ronnie over the next couple of days was remarkable. The colour came back to his cheeks, his eyes sparkled with mischief and no nurse within pinching distance was safe from him, not that it seemed to worry them. Because of the pins in his ankle, he was not deemed fit enough to attend George Mayberry's funeral, which I know was a big disappointment to him. The hospital bent the rules however and allowed Susan and Auntie Marjorie to sit with him for the duration of the service.

Tim Murray did turn up at the crematorium (as I knew he would) and furthermore he brought Ella Thompson with him. Melanie was there, of course, with Brian Chambers and Gavin Partridge, but as Inspector Crabbe was also in attendance I wasn't sure if the Detective Constable was there on duty or as Melanie's escort. That Crabbe should be there when, according to him, he had George Mayberry's murder neatly wrapped up, struck me as odd, but then he was an odd sort of chap.

I didn't see anyone who could have been old George's wife or daughter, which I thought was very sad. The chief mourner was Roland Pembroke and he was sitting all alone in the dimness of the crematorium's little chapel. I didn't expect Tarquin to be there but I did think Marcia could have put in an appearance, if only to give her husband some support. I went and sat by him and when it was all over I walked out with him into the sunlight. His head was bowed and his shoulders slack. He looked old and spent.

We crunched our way back to the car park along the crematorium's extensive gravel drive which was bordered on each side with beds of standard roses, each bearing a plaque at its base, a small, sad memorial for a departed soul.

A loud, female voice suddenly broke the silence. 'I see your wife's not here, Mr Pembroke.' It was Ella Thompson. 'Is it true she didn't get on with George Mayberry?'

Roland screwed up his eyes as if in pain. I looked around for Tim Murray. He wasn't far away. 'Give us a break, Tim,' I called.

He nodded and signalled to his columnist to back off.

'She was right, you know,' Roland said when Ella had gone. 'Marcia didn't like old Mayberry. She resented the time I spent with him and thought him an interfering old busybody — which of course he was — but he had my best interests at heart, bless him.'

I watched Ella rejoin Tim Murray, who by now had Inspector Crabbe cornered by the floral tributes. I wished him luck with the po-faced policeman. I found it strange not to be the one immediately pounced on by the press but I suppose I was old news now, which was a sobering thought.

'But that isn't why she's not here today,' Roland continued, his dark brown voice reduced to a low rumble. 'Recently, I was asked to accept a knighthood. I was delighted at the prospect of having a title but Marcia was absolutely over the moon with the idea of being Lady Pembroke. It was the most wonderful thing that could have possibly ever happened to her.

'I've had to decline the honour, of course, in the light of recent events — which is why I can tell you about it — but the whole affair has upset her deeply.' He paused briefly with his eyes closed as if in prayer before he continued with, 'And that, dear boy, is why she's not here today.'

I remembered how radiant Marcia had looked when she let me in on her big secret. 'Yes,' I said. 'I can appreciate how she feels.'

'Ah, but you don't, Nicholas, Nobody does. It has changed her. She's become completely withdrawn. This cottage I'm renting has a little summer house in the garden and she spends all her time in there, on her own, playing tapes of old Broadway musicals over and over again.'

We split up when we got to the car park. I didn't like leaving my former boss looking so down but what could I do? I got in the Mini and just sat there, thinking. As I watched the old Jaguar drive away I thought about Marcia and what Roland had just told me. With Tarquin's trial coming up, he had no choice but to decline the knighthood. It was either that or face the humiliation of being told he wasn't going to get it after all. I could understand Marcia being mortally disappointed, but to shut herself away, that wasn't like her at all. Marcia had to be with people, to be admired by men and envied by their ladies. I had once likened her to a butterfly because that's how I thought of her, a beautiful, delicate creature flitting from place to place, from one group of people to another. I couldn't think what would make her shut herself away, unless . . . No, that's a crazy thought. I could no more imagine Marcia going to George Mayberry's room with the intention of smothering him in his bed than I could Polly . . . but if the murderer *had* been a woman — and the buttoning of the raincoat suggested it was — then it could only have been one of those two. I drummed my fingers on the steering wheel. I played a detective once, in a shabby little theatre in Leeds. It was a new play by someone who must have been related to the producer. To say it was terrible would be an understatement. The storyline was totally predictable and every character in it a stereotype. The critics panned it and it only ran for three weeks, to houses where on some nights the cast outnumbered the audience. I never refer to it and I try not to think about it but I remember my character always banging on about, Method, Motive and Opportunity.

With George Mayberry's murder the Method and Opportunity bit was easy. The Method being a pillow over the old man's face — and both women were strong enough to do that! Polly had shoulders like a man — and lifted crates of full bottles like one

— and what was it Melanie said about Marcia, that she was once in a chorus line? Well, you don't find any job in the theatre more physically demanding than that!

They both had Opportunity. As the housekeeper, Polly was in and out of the annexe all the time and Marcia's room wasn't far from Mayberry's — in fact, on the night he died I remember Marcia leaving the bar early.

But what about Motive? Well, Polly had a motive of sorts. She knew Mayberry must have found the camera at the place where she *thought* she had killed Ronnie Simmons. Mayberry's recollection of where that place was could provoke an investigation and possibly reveal her crime — but Marcia's motive was stronger. According to Roland, she knew their son was into drugs. He'd actually shown her some ecstasy tablets he'd found in Tarquin's dressing room. She also knew Mayberry took a dedicated interest in what Roland's people were up to, writing it all down in his little red book. On the night he died I was at the bar and so was Marcia when Arthur said the old man would sleep well because he'd sneaked a large vodka into his tonic water. What an opportunity for her to go to his room get a good look at that book! And even if, in his drunken state, he had remembered to lock his door she knew as well as me where Polly kept her pass-key.

But suffocation takes time. Polly was a spur-of-the-moment walloper, would she have had the resolve to go through with something as cold and as calculating as suffocation? I doubt it. Whereas Marcia, being discovered by Mayberry searching for his notebook, could easily have stuffed a pillow over the old man's face to silence him, and then, with her desire for the title having grown to obsession, I could well believe her holding it there until all protestation ceased.

I turned the key in the ignition, put the car into gear and drove off after the Jaguar.

★ ★ ★

The Pembroke's temporary accommodation was Church Cottage, which, as the name implies, was located next to the church. In fact you had to go through the churchyard to get to it. I left the Mini by the gate and walked up to the door. It was a much larger property than the Turner's Rose Cottage and had probably been the home of the verger in times past. In the tiny entrance porch a wrought iron rod hung down from the roof, its end crudely fashioned into a loop. I tugged at it and somewhere within the depths of the house a bell jangled. A few moments later there was the sound of bolts being drawn and the door creaked open fractionally. It was still secured by a chain. An eye peered at me cautiously through the gap. Then, to a shout of, 'My dear Nicholas!' the chain was unhooked and the door was opened wide.

Roland looked surprised but nevertheless pleased to see me. 'Come in, dear boy, come in,' he said.

I stepped into a narrow hallway. There were reception rooms on both sides (it being a double-fronted property) and a flight of stairs at the far end leading up to the bedrooms. A doorway by the side of the stairs presumably took you through to dining room and kitchen. Roland led me to a room where he had obviously been enjoying a drink before I arrived (Scotch, by the look of it) and reading the newspaper. It was a moderately large room and I guessed the one on the other side was of similar proportions.

He mistook my reasons for looking around. 'You don't have to worry, dear boy, Tarquin's out. It seems to me he can do very much as he pleases, so long as he shows up in court when the time comes.'

'And Marcia?'

'Where else?'

'I thought I'd visit her — to cheer her up a

bit,' I said. I thought that sounded really feeble, so I added, 'It was a spur-of-the-moment thing,' which didn't help.

Roland picked up his glass. 'Drink?' he asked, somewhat reluctantly and looked relieved when I shook my head. 'She doesn't relish the idea of company like she used to,' he said sadly. 'Visitors don't cheer her up any more. She's happier left on her own, reliving her early days in the theatre.'

'Can I try?'

He sighed and led me to the door by the stairs, past the dining room and into the kitchen. At the glazed door to the garden he paused. 'The summer house is at the end of the path, you can't miss it. I won't come with you if you don't mind. Seeing me only reminds her of what might have been.'

The gabled front of the wooden hut was faced with pierced and intricately carved wood that reminded me of a Black Forest cuckoo clock. Had Marcia suddenly appeared singing something from *The Sound of Music* I wouldn't have been at all surprised. As it was, the sound that filtered into the garden was, *I Could Have Danced All Night* from *My Fair Lady*. I rapped loudly on the door. The music stopped.

'Who is it?'

'Marcia, it's me, Nick, Nick Carter.'

There was a lengthy pause before the door opened. And then, there she was, although only dressed in jeans and a dark blue fleece her makeup and coiffure was immaculate.

'Nick . . . Darling!' she said, somewhat hesitantly and with nowhere near her customary exuberance.

'May I come in?' I asked.

For a moment she looked uncertain, and then with, 'Of course, darling. It's lovely to see you,' she stepped back and held the door open for me.

The little wooden building may be all *Hansel and Gretel* on the outside but inside it was cobwebby and gloomy, clearly having been used for quite some time as nothing more than a store for empty flower pots, a portable barbecue and sundry garden furniture. Marcia had created a comfortable corner for herself with a sun lounger and a low table, upon which stood a sizeable radio-cum-audiotape player (the summer house was obviously wired for electricity) a bottle of Gordon's, some Schweppes tonic and a scattering of audiotapes in plastic containers.

She flopped down on the recliner and switched the tape back on while I just stood there not quite knowing what to say.

'I played Eliza in Manchester,' she said,

turning the volume down a bit. Not only was I grateful for the reduction in noise but also because here was something I could use to build a conversation.

'And I was *Doolittle* in Skegness,' I replied. I laughed and so did she, which I thought was something of a breakthrough.

She wanted to know about Ronnie, so I readily brought her up to date on his progress. I then went on to tell her about Auntie Marjorie's old cinema in Truro. She lay on the lounger listening to my thoughts on staging musicals while Stanley Holloway sang *Get Me To The Church On Time* in the background. There was a faraway look in her eyes.

'Oh, Nick, just think,' she said. 'We could do *Rose Marie*. Wouldn't dear old Roly just love that?'

I then did something that had to be done.

'Don't move!' I shouted. 'There, on your shoulder. A spider!'

She leapt up with a squeal, tore off the fleece and threw it to the floor. Underneath, all she was wearing was a thin cotton T-shirt.

George Mayberry was an old man but nevertheless I felt sure he would have struggled with his attacker. Polly had a sleeveless top on when I last saw her and other than a vaccination scar and a badly drawn tattoo there were no blemishes on her shoulders or on her arms whereas there were several scratches on Marcia's fair skin and bruises on her upper arms that could well be imprints of thumbs and fingers. I could almost see George Mayberry's gnarled, arthritic fingers gripping them in a desperate and futile attempt to wrench the smothering pillow from his face.

Gathering up the discarded fleece, I gave it a shake and handed it back to her. 'There are no spiders now, Marcia,' I said sadly and walked away, Rex Harrison's unmistakable rendition of, *I've Grown Accustomed To Her Face*, fading into the distance as I retraced my steps back to the house.

17

When I eventually arrived back at *The Grapes*, I found Susan and Auntie Marjorie at a table in the taproom bar. They were both looking very pleased with themselves.

Susan saw me come in and called out excitedly, 'Mr Jones said we should be able to take Ronnie home next week — isn't that wonderful news, Nicky?'

To which, Auntie Marjorie, practical as ever, added, 'I've told the nice landlord here that we will need to keep our rooms on for the weekend at least.'

The 'nice landlord', who was hovering behind the bar, gave me a wink and said, 'Mr Pembroke sent a few quid back with Miss Naylor for everyone to raise a glass to poor old Mr Mayberry. What will yours be, Mr Carter?'

I thought a glass of red wine would be appropriate so I asked for that and waited while it was poured.

'Miss Naylor's staying on for the weekend as well,' he whispered, nodding his head in the direction of the booths. 'She can't bear to be parted from that young copper of hers.'

I hadn't noticed the lovers when I came in

but there they were, sitting in the furthermost corner booth holding hands across the table. I went over to them. Melanie didn't look too pleased when she saw me coming.

'I'm sorry to intrude,' I said. 'But I have some important information for the police.'

Gavin Partridge turned to Melanie and shrugged his shoulders apologetically, she sighed and picked up her drink. 'I'll go and sit with Susan,' she said. 'Don't keep him too long, Nick.'

I waited until Melanie was out of earshot before I began. 'You need to talk to a paramedic by the name of Dave Nuttall.' I said.

'May I ask why, sir?'

'Because what he's got to tell you will clear Eddie Dolan of George Mayberry's murder.'

The young detective looked far from pleased. 'Oh, dear,' he said, a worried frown wrinkling his boyish face. 'Mr Crabbe will not be happy about that. Pinning Mr Mayberry's murder on Eddie Dolan was his last hope.'

'How do you mean?'

'Well, sir. He drew a blank with Caleb Pilcher being Tarquin Pembroke's drugs supplier, didn't he? The anti-terrorist people have more or less taken over the arms smuggling case and Benny Pilcher's evidence has cleared Eddie Dolan of the attempted murder of Mr Simmons. All Mr Crabbe has left is the murder of Mr Mayberry . . . No, sir, he will not be happy, he will not be happy at all.'

'He will be if you give him the real murderer,' I said, and I went on to tell him the whole story from George Mayberry's raincoat buttons to Marcia Fontaine's bruises.

No sooner had I finished than he reached for his mobile and called DI Crabbe, giving him a summary of our conversation. He listened to his master's voice for a moment before saying, 'Yes, sir. Right away, sir.' The young detective put his mobile back in his pocket and downed the last of his drink (straight orange juice, the empty bottle was on the table). 'I'll leave it to you to make my apologies, shall I,' he said with a grin and slipped away.

Melanie was annoyed, of course, but fortunately for me DI Crabbe was the main butt for her anger. 'Even policemen are entitled to a lunch hour,' she said petulantly.

To try and take her mind off her boyfriend's abrupt departure I told her about Auntie Marjorie's gift. The old lady looked mildly embarrassed and said it was just a building that hadn't been used for years, but Susan leaped in and enthused about the project.

'It was built as a cinema over fifty years ago and has stood unused for the past twenty. Mrs Earnshaw's General Manager e-mailed me a recent survey, which describes the structure as sound with no rot or dampness anywhere — and the seating looks all right from the photographs he sent. Obviously we won't know until we see it for ourselves but it sounds promising. The most important thing is it's got a proper stage.'

'And we're going to need a stage manager if you're interested,' I said to Melanie.

Roland Pembroke suddenly came to mind and I saw him as he was in the crematorium that morning, sitting all alone. Life was going to be hard for him with both his son and his wife in prison. 'I wonder if *Rose Marie* would go down well in Cornwall?' I said, thinking aloud.

Arthur came to the table to collect the empty glasses. 'If you're wanting lunch in the dining room I should go through now if I was you,' he said. 'It's filling up fast. Today's special is boiled beef and carrots with pease pudding, it's very popular.'

As we got up to leave my mobile rang, it was Sam. 'You go through,' I said. 'I'll just see what Sam has got to say.'

'Nick, my boy, have I got some good news for you?'

Here it comes, I thought, two weeks playing the back end of a pantomime cow in Weston-super-mare. I'll tell him I'm off to Truro, that'll make him sit up.

'*Blues and Twos* is back on!' he shouted. 'The BBC wants to give you that part you auditioned for.'

What is it they say about London busses, you wait forever for one to come along and then two turn up? One moment I was out of work and then, right out of the blue, I get two fantastic opportunities dumped in my lap. I didn't know what to say. I didn't even know what to think!

'That's great, Sam. Look, I can't speak now. I'll call you back.' I closed the phone and sat motionless, my head buzzing with conflicting thoughts.

Arthur appeared behind the bar wiping his hands on his apron. 'Your party have all gone for the boiled beef and carrots, sir, shall I put you down for the same?'

I stood up. 'Yes, that will be fine,' I said and made my way to the dining room.

The ladies were engaged in a lively conversation. Susan was writing notes and occasionally tapping away on a pocket calculator. The discussion stopped when I got to the table.

She swung round on her chair to face me.

'I'm trying to work out how much money we'll need to keep us going until we open, Nicky. If I can determine a minimum monthly subsistence figure for you, me and Ronnie . . . '

'And me!' Melanie said eagerly, adding, 'If you'll have me.'

I looked at Auntie Marjorie who nodded her head approvingly. 'Of course,' I said, adding, 'But Truro is a long way from Cannford.'

She blushed delightfully. 'Gavin could always apply for a transfer to the Devon and Cornwall Constabulary.'

The notepad and calculator were put to one side as Arthur arrived with our lunch. It may only have been boiled beef and carrots but I don't know when I enjoyed a meal more. I had made up my mind. I knew that I wanted the Truro project more than anything.

I skipped dessert and excused myself saying I had to get back to Sam. I went to my room and made some coffee. I then kicked off my shoes and stretched out on the bed. What I was about to say to my agent could take a long time.

He didn't sound too pleased when he answered. 'Nick, my boy. You took your time. So what do I tell the BBC?'

'I'm not doing it, Sam.'

There was long pause and then he said, quite quietly, 'So you quit? Is that it, Nick, you're quitting the business?'

'Not exactly.'

'What d'you mean, 'not exactly'?' Now he was shouting. 'I get you a plum job with Deejay and you let that arrogant schmuck, Jason Carp snatch it from you. And now, when the opportunity of a lifetime comes along, you say you're not doing it. What's got into you, Nick? I think that bump on the head has made you stupid.'

'I'll tell you what's got into me, Sam, but you must promise to sit quietly and listen. I'm paying for the call, so don't worry.'

I began by explaining how I came to sign up with the Pembroke Players in the first place and went on, taking him briefly through my search for Ronnie and bringing in Tarquin and his drug dealing on the way. When I started to tell him about George Mayberry's murder he forgot his promise and interrupted me.

'*The* George Mayberry?' he spluttered. 'The stage designer?'

'The very same,' I said. 'I can't say anymore. I'm pretty sure who did it but no one has been arrested yet.'

I then told him about the Truro project. This time he listened patiently and when I was finished there was another pause and then he said, 'My cousin Rebecca's son, Ben. His company make programmes for television. He and I don't do business because they don't employ actors; all their stuff is real life. They did that series on a couple who bought a derelict stately home and turned it into a health spa. Did you see it? It was very good. They've just finished another about the re-opening of a disused railway line; I think Channel 4 is due to start showing that in the autumn. I'll tell him about your venture, I think he might well be interested, particularly as you are a TV celebrity.'

Have I mentioned Sam Abrahams' skill in turning a problem into an opportunity? He called me back that evening. Susan and I are due to meet Sam's cousin Rebecca's son, Ben, next week to talk about an eight part TV series. Although Sam doesn't do business with Ben I'd be surprised if there wasn't a little bit of commission in it for him.

I do *love* a happy ending!

We do hope that you have enjoyed reading this large print book.

Did you know that all of our titles are available for purchase?

We publish a wide range of high quality large print books including:
Romances, Mysteries, Classics
General Fiction
Non Fiction and Westerns

Special interest titles available in large print are:
The Little Oxford Dictionary
Music Book
Song Book
Hymn Book
Service Book

Also available from us courtesy of Oxford University Press:
Young Readers' Dictionary
(large print edition)
Young Readers' Thesaurus
(large print edition)

For further information or a free brochure, please contact us at:
Ulverscroft Large Print Books Ltd.,
The Green, Bradgate Road, Anstey,
Leicester, LE7 7FU, England.
Tel: (00 44) 0116 236 4325
Fax: (00 44) 0116 234 0205

Other titles published by
The House of Ulverscroft:

REMAINS FOUND

J.A. O'Brien

Two children find a woman's body which is identified first by a friend called Ruby Cox, as Diane Shaft, and later by another friend, Aiden Brooks, as Cecily Staunton. Why did the dead woman have two names? DI Sally Speckle's problems start when Cox vanishes from Loston police station. Then Brooks, claiming he's a clairvoyant, accurately pinpoints the location of where the body was discovered. Does this mean that Brooks is the killer? But as the investigation gets increasingly complicated by troubles far closer to home, followed by another murder, Sally finds she has more suspects than she wants . . .

A GAME OF MURDER

Ray Alan

Guests arrive at Stafford House for a Saturday evening buffet followed by party games, which include a game of murder. But they are unaware that a real murder has been planned, and that in turn is followed by a second death. Detective Inspector Bill Forward arrives to find there are eighteen suspects at the scene. Only after much patient investigation and strange leads can he bring the case to a surprising, unexpected conclusion.